WENDY DAY

Christmas, Cabernet, and Chaos

A Sally and Pearl Adventure

OPEN SKY
PUBLISHING

First published by Open Sky Publishing 2022

Copyright © 2022 by Wendy Day

This novel is entirely a work of fiction. The names, characters and incidents portrayed in it are the work of the author's imagination. Any resemblance to actual persons, living or dead, events or localities is entirely coincidental.

First edition

This book was professionally typeset on Reedsy. Find out more at reedsy.com

Dedicated to my Mom and Dad, who always made Christmas magical.

Contents

Preface

McKenzie Bridge is tucked in the mountains between Bend and Eugene, Oregon. The two-lane highway stretching up to the riverside mountain village is dotted with small towns and serves as a beacon for tourists year-round. It has been years since I had the pleasure of visiting my family there, but could never forget the beauty of the area.

In 2020 this area was ravaged by wildfires that swept through, burning 173,000 acres of the mountain pass and destroying hundreds of homes and businesses, including Holiday Farms. The scarred land will never be the same.

But since then, the residents of McKenzie Bridge and the surrounding towns have worked together to begin the rebuilding process. Their spirit has been tested but not broken. While some of the buildings are forever gone, the heart of this community lives in the river, forest, and people.

This book features a fictionalized version of McKenzie Bridge and its residents. I loved the area, and it was the perfect place to set this Sally and Pearl adventure. If you are ever able to visit, you will find unparalleled natural beauty and down-to-earth, friendly people.

1

Christmas is Coming

Sally Johnson pulled her fuzzy pink blanket up over her legs, not taking her eyes off the glint of the knife blade. This was going to end badly. She squeezed the corner of the blanket until her knuckles turned white, her heart racing as ominous music rose to a crescendo.

"Oh, you know she ain't gettin' away," said Pearl, her feisty best friend.

"Wouldn't be a good show if she did," Sally said, biting her thumbnail.

Pearl leaned forward, adjusting her bifocals. "Whew, he's sure quick with a knife."

Sally nodded as screams filled the room. "I knew it was him. He should've burned that jacket instead of stuffing it in the dumpster."

"Sloppy," Pearl agreed. "And tryin' to blame it on her brother. He's as windy as a sack full of farts." As the program ended, Pearl clicked off the remote and clapped her hands together "Alrighty, let's get goin'. It's Drinksgivin', my favorite night of the year."

Sally folded her blanket and draped it over the back of the couch. A year ago, she never could have guessed she'd be roommates with Pearl, watching true crime and going out to the bar, especially at her age. "Hold on. I need to run a brush through my hair."

Pearl pulled her chin into her neck. "You sure you wanna brush that hair? It's gonna be stickin' up like the Fourth of July."

Sally patted her curls. Michigan's humidity could change on a dime, and it was never exactly kind to her curly hair. "If I say you're right, will you drive?"

"Sure. That way, you can have a margarita or two before you get up to sing."

The day before Thanksgiving was an unofficial holiday celebrated as the biggest bar night of the year. Sammy's would be packed.

Sally pulled on her brown cropped boots over her black leggings and switched out of her Michigan State sweatshirt into a long, thin, cream sweater. When she returned to the living room, Pearl was grinning, dressed in a bright pink sweatshirt that said *I Solved a Murder, and All I Got Was This Lousy Sweatshirt.*"

"Where did you get that?" Sally asked, eyes wide.

"Special order. Thought you'd like it." Pearl held out the bottom of the sweatshirt to make sure Sally could read it clearly. "Got you one too. But it's a Christmas gift, so you gotta wait."

Sally shook her head and smiled at her friend. She had no desire to parade around town inviting more attention to their time in Mexico. It has been fun at first, being local celebrities, but it had quickly worn on her. Luckily, people tended to move on from their interest in the senior sleuths after the initial intrigue, but it could have its advantages. Tonight, Pearl was probably just looking for free drinks.

They hopped into Pearl's yellow convertible with her signature dancing daisy stuck to the dashboard. Ten minutes later, they pulled into the Sammy's parking lot.

"Everybody and their cousins are here," Pearl said, climbing out of the car and surveying the smokers huddled together near the door.

Sally pulled her coat up around her ears for the short walk from the car. "Remember that we can't stay out too late. I have a ton of cooking to do in the morning."

As they headed towards the entrance at a quick clip, Pearl waved her off. "Yeah, yeah. Karaoke starts at eight. Should be able to sing at least one song and be home by ten."

"Wish it wasn't so crowded." Sally licked her lips. She needed lip balm. Maybe Pearl had some. She would have to ask once they got settled.

"I hate this time of year. Busy as a cat coverin' crap on a marble floor." Pearl huffed.

Sally stopped with her hand on the door under the neon sign and turned to Pearl. "Now listen, you'd better find your holiday spirit because tomorrow is Thanksgiving, and after that, it's officially time to get excited for Christmas. I intend on making this the best one ever."

"Sally, darlin', you done told me this a million times. Keep buggin' me about it, and I'm gonna paint myself green and start swipin' presents." She waggled her eyebrows. "You ain't gonna make this old heart grow three sizes. It ain't natural."

Sally frowned and pulled open the door. The revelry was already in full swing. Kids home from college were meeting up and swapping stories, and new divorcees were looking for some fun before plunging into their first holiday on their own. Sally and Pearl headed straight for the DJ booth. The karaoke host, Terry, saw them and grinned. Pushing his glasses up on his nose, he said, "Hey, ladies. Are you finally going to sing tonight, Miss Pearl?"

"You ever hear two cats fightin' after midnight on a full moon?" Pearl asked.

Terry shook his head, biting back a grin.

"You ain't gonna hear it tonight, either."

Terry laughed and turned to Sally. "What about you? The usual?"

Sally tugged at the hem of her sweater and looked around. She had been practicing a different song all week but hadn't considered how many people would be there. She flinched as Pearl elbowed her in the side and said, "You ain't gonna chicken out now."

Sally rolled her shoulders back, took a breath, and said, "I've been practicing a new song." She leaned over and whispered in Terry's ear. His eyebrows shot up. "Alright then. Got about 12 singers in front of you, so get cozy."

"Ain't fussin' about the wait. Gotta get our margaritas on," Pearl said. She looped her arm through Sally's and headed to two open seats at the bar. Sliding onto a bar stool, Pearl said, "Don't be goin' wild. I ain't interested in a repeat of you gettin' dragged out to the car by Terry."

"Why do you have to bring that up?" Sally's face flushed with the memory, or lack thereof, of that night. She was still mortified every time she thought about it.

When they had returned from Mexico after busting a drug ring posing as a group of vacationing singles, their small town had been full of gossip about their adventure. They had become sort of local celebrities. When they decided to go to karaoke, patrons of the tavern were all too happy to supply them with free drinks. While Pearl could always hold her liquor, Sally had not fared as well that night. After a drunk rendition of Madonna's "Material Girl," she had thrown up in the bathroom. Not a great look for a grandma. Now she had a strict two-drink limit whenever they went out. Pearl, thinking this was hilarious, was never going to let her live it down.

"Hello, ladies." An older man with his belt hitched high and a long, toothy grin approached them holding a bottle of beer. "Nice sweatshirt, Pearl. Staying warm after getting back from Mexico? I could help you out, you know."

"Jack, shouldn't you be off pluckin' a turkey or somethin'?" Pearl scolded.

"I'd pluck a turkey for you." He said, leaning an elbow on the bar and winking.

"Oh, my stars. You been flirtin' with me for months. Think you'd about give up."

"Never, my dear." He replied before giving her a deep bow and backing away dramatically.

Pearl rolled her eyes. "Real charmin'."

"You could do worse," Sally said, then sipped her drink.

"That old fool has been sniffin' around as long as we been comin' here. I ain't lookin' for no ball and chain," Pearl said.

"There are other nice men in town."

"You can do better than the men here. Heck, you *have* done better. Mike could bench-press ten of him on a Tuesday." Pearl lifted her chin in the direction of Jack, who was leaning over, balancing on his heels, talking to two uninterested young ladies.

Sally laughed despite herself. "You think so? It's probably

5

true."

Pearl ignored her and continued, "I'll do you one better. He could fry up Creepy McCrusterpants over there and eat him over eggs."

Sally laughed more loudly this time. This was why she loved going out with Pearl. Every time she thought she'd seen or heard it all, Pearl surprised her yet again.

"Pearl, do you think I'm too old to sing a song with a rap? The board says there are two singers until I'm up. I still have time to change my song."

Pearl scoffed. "If Old Creepy can flirt like a boy messin' his knickers when he sees bras in the Sears catalog, you can sing your rap. I'll clap loud because whatever happens, you can count on me to be your fan."

"You really are my best friend," Sally mumbled, sipping her margarita.

"I know it," Pearl replied. "Better start those warm-ups. It sounds like that drunk 'Mr. Roboto' is just about to Kilroy himself."

Sally took a deep gulp of her margarita before reaching over to hug Pearl tightly.

"Hey now," Pearl said, untangling herself, "Don't want people gettin' the wrong idea. And besides, I'm still in danger of grinchin' out if you get too mushy."

"Noted," Sally giggled.

"Hey, wait," Pearl said, opening her purse and brandishing a new stick of chapstick. "Figured you'd want this."

"You're a lifesaver," Sally said, taking it and smearing it on as she moved toward the DJ booth now that she was on deck. "Clap loud, Pearl!"

"Like thunder," Pearl said seriously, slapping the bartop for emphasis. Sally had been quietly practicing all week, listening to the song on repeat in her headphones so that even Pearl could be surprised.

As soon as the lights hit her face and she pulled the microphone from the stand, the rest of the world seemed to slip away. Sally turned her eyes to the blue screen, waiting for the first bars of the popular song to begin. The weight of the microphone in her hand felt good. She twirled the cord around her hand to make sure she didn't trip on it and took a deep breath. When the opening bar of "Lady Marmalade" played, the crowd went wild.

After the first line, she searched for her friend, who had slipped off the bar stool and was jumping up and down. Sally smiled and closed her eyes, hitting a high note easily. The song was a bit risqué but so fun to sing. She did modify the rap section a little. It was one thing to sing about sex in French, and it was another to brag about it in English.

On the final note, Sally took a deep bow, grinning sheepishly during the raucous applause. Some people were laughing, and some were whooping. Everyone appreciated her vocal talent combined with the unexpected novelty of her song choice. "You go, girl!" shouted one of the visiting college students, and Sally blushed deeply, dipping her head in embarrassment and gratitude.

Pearl was clapping and hollering loudest of all. When Sally stepped down in triumph, she wobbled a bit. What in the world? How many drinks did she have? Had the bartender doubled up on the tequila in her margarita? Either way, it went to her head far faster than she thought it would. She made a beeline for her stool.

"Thank goodness," she said after asking for water and taking a long drink.

"That you have a best friend like me?" Pearl asked.

"Yes, and also that you're driving."

"Lightweight," Pearl teased. "That's what you get for drinkin' on an empty stomach. I'll put in an order for some chips and guac and get us some of them mozzarella sticks."

"Tomorrow is Thanksgiving. I always skip dinner the night before Thanksgiving," Sally mumbled, tugging anxiously at the hem of her shirt.

"First, that don't make no sense. Second, you ain't gotta do nothin' you don't wanna do."

"I know it's strange. I just want everything to go perfectly tomorrow. It's been a hard year for all of us, and Lauren needs to know she can count on me. Even though things have changed, it will be okay."

"My stars, Sally Johnson, we done learned that lesson in Mexico."

"The kids weren't in Mexico, and I'm still their mother. It's my job to make Christmas magical for them, and also you."

"Sounds like it ain't for them, is all," Pearl pointed out. "Eat some chips, at least, so that your Christmas spirit stops eatin' you."

Sally snorted, reaching for a chip. "I'll stop trying to make your heart grow three sizes. I promise. Just at least give me a chance to really wow you at Christmas. I know you'll understand why all the worry was worth it when it turns out perfectly."

"Seems like gettin' through Thanksgiving without a hangover might be a more pressin' concern," Pearl said, "but you're always somethin' else when you've got a fire lit under you. I'm sure Christmas with you will be just dandy."

"It'll be *perfect*," Sally emphasized, scooping up a hearty helping of guacamole.

2

Happy Thanksgiving?

Sally buzzed around the crowded kitchen in her orange and brown turkey apron. A sheen of sweat gleamed on Sally's forehead, and the windows steamed as an early snowfall blanketed the yard. Pearl sat at the little kitchen table, where she had finally settled to wipe down the china with a damp cloth. All morning the two of them jockeyed for position as they prepared dinner in the small, cheery kitchen. This was the one area of the house they had not figured out how to share. Pearl didn't love cooking, but she loved being in charge. Sally loved cooking and didn't like being told what to do in her own kitchen. The clash was especially noticeable today, with so much left to do and Lauren's family due to arrive in an hour.

Sally did her best to even out her breathing and focus. Today was all about the golden turkey baking in the new oven Pearl had purchased with the proceeds from the sale of her house. Sally's family would gather and give thanks around the table, and she would reflect afterward on a holiday well done.

In addition to the oven, Pearl had insisted on a few other flashy upgrades when she'd moved in. Sally had relented when it came to the stove, the TV, the luxurious leather couches, and even a hot tub for the back porch. Pearl was still trying to bring her around to installing a tiki bar to go with it.

"Are you still gonna decorate these cookies?" Pearl asked, fetching a miniature tray out of the toaster oven and setting it on the cooling rack. "You know I ain't got a head for that stuff. I ain't got the patience for it, either."

"Of course I'll decorate the cookies," Sally chuckled. "Are you ever going to share the secret recipe for your sugar cookies with me, or are you just going to mysteriously mix them all up in a bowl with your back turned?"

"Sally, I'd trust you with my life," Pearl said seriously. "Don't reckon I'd trust anyone with my recipe for sugar cookies. These are the best cookies where I'm from and where you're from put together."

"Fair enough," Sally chuckled. "But like you said, there's a reason you ask me to decorate."

"Of course, there is," Pearl said shortly. "I've always known my strengths and where I got to delegate. Ain't no shame in that."

"Personally, I like being part of a team," Sally said, smiling and getting her frosting pipettes ready.

"Heck, ain't we known that for a while, now?"

"It wasn't true when it came to the deviled eggs," Sally grumbled. "How did we mess those up so badly? Do me a favor and just don't tell Lauren."

"I won't, as long as you make these little angel cookies real pretty."

After Sally finished frosting the cookies, they set the dining table with Sally's china and Pearl's favorite red tablecloth. Sally had insisted on ironing it the night before. Pearl had

11

wanted candles, but Sally reminded her that there would be a toddler at the table and that it wasn't nice to make firefighters work on Thanksgiving. Pearl had grumbled mildly, but even without the candles, the dining room looked like a Norman Rockwell painting.

"It's been a while since I've seen that tablecloth with so many place settings," Pearl said, planting her hands on her hips. "I almost wanna look at it for a spell before your little doll of a granddaughter starts throwin' drumsticks and gravy all over the place. What's her name, again? Aubergine?"

"Amelia!" Sally laughed, then said gently, "Go ahead. Look as long as you like." Sally was relieved Pearl was no longer bustling around and getting underfoot. "I still have some side dishes simmering on the stove, but we're almost ready. We should take a load off until the kids arrive and watch the Macy's Thanksgiving Day Parade."

Pearl waved her off. "Nah, I've seen enough floatin' balloons and marchin' bands. I care more about what happened to the Pine Creek Ax Murderer. But that ain't exactly festive, I suppose."

Sally smiled and squeezed her hand. "Watch whatever you'd like to, Pearl. Just make sure you turn it off before the baby might get scared." She handed Pearl the remote and went to watch for Lauren's minivan.

An hour later, they were gathered around the table. Lauren's husband, Brad, prayed over the food and family. Sally's heart soared listening to his sincere gratitude. She offered up her own silent prayer of thanks that Lauren had found such a nice man to marry. The next few minutes were spent catching up on Brad's job and Amelia's preschool plans.

"Mom, I have something to tell you," Lauren said, swallowing a bite of mashed potato that seemed to stick in her throat. Sally was slicing a piece of turkey and paused. Lauren's throat bobbed, and she glanced at Sally's knife briefly and then back at her mom's face. "This is hard to say, and I wanted to put it off as long as possible so that Thanksgiving would still be wonderful, but we won't be here for Christmas."

Sally rested her wrist on the table and cocked her head to the side, trying to process what she'd just heard. "What?" What was Lauren talking about? She must have misunderstood because it wasn't possible that Lauren could miss Christmas. Sally tried to swallow. Had she ingested a turkey bone?

"We spent last year here and promised Brad's family we would spend Christmas Eve with them. They moved to Florida, so we can't do both." Her husband looked at the table. Amelia clapped her hands and babbled, uneasy with the sudden somber mood shift and trying to restore the smiles to the adult faces around her.

Pearl gnawed at a turkey leg. "Fair's fair, I reckon."

Sally frowned. Pearl shrugged. "Just sayin'."

Sally went back to slicing her turkey. She wasn't sure how to respond. Pearl was right. It was only fair, but Sally's heart ached. She had lain in bed last night after karaoke, thinking about Christmas morning, having her family gathered around the tree, and opening the presents she had so carefully selected. Now it wouldn't be complete, so it wouldn't be perfect. What could she do? Sally sighed, trying to cling to the bright side of the matter. At least her boys would be home. "I understand, honey." Her mind understood, but her heart was roaring in protest.

Lauren still hadn't moved. She chewed her lower lip, brows furrowed. "Mom, I'm so sorry. I know how important Christmas is to you. Maybe we can celebrate early or something."

Sally waved her off, blinking rapidly to keep the tears from forming. She didn't want to be petty but couldn't quite muster graciousness after such a painful blow. "It's alright. At least I'll have my boys here. I am sure you'll have fun in Florida." Sally focused on cutting her turkey. She would need a spoon if the pieces got any smaller.

"About that, Mom. I talked to Joel yesterday. He has a huge project deadline and can't get away long enough to come home for Christmas."

Sally's head snapped up, and her knife clattered to her plate, causing everyone at the table to jump. "What? Joel's not coming either?"

Lauren's lip quivered. She shook her head.

Sally sat back. "Henry?"

Lauren rolled her eyes. "So, Henry's wife got him to cave and sign up for a couples' yoga retreat in the Mojave Desert. It's nonrefundable and, in her words, 'super important for their spiritual health as soul-bonded partners in the fluid dream of life.'"

Pearl sucked in a breath. "Didn't she change her name? Henry married a Wanda but ended up with a 'Windbag' or some-such?"

"Wind*song*," Lauren corrected dully. Her husband Brad snorted, trying to disguise it as a cough.

Sally smacked her hand on the table with sudden, unexpected force, causing everyone to jump. "That's just great. I can't believe I will be alone for Christmas."

Pearl pulled her chin into her neck. "Oh my stars, what am I, chopped liver?"

"Of course not. But I wanted the perfect Christmas with my

children, and now they apparently have better things to do."

"That's not fair," Lauren said. Brad covered her hand with his own. "Things just didn't line up this year. We can still celebrate early or around the new year, and all of us are committed to making it, no matter what."

Sally sat still and contemplated the situation. She'd never had a Christmas without any of her children at home. This would also be her second Christmas without her husband Harold, who had died a year and a half ago after having a heart attack and dropping dead in their living room after yelling at the TV. Even if their marriage hadn't been ideal, there was nothing like staring down the barrel of a silent, empty Christmas to make her miss him so much that it ached.

The last year had been clouded with the fog of grief. Sally hadn't even bothered with a tree for the previous Christmas, opting instead to go to Lauren's for dinner. This year she was finally feeling better and ready to start decorating the day after Thanksgiving, making up for lost time, finding joy in the holiday just like she used to before Harold died. But if Lauren and the rest weren't going to be here, what was the point? Maybe she could go visit one of the boys. But that would leave Pearl here alone. It was hopeless.

Lauren reached for Sally's hand, reminding her again that there was a backup plan to soften the blow. Lauren had always been like that. She'd say it today, tomorrow, a week from now, to ensure that Sally knew she wasn't forgotten. "Mom, you can still decorate and everything. I'll even help you while we're here. We can celebrate a week early or a week late. It'll be fine."

"Of course," Sally said, primarily out of habit. She didn't want to rock the boat and understood that she had to share Lauren with Brad's family sometimes. It was just that there had been times in the last year when she didn't think she would make it through the grief. She would lie in her bed feeling numb. While those days were coming less frequently now, they still happened, and it wasn't just because of Harold. It was everything. It was how she had imagined her life turning out, and all the wasted time spent trying to please an unhappy man. It was the time she could have spent traveling, nurturing friendships, and loving her family without limits or regrets.

The rest of the meal was subdued as if the collective turkey coma had descended early. Amelia's head even drooped forward onto her bib, and she started snoring. Not wanting to pout and needing a distraction, Sally stood to fuss over her granddaughter, snuggling her chubby, satisfied little body close and trying not to think of how she wouldn't have this chance on Christmas. As Sally rocked Amelia and shuffled around the kitchen, she could hear polite compliments over her shoulder as the others finished their pie. Lauren and Brad offered to wash the dishes, perhaps just as much out of guilt as wanting to help out. Sally might have insisted she could handle the cleanup any other day, but for now, she was just happy to get off her feet and snuggle with a sleepy Amelia on the couch under her fuzzy blanket, where no one could see her wet eyes and quivering lip. What was she going to do?

3

A Modest Proposal

"I ain't fussed if we skip Christmas this year. Never been a big fan anyhow," Pearl said later that evening after Lauren, Brad, and Amelia had left. She glanced up briefly from the pumpkin pie she was slicing for herself, then back so she could scoop it onto a plate without mishap.

Sally closed the refrigerator and hugged a tub of whipped cream to her chest. "We can't just skip Christmas. It's my favorite time of year."

"Okay," Pearl said, taking the whipped cream from Sally. "So what do you wanna do about it?"

Sally sighed. "I don't know. Maybe they'll change their minds." She leaned against the counter and folded her arms. Today had been a good day in so many ways. It was peaceful and busy, and there was easy laughter around the dinner table before Lauren dropped her bombshell. Sally had held it together relatively well even after that point, but now, her edges began to fray with noticeable melancholy. There were no loud football games to be watched. There was no pecan pie, which everyone hated except Harold. And now, instead of having a month to prepare the details of a perfect day, lining up the edges of wrapping paper, tying bows, and trimming trees, she was lost.

Pearl peeled the lid off the plastic tub and scooped three spoons full of whipped cream onto her pie.

"That's an absurd amount of whipped cream. I can't even see the pie," Sally said, raising an eyebrow.

Pearl pointed the spoon at her. "You eat pie your way, and I'll eat pie my way."

Sally shook her head, her face melting into a smile despite herself. Pearl always provided some levity, even at her lowest points. She walked over to the counter where she kept a running grocery list and added another tub of topping. As she wrote, Sally's phone buzzed. She plucked it from her pocket. Hope sprang anew. Maybe it was the kids calling to say they had changed their minds. It wasn't. Scanning the caller ID, she saw an Oregon area code and found herself grinning anyway.

It was Mike.

The last time she saw Mike was the morning they had left Mexico. Her vacation with Pearl had dramatically turned into an international drug bust. Mike had been an undercover DEA agent, although they hadn't known that until shortly before the end of their adventure. Sally's mind flooded with memories of dancing close to him, margarita salt on her lips, his skin smelling like coconuts and sea spray.

"Happy Thanksgiving," she said, slipping into the living room to take the call.

"Happy Thanksgiving to you, too. How was your day?" Mike's voice sounded warm on the other end of the line.

They slipped into a relaxed conversation. She told him about their disastrous deviled eggs and Pearl's overuse of whipped topping, and they laughed easily together. Mike said that he had spent the day with the local pastor's family in McKenzie Bridge, where he'd recently taken a new job as the chief of police.

"Now that Thanksgiving is out of the way, I'm already hearing 'Sleigh Ride' every five minutes on the radio. I guess it's officially time to start getting ready for Christmas," Mike joked. Sally felt an aching swell in her chest. It burst open, and the words tumbled out as she shared her disappointment about spending the holiday at home without her family.

"I'm sorry, Sally. I know how much you were looking forward to this," he said softly. Sally dabbed at her eyes, but the tears flowed from relief rather than pain. Pearl, for all her dry wit and no-nonsense toughness, was terrible at offering comfort.

"Thank you for saying so, Mike. It's nice to think that someone understands."

"No one wants to be alone on Christmas. Of course I understand. I also have an idea, and a modest proposal, if you will."

"Oh, my," Sally chuckled. "A proposal? How very forward."

"There's that smile," Mike said.

Sally smiled even wider. How could he know her so well that he could even hear her smile over the phone?

Mike continued, "You know that I live in McKenzie Bridge, Oregon. It's a destination for people who love to travel and love Christmas, and that sounds just like someone I know."

"You might know someone like that," Sally said slyly.

"So what do you think? Do you want to come to the Christmas Capital of the Northwest for Christmas? Pearl should come too, of course. I'd never dream of splitting up the dream team."

Sally sat down in the new floral armchair she had purchased to replace Harold's old recliner and swung her feet onto the ottoman. "That sounds perfect. If it's a choice between sitting at home or being in the Christmas Capital of the Northwest, how can I say no?"

"Sounds great. You guys are welcome to stay with me, but there's also a nice little resort in town with a hotel. They are usually pretty full this time of year, but I might be able to pull some strings."

"Oh, I don't know. Could you? I don't want to be a bother." Sally picked a piece of lint off her sweater and continued, "Actually, this might be just the ticket. I need to talk to Pearl. I'll get back to you as soon as I can, if that's alright."

After they hung up, she let the phone fall to her lap and considered her options. She could celebrate later with the kids. That was the easy part. How would it feel to see Mike again? Her face flushed at the thought of kissing him beneath the mistletoe. She shook her head. That was stupid. When they'd last parted, she had been unequivocal about not looking for romance. But a year had passed since then, and a lot had changed. To temper herself, she remembered that her housemate was a bit of a grinch. Pearl could shoot down the whole idea, so it might not even matter.

She returned to the kitchen, leaning against the door frame and explaining the plan to Pearl, who was sorting through a mountain of laundry and matching up socks at the kitchen table. "It'd be nice to see Mike," Pearl said, "but wouldn't you rather go someplace warm? We could go back to Mexico or maybe to a topless beach somewhere."

"I can't spend Christmas without snow," Sally said.

"Half the time, there ain't even snow here in Michigan on

20

Christmas, yet you've survived."

Sally pursed her lips. "You know what I mean. Why would we ever give up a chance to visit the perfect Christmas town?"

"You just wanna go see Mike." Pearl frowned, held her arms out, and spun around. "Better practice my role as the third wheel. Besides, if I say it once, I've said it a hundred times, I ain't the biggest fan of Christmas."

Sally stepped into the room, grabbing some socks and starting to pair them up. "Oh, come on, it wouldn't be like that. Mike and I are just friends. And you are my best friend, even if you're a little bit of a grinch. You won't be a third wheel."

Pearl waved her off. Then she looked at Sally and sighed. "Fine. The Three Amigos are gonna have a reunion, but I ain't carolin', and I ain't wearin' some stupid Santa hat."

Sally laughed because, despite Pearl's grumpiness, she could see her friend's eyes shining with excitement at the prospect of traveling together again. "Deal."

4

Welcome to McKenzie Bridge

December 15th

Mike navigated his red Ford pickup truck up the winding road from Eugene to the mountain town of McKenzie Bridge, also known as the Christmas Capital of the Northwest. Sally insisted that Pearl sit in the middle of the bench seat. She didn't want Mike to get the wrong idea. And, if she was being honest, she was nervous. He had tried to kiss her in Mexico, and it had ended in minor disaster. But his eyes were still that cerulean shade of blue, and his smile still came easily. And now here he was, ferrying them up a mountain to his perfect Christmas town.

"How do you like being a police chief?" Sally asked, glancing in the passenger side's rear-view mirror to ensure that their luggage was still in the pickup truck's bed.

"It isn't drug enforcement, but I like it. It beats the heck out of chasing the cartel, at my age."

"How'd you get the job?" Pearl asked. "Don't reckon you challenged the previous chief of police to a shootout and drew from the hip."

Mike laughed. "Not exactly. Even sheriffs stopped settling things that way after it became an elected position."

"Rats, I was hopin' for somethin' a little more excitin'," Pearl grumbled.

"A college friend of mine lives up here and sent me the notice. I was so tired of filling my days with golf and television that I almost went to work at the post office for something to do. But this seemed like a better use of my time."

"Can't be much crime up here," Pearl commented. "I bet y'all got a 'Code Candycane' for when the decorations are too far apart on the trees, or somethin', just to keep you busy."

"You'd be surprised," Mike said with a quick sideways glance. "We have our share of naked hippies who like to camp in the woods near the hot springs and get stoned. Sometimes the harder drugs trickle in, and our shops get some petty theft. But compared to my last job, this place might as well be Mayberry."

Sally watched the scenery as they drove, only half-listening to their conversation. She had never seen these kinds of mountains before. Michigan was pretty flat, at least where she lived, but here, green pines seemed to touch the sky on one side of the road as they climbed the mountain. The McKenzie river flowed beside them on the other side, winding along parallel with the road. Occasionally a waterfall would appear out of nowhere, sliding down the mountain and disappearing into the ground. Houses dotted the way and blocked their view of the river as they passed through little villages. Wood-covered bridges crossed the river periodically, painted red, blue, and green.

The trio rode in comfortable silence for a while, listening to the Christmas songs on the radio, which Sally occasionally hummed along to. As they climbed past the snow line, the world started to turn white. The trees were heavy with their fluffy winter coat. It was a beautiful sight, and Sally couldn't stop staring. She grunted when Pearl elbowed her. "Are you even payin' attention?"

"Oh," Sally said, rubbing her side. "Sorry, I was caught up in the view. It's so breathtaking."

Mike smiled and nodded in agreement.

"Sorry. What were you saying?" Sally asked, pulling at the hem of her jacket.

Mike glanced over at her. "I was asking what you two have been up to back home? Anything you might not have told me over the phone."

Sally cleared her throat. "It's been a bit of a crazy year. You already know Pearl sold her house and moved in with me. We renovated the kitchen, and last month we put a hot tub on the back deck."

"I read it was good for joint pain," Pearl interjected defensively. "Still tryin' to figure out how to write it off as a health-related expense, but I got some ideas."

"We've been playing bingo and volunteering at the local church." Sally added.

"Sally here is tryin' to get my soul saved before I kick the bucket." Pearl flashed her a toothy grin.

Sally pursed her lips in response.

Pearl continued. "What? I know Jesus. I have my whole life. I just don't feel the need to go around talkin' about him all the time, and Jesus probably ain't insecure enough to need me to."

Mike chucked but didn't comment.

"Anyhow, since movin' in together, we've been havin' more fun than foxes in a hen house. Gonna travel the world if we can stand to leave the Jacuzzi for that long, right Sally?"

A smile spread across Sally's face, and she nodded. "I would like that. I got my passport renewed and everything. It would be fun to see some of the places I've only ever heard about."

"Where are you planning to go?" Mike said, slowing down to let someone turn off the main road.

"We got a map up in the spare bedroom. We're still decidin' if we wanna do one of those cruises, a group tour, or just set off on our own and see what happens," Pearl said.

"I vote for a cruise. I used to watch *The Love Boat,* and I've always wanted to go on a cruise," Sally said, taking out lip balm from her purse and swiping it across her lips.

"She's got a thing for that Gopher," Pearl chortled.

Sally scoffed, "I do not. The Ship's Doctor was always my favorite. Smart and distinguished."

"That Ship's Doctor was a cad."

"Well, no matter. This is our first trip since coming back from Mexico, and we are just so glad you invited us. I've always read about Christmas in McKenzie Bridge, and now I get to be a part of it." Sally beamed at Mike, who smiled back at her. Pearl sat in the middle and rolled her eyes.

When they'd all met in Mexico, Sally and Mike had shared a mutual attraction and undeniable chemistry. But after the awkward attempt to kiss her, she had put him off. While they were friendly, Sally was still trying to gauge how much of that awkwardness might remain.

"Are you sure you wouldn't rather stay with me at my home? I have plenty of room," Mike said.

"Oh no," Sally said. "We don't want to be a bother. We rented a nice room at that resort hotel you recommended. I heard they have a good restaurant too."

"That's true. It's a local favorite." Mike nodded.

25

"Hope they got good Wi-Fi," Pearl said, holding her phone in the air and moving it around in slow circles. "I got no bars, and I need bars for streamin' *Unsolved Mysteries*."

"Service is pretty spotty up here. But I have a landline at the station and my house if you need it."

Pearl slumped, disappointment pursing her lips.

"What if there's an emergency? How would anyone get in touch with us?" Sally asked, anxiety pricking her skin.

"What do you think's gonna happen? That you'll get trapped in a chimney?" Pearl asked. "Run over by a reindeer?"

"Stop it." Sally waved her off.

"Get tangled in a string of lights?

"I'm just being cautious."

"Choke on a fruitcake?"

"Now, really..."

"Get knocked out by the town Christmas tree fallin' on your head?" Pearl bit back a laugh.

Mike leaned over, turned up the music, and started singing off-key, sending Sally and Pearl into a fit of laughter before they started singing along with him. Sally was quick to join the chorus, and while Pearl was a little slower, she caved after a few measures, trying to match Mike's off-key notes rather than the correct ones sung by Sally and the radio.

5

Reindeer Games

It was dusk when Mike turned right and headed over the covered bridge spanning the river. As the road curved around the mountain, snow drifts gave way to buildings lining both sides of the main road through town.

Lights were strung between the street lamps down the main drag, creating a cascade of color and Christmas joy. It was just like *It's a Wonderful Life*, Sally thought. Lights on the buildings began to flicker to life, casting a soft glow over the entire town. Sally sucked in her breath and clapped her hands together in delight.

"Oh, my stars. Call me George Bailey and keep me away from the bridge," Pearl said, smacking the dashboard. "I feel like I done just stepped into a movie."

"I know," Sally said. "Isn't it glorious?"

Mike chuckled. "You ladies will liven up this town, that's for sure."

"So, what do you have planned?" Sally asked.

"There are activities all week. There's always an electric light parade with a prize for the best float. There's a baking

27

contest, a tree lighting, and all sorts of little gems hidden in businesses and on side streets."

"You're not gonna try to hook us up with another singles group, are you?" Pearl asked, her eyes twinkling with mischief.

"No," Mike said, chuckling and shaking his head. "You'll be glad to know that there are no Santa's Elves Singles that are secretly running drugs. This actually is all about Christmas. When I heard our Sally was such a huge fan, I knew I had to invite you girls out to visit."

Sally's eyes reflected the Christmas lights, completely dazzled. "Oh yes, I'm a huge Christmas fan. This is a dream come true." She swallowed the melancholy threatening to creep in, trying not to think of how much she wished her kids were here. Instead, she focused on what she did have: two wonderful friends in the festive, glimmering Christmas Capital of the Northwest.

The shops were bustling with visitors. Cars inched their way down the street, looking for coveted parking spots made even scarcer by the busy tourist season. Sally scanned the activity and then sucked in a breath. A split rail pen was set up in a parking lot between the coffee house and the antique shop. Inside the pen, three reindeer wandered around, nosing at carrots held out by small hands.

"Oh, can we stop?" Sally asked. Those were real reindeer, and she couldn't think of a more perfect way to start their adventure.

"Don't you wanna go check in to the bed and breakfast?" Pearl asked.

"We can do that later. You promised me all the Christmas spirit in one place. Reindeer are a perfect place to start."

"If you say so. But I am startin' to get hungry, and you know

28

that hangry is right behind."

Mike pulled next to a car and backed into a spot, parallel parking just beyond the coffee shop. The passenger door creaked as Sally pushed it open and climbed out. She had to step over the snowbank and was glad she had worn her boots. Pearl slid to the end and looked down. Then, without comment, she jumped, landing on the sidewalk beyond the snow bank. Miraculously, she did not slip on impact.

"Let's get some coffee while we're here. My fingers are gonna freeze right off." Pearl said, heading towards a cheery decorated café just two doors down from the reindeer pen.

As they reached for the door handle, a fretful, frail-looking older woman met them on her way out. "Oh, Chief Cunningham, I am so glad I ran into you." A bulky black coat and a fur-trimmed hat seemed to be all that kept her from blowing away in the wind. Thick-rimmed black glasses sat on her tiny, sculpted nose, making her large eyes appear even larger and more alarmed. A jittery Pomeranian wearing a black sweater was tucked under her arm beside her sleek Birkin handbag. She pushed forward, and Mike and the girls backed up quickly to make space for the advance, ending up down the steps and back on the sidewalk.

Mike sucked in a breath, exhaling slowly as though bracing himself. "Sure. What can I do for you, Birdie?"

"That woman next door to my house is destroying the neighborhood."

"Is that so?"

She nodded, reaching up to push a strand of stray hair back under her hat and away from her pert little face. "Her boys set up an ice rink in the front yard, and it's an eyesore. Not only that, the yard is full of noisy kids all day and late into the night.

It could be a safety hazard for them, not to mention decent folk!"

Mike shoved his hands into his pockets, and Sally recognized his tone as one of forced patience. "Now, I don't know any law against ice rinks on private property."

"But it's a public nuisance."

Sally's mouth hung open. How could this woman think kids having clean, honest fun in their parents' own yard was a public nuisance? And who could be this grumpy in McKenzie Bridge at Christmastime? Maybe there was more to the story.

Mike stroked his chin in thought. "Are they charging for access to the rink, or have they built a permanent structure around or near it?"

Birdie scoffed, "No. It was some sort of clear plastic they filled with water, let it freeze, and cut it open like a stuffed pig. But Chief Cunningham, the knife might still be out in the yard, waiting to cause severe injury. Next thing you know, they'll be putting up stadium lighting and selling popcorn long after dark."

"Isn't the yard already full of snow?" Mike raised his eyebrows, and Sally nodded despite herself. She was trying to picture what made the kids' actions so offensive and couldn't see the issue.

"Yes, what does that have to do with anything?" Birdie asked, blinking rapidly behind her glasses.

"Excuse me, what exactly is your problem with those kids?" Pearl asked, voicing exactly what Sally had been wondering. Some people had no real problems, so had to create them just to cause trouble. Sally tried to avoid people like that. Wherever they went, conflict wasn't far behind.

The fretful woman's eyes narrowed and looked at Pearl.

"And just who are you?"

"A friend of Mike, here." Pearl pointed to Mike. "I ain't never heard of someone complainin' about an ice rink full of children, especially at Christmas. Seems a bit silly if you ask me."

"Well, maybe you haven't, and I'm not asking you. This is McKenzie Bridge, and we do things a certain way here. We have standards to maintain."

She turned back to Mike and pointed at him, her lip quivering as she tried to affect wrath as well as anyone with a Pomeranian smaller than her purse possibly could. "I expect you to do your job and investigate this. Consider this my formal complaint."

Mike nodded and gave her a practiced smile. "Of course, Birdie. I will be on duty in the morning and take care of it then."

"You can't go make them take it down now?"

Mike glanced at Sally and Pearl, then back to Birdie. "No, ma'am. Now, Gavin is on duty tonight, and if anything happens where you have cause to believe your safety is directly threatened, please call, and we will send someone out."

Birdie ran her gloved hand over her sweater-clad dog's head. "We'll see what the city council has to say about this. You're new here, Chief Cunningham, and I thought you'd want to do a better job making friends."

"I'll keep that in mind," Mike said curtly. She huffed and pushed past them to a black car at the curb, its driver waiting by the open back door.

Pearl shook her head. Sally bit her lip. That woman seemed awful, and certainly like she didn't belong in this picturesque Christmas town. Maybe she'd be better suited to a cave on a mountain.

"She should take her own advice about makin' friends," Pearl muttered to Sally.

As soon as the car pulled away, Mike released his breath and shook his head.

"Are you actually going to go investigate the ice rink in the morning?" Sally asked Mike.

"Heck, no," Mike said. "Birdie Grassley is the town's busybody. Every time I see her, she has a complaint, and it's never anything significant. She'll fixate on a new molehill tomorrow. I guarantee it."

"Well, ain't she a peach?" Pearl said, pushing the door open to the coffee shop. A bell tinkled above them, and the aroma of fresh ground coffee beans greeted them. Pearl slipped off her gloves, shoved them into her coat pocket, and rubbed her hands together to warm them. Sally followed behind her, and Mike brought up the rear, letting the door smack shut behind them. The wood creaked under her feet as Sally stepped forward to get a better look at the menu written in chalk on the wall behind the baristas.

A jovial older woman dressed in a festive red sweater and a Santa hat smiled broadly. "Welcome. What can I get for you?" She looked at Sally and Pearl and then noticed Mike. "Hey, Chief. Day off?"

"Sort of." He ran a hand through his hair.

"Saw Birdie giving you the business on the sidewalk," the woman chuckled. "You deserve a coffee on the house for dealing with that woman so close to Christmas." She smiled and went to fill a cup for him before taking Pearl and Sally's orders.

"It seems like she has quite the reputation," Sally commented to Mike as the baristas prepared their drinks.

"Birdie's family has been here since before the town was founded. Her McKenzie Bridge spirit is a little... intense." Pearl snorted at the carefully chosen word. "Just about everyone in this town has been on the receiving end of it, and people form intense opinions after enough of that."

A few minutes later, they headed outside to see the reindeer, cozy cups of coffee warming their chilly hands. Sally led the way, heading for a man dressed in a brown leather hat and a canvas farmer jacket with *Steve* embroidered near the collar. He was selling carrots for a dollar. Sally dug through her purse for two dollar bills as they waited in line behind a dark-haired little girl in a red beret with a pair of expensively dressed, tired-looking parents. Her mother was an elegant woman near 40, with black hair pulled back into a sleek bun and a red Louis Vuitton scarf. Her father was a paunchy man, several years older, with a receding hairline and a brown plaid coat.

Once Sally paid for her carrots, she giggled as she headed to the edge of the fence. One of the reindeer eyed her and then moved in her direction as she stretched her hand out with one of her carrots. His fuzzy antlers were still growing, and his brown eyes were flat but thoughtful. He pulled his lips back, revealing alarmingly big teeth. Sally gulped and looked back over her shoulder. "Reindeer are vegetarians, right?" she asked Steve.

Standing on the other side of the enclosure, the little girl in the red beret froze, eyes widening as she overheard the question. She tugged on her father's jacket as if she wanted to verify this with him, but her father waved her off in favor of what seemed to be a quiet argument with her mother.

Steve shifted the carrots in his arms, smiled, and winked. "As long as you aren't a carrot, you are in no danger of getting

33

eaten."

"Did you know that they're technically caribou?" Mike asked, leaning on the railing next to Sally.

"I didn't. They're so adorable." Sally leaned on the fence and smiled, thoroughly enchanted.

"She packed her light-up Santa hat, you know. She wanted to wear it on the plane, but I threatened to turn her in to airport security if it even poked out of her carry-on," Pearl chortled.

"Did you forget to add 'bah, humbug' to the end of that sentence?" Sally asked.

"Look here, I am doin' my best to dredge up some Christmas spirit on account of your kids leavin' you all alone. Heck, I even traded sunny tropical weather for this snow-capped tinsel-trimmed hellhole that–"

Mike interrupted. "Ladies! You're here now, and McKenzie Bridge has a way of rewarding a great attitude."

"Yeah, well, I'll do my best," Pearl said, crossing her arms.

"Will you be able to join in the festivities with us?" Sally asked.

"I should be able to take a fair amount of time off as long as things stay quiet, but I'll still have to keep an eye on things. If you get bored or start to miss me too much, a ride-along in my cruiser is always an option." He winked.

"Ride-along? Like to crime scenes?" Pearl asked, her surly mood seeming to melt with the curious draw of true crime in real time.

"Well... more likely, we would be sitting by the side of the road in an obvious spot to encourage people to slow down," Mike admitted.

"Sure am glad we flew across the country to sit in the back of a cop car on the side of the road," Pearl quipped.

Mike grinned. "Pearl, I've missed you. What do you say we get you girls settled?"

"Wait, I have one more carrot to feed the deer." Sally waved the carrot around and then stuck her arm out. Another reindeer, larger with huge antlers, sauntered up and sniffed the carrot. Then he turned to walk away. "Hey. He turned me down. What a carrot snob."

Another reindeer was still chewing the last carrot he had scored from the little girl in the beret. Empty-handed, she was now staring wistfully at the animals while her parents bickered. In search of another prospect, the reindeer made his way over to Sally and snatched the carrot out of her hand in three chomps.

Sally wiped her hands on her jeans and beamed. "What a wonderful way to start our visit. Thank you for stopping."

Heading back to the truck, Sally noticed that a news team seemed to be setting up across the street.

"What's all this about?" Pearl asked, pointing to the media presence. "Did someone overdose on eggnog or get shot or somethin'?" She shook her finger at Mike. "I'd rather sit bored in the back of your cop car than wind up on the wrong end of another criminal enterprise."

6

Holiday Farms

The trio drew nearer, pausing to watch two reporters who seemed to be preparing for a live shot. The pretty young blonde and older dark-haired man struggled to pull microphone cords through the back of their festive sweaters before clipping the mics to their collars. Outside a television-branded trailer, a green awning had been pulled out to shelter their temporary studio. Their team had created a set that looked like a cozy cabin, complete with a fireplace and plush armchairs for the reporters.

"They set up here every year. It's a station out of Portland, and they camp out in town and do live reports throughout the week before Christmas," said Mike.

Sally was mesmerized. She had never seen a television show of any kind being produced live.

"They always wear all those cosmetics?" Pearl asked, wrinkling her nose. "They look like Oompa Loompas."

Mike chuckled. "I think it's stage makeup. All those production lights will wash you out and make you look like a ghost unless you've done it a certain way."

Pearl scoffed. "I still don't trust anybody wearin' that much makeup. It ain't natural."

"I think that's the point." Sally offered.

After a quick mic test, the reporters smoothed their clothing, settled into their armchairs, and smiled. "We are broadcasting live from the Christmas Capital of the Northwest," said the bleached blonde in a practiced, polished lilt. Her heavily lined eyes sparkled with excitement.

"That's right, Brenda, and it is picture-perfect as always, just like you." Her counterpart leaned forward and playfully swatted her leg. He was on the outer edge of television-worthy looks. The wrinkles in his forehead had been smoothed by Botox, and his hair was dyed black, but the lines around his mouth and on his neck couldn't lie. He was clearly a fair bit older than he was trying to look and behave.

"Richard." Brenda swatted his arm in return. "You old charmer. What do we have on the schedule this week?"

"Hey, who are you calling old?" Richard said, smiling at the camera.

Sally, Pearl, and Mike watched for a few minutes as the reporters bantered about the upcoming quilt show and possible inclement weather on the horizon. While it was interesting to see the process of live television in person, Sally realized after a few minutes that it wasn't terribly different from watching it at home or in a hotel room, except that those places were far warmer.

Mike noticed Sally shivering and touched her arm. "Sun's getting low, and the temperature with it. Let's get you and Pearl out to the resort where your hotel room's waiting for you." They wove their way through the crowd back to Mike's truck.

"I hope Holiday Farms ain't an actual farm," Pearl said, buckling her seat belt. "The only kind of manger I wanna get close to is a nice and clean one with Wise Men and baby Jesus."

Mike put on a serious face. "I hate to disappoint you, but it is, actually, a farm."

Sally turned to Mike to see if he was joking. She pictured lots of mud, pigs, and chickens wandering the ground. Were they going to be asked to sleep somewhere they could smell hay and manure? This was going to be a disaster.

Mike wiped his mouth and chuckled. "It's a Christmas tree farm."

"Oh," Pearl sputtered. "Suppose that sounds perfect, given this town's whole theme and all."

Mike pulled out and drove two blocks down, turning right at the corner of the bakery. He headed south to the edge of town. On the right-hand side of the road, a large three-story farmhouse stood sentinel in a sea of green and white. The entire place was lit up with colored twinkle lights. The split rail fence marking the entrance and parking area was draped in rich garlands and white lights. On either side of the main building, along the river, small cabins dotted the landscape.

Mike pulled into the closest parking spot to the front door and hopped out. Sally and Pearl climbed out of the passenger side, and by the time both their feet were on the ground, Mike had their suitcases out of the back of the truck and ready to tow into the lobby just next to the restaurant.

"Where is the hotel?" Sally asked, confused. She'd expected to see their lodgings before anything else after they'd parked.

"The first floor is the restaurant with a gift shop off to the side," Mike explained. "The second floor is a spa with a salon. The third floor is where the owners, Craig and Carol, live.

Through to the back is the new addition that has brand new rooms for guests."

"It's just like a Hallmark movie," Sally said, eyes shining.

"Maybe there is a small-town lumberjack lookin' for love," Pearl whispered, elbowing her in the side.

"Stop it. You are the one who needs a passionate love affair, not me."

"Oh my stars, no, thank you."

Sally caught Mike smirking. He had heard their conversation. She pulled on the hem of her coat. So far, their visit hadn't been awkward, and she didn't want that to change. He had become such a good friend to both Sally and Pearl in the year since their adventure in Mexico, and it would be terrible to spoil something so wonderful.

After they enjoyed a delicious dinner at the restaurant, Sally and Pearl said goodbye to Mike for the evening and found their room. Even though it was a new addition to the resort, it was decorated in a homey and rustic style that made it look lived-in. Gingerbread men dotted the quilted coverlets on the beds. A batch of fresh-baked cookies had been set out for them. Best of all, there was a small, slender, decorated Christmas tree in the corner, its gentle light winking out across the room.

"They thought of everything," Sally breathed, clasping her hands. "Isn't it beautiful, Pearl?"

"Yeah, real pretty," Pearl said, unzipping her suitcase and rifling around for her palm tree-printed pajamas. "I'm unpluggin' that thing at 10 PM sharp, though, on account of my single-ply eyelids and wantin' to get some sleep."

"Alright, you grinch," Sally said with a laugh. As she settled into bed with her book, she glanced across at Pearl to ensure she wasn't the only one hearing the sound of a man and woman arguing, the tones rising and falling tersely in the room beside them.

"Guess someone's grumpier than I am, after all," Pearl said."Even in the Holiday Whoville lah-dee-dah Capital of the Northwest." When she got up to unplug the Christmas tree, she thumped on the wall with her balled-up fist several times, and abruptly, the voices went quiet. "Hope they leave soon. Ain't interested in listenin' to that all week."

7

A Piece of Work

December 16th

The following day, Sally and Pearl were up early. Their comfy hotel beds, along with the time change, left them well-rested and itching for something to do. Luckily, Mike had a plan. Light snow fell and softened the world as they met Mike at the hotel's door. Sally couldn't get over how many times the word "perfect" had already run through her mind since they landed yesterday.

After a short ride across town, Mike parked his truck behind a small one-story brick police station three blocks from downtown. The three of them got out, and he moved towards a pole building on the property to slide open the door.

"Are you sure you girls are up for helping?" Mike turned and asked before stepping into the building. "It's not your project to worry about, and I'd just hate to turn your vacation into an obligation."

"We're sure," Sally said, beaming at Pearl. Sally had always wanted to be part of a project like this. Light parades had been a tradition in her hometown, but she had never had the

41

opportunity to help build a float for one.

"Well, heck. It beats fightin' the crowds downtown. So as long as this place has a heater and a bathroom, I'm as ready as a virgin on his weddin' night." Pearl pulled off her gloves and glanced around the building. Then she walked over to the wood-burning stove in the corner and put her hands up to warm them. "That'll do. Gotta toast my little marshmallows."

Sally followed Mike over to a hay wagon. "What are we making for the parade?"

"Well, that's just the thing. I don't know. Gavin and his wife, Kelly, will be here to help later, but I'm supposed to start the thing. I'm not creative, though, and you have such an eye for color and design that you might be saving my skin here."

"You got any supplies, or are we goin' to build an imaginary float?" Pearl said, wandering in their direction. "Could pile some boxes on a flatbed, drape a big sheet over the whole shebang, and call it a day. We could say we made a 'Holy Ghost.'"

"Pearl!" Sally snorted, disapproval and amusement fighting with each other in her tone.

Mike pointed to a stack of cardboard boxes leaning precariously against the wall. "We have lights, tinsel, and all kinds of other stuff. There's also some chicken wire and wood. I have tools, and I am ready to follow orders."

Sally pulled a notepad out of her purse and dug through the inner pockets for a pen. "We need to draw out a design to start. What's the theme?"

"'Christmas Through the Decades,'" Mike said flatly, as though reciting from rote.

"What the heck does that mean?" Pearl asked.

"Who chose that theme?" said Sally, staring.

Mike carried a box to the trailer and set it down with a thump. "The committee, which used to be headed up by the delightful Mrs. Birdie Grassley. We met her in town yesterday, if you recall."

"Well, that explains it," Pearl said. "Why does a parade float need a theme at all? Christmas is just Christmas."

"Honestly, I have no idea," Mike said, scratching the back of his neck. "I guess it's open to interpretation."

"Let's see what we've got in those boxes and go from there," Sally suggested, lifting the lid off of one.

Pulling out a plastic Santa and several reindeer, she smiled slightly. Things weren't so bad. "We can use these," Sally said, standing them up in a line.

Two hours later, Pearl planted her hands on her hips, frowning. "Well, I guess it's startin' to look like Christmas," she said doubtfully, surveying the float. They had constructed gift boxes and a tree out of wood and chicken wire, but they still needed to add tinsel and lights.

"It's not finished," Sally chided. "As you said before, Christmas is Christmas!"

"Christmas is Christmas, but this is a few chords short of a carol," Pearl said, hardly sounding impressed.

"Oh, stop that humbugging. It's going to be great," Sally said. Turning to Mike, she asked, "Didn't you say Gavin and his wife were coming to help later? How much later did you mean?"

Mike ran a hand over his hair. "They were supposed to be here already. Not sure. Maybe he's dealing with Birdie's ice rink crisis," he joked dryly.

Sally continued rummaging through the boxes. She pointed to a box of tangled lights and said to Pearl, "Here. Untangle these and test them, please."

Pearl huffed but dragged the box over to an outlet and grabbed a folding chair leaning against the wall. Then she got to work.

A blast of cold air temporarily displaced the heat from the wood stove as a young couple entered, quickly pulling the door closed behind them. "About time," Mike said, walking over to shake their hands.

The young man, Sally guessed, was Gavin. He was wearing his police uniform with a thick coat on top."Sorry boss, the twins were up a lot last night."

"I get it. Just glad you're here." Mike introduced Sally and Pearl to Gavin and his wife, Kelly. The pretty girl had sandy brown hair pulled back in a braid and the weary eyes of a new mother. She held out a tin of cookies. "Peace offering," she smiled.

Sally's heart melted. She remembered the days of walking her own babies around the living room, willing them back to sleep. "Thank you, dear."

Kelly set the tin down on the edge of the float trailer and surveyed the progress. Then she headed over to where Pearl was fighting with the ball of lights and offered to help. Pearl was thrilled to hand over the lights for a few minutes and immediately went to grab a cookie. After eating a few more cookies than they meant to, they all worked with a renewed sense of vigor. Gavin and Mike secured the frame to the trailer. While the girls worked on adding tinsel and lights, Kelly gave them a little more insight into the workings of the small town.

"I've been telling Mike," she said, reloading the staple gun, "that it's all about getting cozy with the old money and the residents whose families have been here forever. If you're good with them, the rest of the town will follow."

"Like who?" Sally asked innocently. "Who would you say we should try to get in good with?"

"I heard you guys met Birdie," Kelly said bluntly, pouring herself a cup of coffee from the thermos she had pulled out of a plaid tote bag. "That sure would be a start when it comes to old money and a family here for generations."

"I don't like to talk badly about anybody, but rich or not, that woman is one feather short of a duck," Pearl said.

Kelly held her coffee cup to her lips and smiled, giving Pearl a quick, brisk nod.

"You'll have to excuse Pearl for being rude," Sally said, giving Pearl a stern look. For all they knew, Kelly could be friends with Birdie.

"Oh, don't worry about me. I live here. I know she's cuckoo for Cocoa Puffs."

"Really?" Sally asked, staring. It seemed like Mike hadn't been exaggerating about that reputation.

Kelly nodded. "She thinks everybody's out to get her. If anything happens in this town and she's remotely close to it, she is sure it was aimed at her. According to Birdie, she's always the target of some revenge plot or conspiracy if she's not catching her death of some new and awful disease." She rolled her eyes before taking a sip of coffee.

Gavin chuckled. "Remember when the house next to hers caught fire? She was sure somebody had done it, hoping the flames would jump over to her place and burn it to the ground."

Gavin, Kelly, and Mike all laughed.

"Has she always been like that?" Sally asked, feeling a little bad for the paranoid older woman.

"She was always a bit eccentric, but after her husband died, she went off the deep end. They had one of those marriages you dream about. They'd walk around holding hands even as adults. Guess a Pomeranian isn't the same."

"How sad," Sally said under her breath, feeling even worse. While the antics of the town crazy lady were funny on the surface, she understood the grief that came along with losing a spouse. How painful must it have been for Birdie to lose her husband after being best friends with him?

"Come on, Sally. Both of us lost our husbands, and we done managed to stay mostly sweet and pleasant," Pearl said.

"Both of us?" Sally asked skeptically.

"Hey, I say it like it is and speak my mind. Always have, ain't changin' now," Pearl said defensively.

Gavin chuckled. "Don't worry about it. Birdie's paranoia is legendary. Most people have heard her cry wolf a hundred times. If her old money didn't go so far back, people wouldn't indulge her as much as they do, and even so, there are limits for any reasonable person."

"I am an extremely reasonable person, and as much as I want to put her mind at ease, I have to agree," admitted Mike. "Even in a quiet town, there's such a thing as wasting law enforcement's time. If she'd spent half as many minutes knitting as she spent filing complaints against her neighbors, she'd have a whole shop full of Christmas sweaters by now."

"Ugly ones, probably," Pearl snickered. "If she's makin' a float for this parade, what do you reckon the theme is? 'Little Dogs Dressed in Chanel?'"

Sally laughed along with the others, but the sound was significantly less hearty. She wondered what the fretful woman was doing now. Was she surrounded by her expensive things but otherwise all alone for Christmas?

"Doesn't she have anyone besides the dog?" Sally asked.

"Her nephew Trevor lives with her. Don't even get me started on him. He's a real piece of work," Kelly said, rolling her eyes.

Eventually, they decided to stop for the night. Sally's back ached from bending over to staple lights. Sally was grateful when Mike insisted on treating them to dinner at the hotel restaurant. As they passed around plates of roasted potatoes, green beans, and perfectly-fried chicken, Mike presented them with an idea. "I was thinking that tomorrow we could go get a tree."

"We got a tree. It's about yay high and sittin' in the corner of our room," Pearl said, holding her chicken leg up over the table before biting into it.

"I mean a real tree, for my house. "

Sally set her glass of wine down. "Really? Can we cut our own? I've always wanted to do that at a tree farm in Michigan."

"We're not getting it from the tree farm," Mike smiled, a twinkle in his eye.

8

Good Place to Dump a Body

December 17th

Sally and Pearl shared a look of concern when Mike pulled his truck over to the side of the mountain road and turned off the engine.

"You run outta gas or somethin'?" Pearl asked.

Mike chuckled, "No. We are going to cut down a fresh tree. Come on." Without another word, he climbed out of the truck and walked to the back. Sally and Pearl sat frozen for a moment before he appeared next to the passenger side window holding up a chainsaw, grinning like a madman.

"Great. Your boyfriend is gonna chop us up into pieces and leave us for the vultures."

"Oh, stop it," Sally said, swallowing hard and opening the door to climb down. Sally looked at the sweeping valley to one side and the gentle incline leading to the treeline on the other. She couldn't help but think that this would be a great place to dump a body. It was a good thing she trusted Mike. Otherwise, there was no way she'd be out here.

Pearl took the whole thing in stride. "This is my kinda

adventure," she said, stomping through the knee-deep snow in her high-topped, heavy-duty boots.

"Are you sure this is legal?" Sally asked, looking up at the towering pine trees heavy with snow. The only sound aside from their voices was the crunch of the snow under their feet.

Mike trailed behind them carrying a chainsaw. "You'd best believe that the chief of police is sure. You have to buy a permit, but I happen to have ours here in my pocket." He patted the breast of his coat.

"But who owns the trees?" Sally asked.

"This is state property, so we all do."

"Is that why the tree farm turned into a resort instead? Cheap trees?" Pearl asked, swatting the snow off of a low-hanging branch.

"They still run a small tree farm, but it's nothing like it used to be. People come to McKenzie Bridge for the Christmas spirit, but they generally don't feel like trudging up a mountain to cut down a tree. Which is good news, because most of the city-dwellers have no idea how to use a chainsaw, and we'd end up with a lot of injuries or torn-off bumpers if they tried to Griswald their own tree."

"I see what you mean," Sally said, biting the inside of her cheek as she tried to picture the family they'd seen at the reindeer enclosure trying to chop down a Christmas tree. The father's expensive silk tie could get tangled up in the chainsaw. The mother's fur-trimmed coat might get snagged on the branches as they tried to carry it off. Sally supposed that the little dark-haired girl in the red beret might have fun if her parents could get along for more than four seconds.

"Any bears out here? Or wolves? Bigfoot?" Pearl asked.

"Don't worry about that. Bears are hibernating. We could

run into an elk or a cougar. But it's unlikely." Mike paused before adding, "Bigfoot's even more unlikely."

Sally tugged on the hem of her jacket. Her eyes darted around. Elk? Cougars? She wasn't worried about Bigfoot, but running across a cougar would be terrifying.

"Shoulda brought my gun," Pearl said. "Why do I never got my gun with me when I need it?"

Pearl and her gun. She'd griped about not having it in Mexico, too. Pearl had been trying to talk Sally into getting a handgun for months, but she had no interest in carrying one. Why should she? As long as she had Dirty Harriet living with her, she was covered.

"Pearl, you don't need your gun!" Sally fought the urge to roll her eyes, offering a tense smile. "You need some Christmas spirit. That's why we're here, remember?"

"Yeah, yeah. My memory ain't going," Pearl grumbled. "Gonna listen over here for cougars."

Mike turned to Sally. "What kind of tree should we get? If you're wondering, we can go much bigger than your hotel room's decoration or anything growing at Holiday Farms."

"The biggest one that will fit in your living room, of course." Sally wondered if Mike had enough lights and ornaments for a tree of her ideal size. If he didn't, they would have to buy more, all in the name of perfection.

Mike smiled. "Alright then. Let me know when you see one you like, and I'll let you know if the ceiling is high enough."

Sally nodded. Chopping down a tree for Christmas had been a dream of hers since she was a little girl, and it had taken until she was in her sixties for her to finally have the chance. She rubbed her hands together, thankful for the heating packets she had shoved into her boots and gloves before they left.

Between the passing clouds, the sun shimmered off the snow like diamonds. It was so bright her eyes chased the shadows of the trees to avoid the reflected light. She should've brought sunglasses.

When Mike stopped, Sally looked up. Shielding her eyes, she surveyed the line of trees in front of them. There it was. A ray of sunshine broke through the clouds and shined directly on the tree. It was as if heaven had opened up and bestowed its blessing. She stomped through the snow to lean in and sniff the branches, running her fingers along the needles. It all came together in a perfect blend of soft needles and strong branches. "Is this one too tall?"

Mike surveyed the tree, walking around the bottom. Then his eyes traveled up to the single branch, stretching out at an awkward angle. He squinted one eye. "It might be a little tall."

"A little? That tree is halfway to heaven," Pearl pointed out. "Unless you live in a castle, might be best to find somethin' else."

Sally looked over at her and frowned. "You just think that because you're so short."

Mike squatted and pulled the branches apart, examining the trunk and several entry points. "It's a little tall, but we can just cut up from the ground a bit."

"That's a great idea," Sally said as Mike fired up the chainsaw and started cutting a few feet up from the ground. Pearl and Sally huddled together, watching Mike work.

After a few minutes, he called out, "Timber!" Sally and Pearl jumped back as the tree fell onto a plush, powdery cushion of snow.

Mike grunted as he leaned down to grasp the tree's trunk, preparing to drag it back to the pickup truck. "It's going to look great on the stand," he said. "We'll drill a hole in it and set it right up."

As they made their way back through the snow, they caught a glimpse of red through the trees.

"Good grief," Pearl said. "Didn't think we'd see anyone else out here stompin' through the snow. Think I recognize 'em, though."

Sally stared as the small group drew closer. Sure enough, it was the family from the reindeer enclosure. Her eyebrows shot up.

"Well, butter my butt and call me a biscuit. Never thought I'd see those prissy city folks out here," Pearl said, as though she'd read Sally's mind a few minutes earlier.

They paused and watched the man and woman arguing about whose turn it was to drag the tree. The little girl in the red beret caught sight of them staring. She raised her mittened hand to wave, and Pearl waved back, exaggerating the motion of her arm to the point where her whole body was almost swinging around like she was using a hula hoop.

"Pearl, you look silly," Sally chuckled.

"I don't give a damn," Pearl said, continuing to wave. "Ain't no other adult's been happy to see that child in the last few days, I can tell you."

"Do you think so?" Sally asked, timidly raising her hand to wave back at the little girl.

"Heck, I know it. She's got eyes for what's happenin' all around her, and her mommy and daddy just got eyes for what ain't."

They trudged back to the road. Pearl was quiet, and Sally thought she must be thinking about the little girl. Sally draped her arm around her friend and squeezed her close. As much as she had loved their outing, she sighed in relief when she saw the truck. The cold had worn through her defenses right down to her bones.

Mike heaved the tree into the pickup truck's bed while Sally and Pearl watched. Sally had offered to help, worried about the effect all this physical labor in the cold might have on his heart, but he'd waved her off, insisting on handling it by himself. "You girls warm up," he said as he climbed into the car and started it, turning the heat on high. While Sally and Pearl settled into their warming seats and waited for the heat to thaw their feet and fingers, Mike tied down the tree with bungee cords, brushing off a bit of additional snow. Finally, he climbed back into the truck and smiled. "I think it's safe to say we got a good one."

"This was so fun," Sally said. She had always wanted to do this, and it was just as she imagined, maybe minus that strange, sad family. Her nose was runny from the cold, and her fingers started to warm up as she rubbed her hands together in front of the vent.

"It was more satisfyin' than goin' to the town tree lot or unboxin' a plastic tree, that's for sure," Pearl added, pressing her hands to the vents.

They crept back down the mountain, Mike driving with the slippery conditions in mind. The tires occasionally caught on patches of ice and sent them sliding. Each time, Sally would reach out to brace herself on the dashboard, wide-eyed and sure they would slip right off the mountain.

"Sorry ladies, occupational hazard," Mike said apologetically, pumping the brakes to test their traction.

"Oh my stars, I can't imagine having to drive in this for months every year." Pearl shook her head.

After what seemed like an eternity, they finally made it back to town, where the roads were clearer and better lit, even in the rare places where they weren't downright festive. "Let me take the tree home, and you can hang out for a little while and get warmed up," Mike said, turning onto a street they hadn't been down yet during their stay. "If you're feeling up to it, you can stay and decorate for a bit and I'll fix dinner. When you're ready, I can drive you back to the hotel."

"Ain't you glad your boyfriend is such a gentleman?" Pearl whispered in Sally's ear. Sally nudged her back none too gently.

"He's *not* my boyfriend," she hissed.

"Fine, 'gentleman caller,' or whatever floats your boat," Pearl snorted. Sally nudged her again a little harder, worried that Mike might hear.

9

The Third Wheel

"This is amazing," Sally said, stepping into Mike's A-frame log cabin. There was a stone fireplace reaching to the ceiling and flanked by floor-to-ceiling windows looking over the valley. A large painting of a deer in the snow hung over the mantel. An overstuffed brown leather sectional with a red plaid wool blanket thrown over the arm sat in front of the hearth. The whole place had a masculine, lodge-like feel to it. It smelled like cedar and eucalyptus. Low, ambient Christmas music was playing from discreet, well-placed speakers, and in the corner next to the fireplace was the perfect spot for the tree.

Mike dropped his keys on the small oak table by the front door and pushed the door shut. "Thanks. It has a great kitchen too. It's the reason I bought this place."

"You like to cook?" Pearl asked, not trying to hide her surprise. "Most men I've met only boil water, and even then, only when the situation is dire."

Mike grinned. "I do. My grandma taught me. I'm not much of a baker, but I never met a cut of meat I couldn't turn into a five-star roast. If you want a five-star breakfast, I can also

55

pull that together, even if most days I just end up starting my day with oatmeal and fruit."

Pearl kicked off her boots. "Well, ya learn somethin' new every day. Guess I gotta start callin' you Chef Ramsay."

Mike rubbed his hands together. "It's chilly in here. Let me drag that tree in, and then I'll get a fire going."

"I'll help," Sally said.

Ten minutes later, Sally sat on the wood bench next to the door and pulled her boots off. She slid out of her coat and looped it on the hook next to Mike's. Tiptoeing around the slush melting on the tiled floor of the foyer, she followed Mike to the fireplace, where he squatted, pulling logs from a pile next to the mantle and stacking them inside. She shifted her gaze to the window and beyond. The fading sunlight was casting long shadows over the mountain. Trees hung heavy with snow, lower branches kissing the ground. The view was like a postcard.

Meanwhile, Pearl parked herself on the couch and pulled the red blanket around her shoulders, scrolling through her phone.

Sally turned from the window when she heard the sound of a crackling fire coming to life. Mike stood with a satisfied smile, planting his hands on his hips. Sally moved beside him and held her arms out to be warmed by the heat of the flames.

"What's that smell?" Pearl asked from the couch. Sally wondered the same thing. She was famished from the long day in the woods and at the station. It smelled like spices and simmering meat and potatoes.

"I told you I could make a mean roast, didn't I? It's been slow-cooking in the crock pot all day. It should almost be ready," Mike said, turning to Pearl.

"I suggest we drink, eat, and decorate, in that order," Pearl said, looking up from her phone. "Then maybe drink some more," she added as an afterthought.

Sally looked to Mike, who smiled. "Your wish is my command. Sally, what do you say we go open a bottle of wine?"

Sally smiled back at him. "Sounds great." She patted her hair and straightened her sweater, her mouth suddenly dry. She hadn't been alone with Mike since they arrived, and something about being alone with him in his kitchen seemed extra intimate. Was this what her life would have been like if she had married someone like Mike instead of Harold?

Things didn't work that way, of course. They wouldn't be the people they were if they hadn't lived their lives up to this point. Maybe they would have grown just as grating to each other as the worst parts of her marriage with Harold, though Sally needed to actively try to make herself believe it when her feet and her heart felt so light in his presence.

Mike headed for the kitchen, glancing over his shoulder to see that she was following. She hesitated only briefly as she trailed after him, her socks quiet on the wide-planked wood floor. They rounded the corner and came to a beautiful kitchen with dark green lower cabinets and unfinished, rustic birch upper cabinets. It was stunning.

Mike opened the door of a wine fridge tucked under one of the cabinets and pulled out a bottle. He read the label, frowned, and slid it back inside before choosing another bottle. "Ah, this is what I was looking for." He held the bottle up for Sally to see, and she leaned closer.

She didn't recognize the label but trusted Mike's taste in wine. "Looks perfect."

Mike smelled like musk and cedar. His eyes glowed in the

reflection of the firelight bouncing off the window. He pulled three glasses down from the cabinet and poured them each a generous amount. He handed Sally a glass and lifted his own. "To a very memorable Christmas." His eyes smoldered as he looked at Sally.

Sally lifted her glass and focused on keeping her hand steady. Her breaths were fluttery and shallow. She looked up at him from under her lashes. "To a perfect Christmas," she revised, raising her glass.

"Hey, are y'all gonna bring me a glass of wine, or are you just gonna leave me here to die of thirst?"

Mike cleared his throat and broke their shared gaze, chuckling. "We'd better get back in there to rescue Pearl." He flashed a regretful smile, and Sally nodded. She pushed a curl behind her ear and followed Mike back into the living room.

Mike handed Pearl her glass of wine and then excused himself to plate the roast and set the table for the three of them.

"Ain't gonna be a third wheel, my foot," Pearl mumbled. "If I'd known y'all were gonna get all cozy in a mountain lodge, I might have stayed home with my murder shows."

"Why would you say that?" Sally asked, cupping her wine glass with both hands. "I'm sorry you're feeling left out. Maybe tomorrow you and I should do something, just the two of us."

Pearl shifted uncomfortably. "I always thought you and Mike would be cute as a couple of doodlebugs together. That's the truth. Guess that grinch attitude I got is makin' me a bit selfish."

"Never," Sally said, sitting next to Pearl and taking a sip of wine. "I promise not to slip off too much without you as long as you promise to let me know when things are bothering you. You always speak your mind, remember?"

"And you always take teasin' like it's gospel. Have your whirlwind romance. It ain't hurtin' me none."

"Can you help me strike a balance?" Sally asked with a smile, even if she would hardly call what she had with Mike a "romance."

"Only if you let me help trim that unreasonably gigantic tree," Pearl agreed, letting Sally hug her. "After gettin' a belly full of that tasty-smellin' man meat, of course."

"Oh, stop it," Sally laughed, swatting at her playfully.

10

To the Salon

December 18th

"Maybe I'll get my hair done before we go shopping," Sally said the next morning, standing in front of the mirror in their room and running her fingers through her locks. She had meant to get it cut before they left, but had run out of time. The curls reached beyond the nape of her neck and were starting to look unkempt.

"Where you gonna get it cut?" Pearl asked before chuckling, "Maybe we could find Birdie and ask who does hers."

"Mike said there was a spa upstairs. Maybe they have an opening," Sally suggested.

"You can't let just anybody take scissors to your head. You could end up bald."

"I'm willing to risk it. My hair is so curly that if they mess it up, the curls will hide the worst of it anyway. And I need to cover this gray."

Even though Sally's hair had long since turned gray, the world would never know as she had faithfully dyed it blonde since the first strands of gray showed up in her thirties. For years she had used box dye, but lately, she had started going to the salon to let a young woman with a nose ring shampoo, color, and cut it for her. It was a luxury she thoroughly enjoyed.

Sally lifted the receiver and dialed the yellowed-with-age push-button hotel phone. She was transferred to the salon and found out they'd had a cancellation for that morning. "I'll take it," she said, smiling. "Thank you so much."

Sally hung up the phone. "What luck. I don't know how my hair got so out of hand, and now I don't have to deal with that mess for our perfect Christmas." She absently patted her hair and turned to grab her sweater.

Pearl was lying on the bed, her ankles crossed, flipping through a magazine she had grabbed at the gift shop's news-stand. "How long you gonna be gone?"

"It'll probably take an hour or so." She slid on her sneakers. "Who knows, though? I might even get a manicure if they have time for me."

Pearl stared at her. "Just make sure you knock before you walk in. I may not recognize you, and that goofy little tree in the corner would be good for clobberin' intruders." She grinned mischievously.

"Oh, stop it," Sally giggled, waving her off and grabbing her purse from the bed. She pulled the door open and stepped into the hallway. The faint scent of new paint and carpet still lingered in the air. Sally felt like she was floating as she headed to the hotel lobby. She hummed a favorite Christmas tune and tried to decide how she wanted her hair to look. She'd never been particularly good at communicating exactly what she was going for, especially at the salon. Maybe Pearl was right, and without her usual girl with the nose ring, she'd fail here and end up with something ridiculous. She girded herself, deciding

61

that it would be fine as long as she organized her thoughts before speaking.

At the front of the restaurant, she ascended the wide oak staircase to the second floor. Upstairs, the space had been split into two separate areas. On the left was a waiting room with an open railing looking down on the lower level. Oversized, comfortable chairs with vintage floral fabric were gathered around a white shabby-chic coffee table. Behind two of the chairs was a glass door with an *Open* sign hanging at an off-kilter angle. Above that, it said *Style by Sheila* in bubble letters. Inside, a trendy-looking woman in her late 20s was talking loudly on her cell phone. She wore dark eyeliner under heavy bangs, and leaned against the back of one of the salon chairs with her hip popped out. "I don't care what he says. I can't wait forever for a ring," she said, seeming heedless of who might be overhearing her.

Sally took a step towards the door and then paused. Should she knock on the glass? Maybe she should wait. She moved to one of the chairs facing the glass door and sank into the seat, waiting for the girl to notice her. But she kept talking and started to pace, her heels clicking over the tile floor.

"I know he says he wants to wait till he gets the money, but that could be 100 years from now, and I am not getting any younger. He promised to get us out of this town. Can you picture me wearing shorts year-round, with my own salon in Los Angeles? That's where I belong, not some isolated tourist trap in the mountains."

Sally tugged on the hem of her jacket, trying to decide what to do. She surveyed the magazine selection on the coffee table and slipped an outdated gossip magazine out of the stack.

"Yeah, and I'm gonna talk with him about it tonight,"

the woman continued after a pause just long enough for her conversation partner to get a few words in edgewise. When she noticed Sally sitting out in the lobby, she stopped mid-sentence. "Shoot, I'm sorry. I have a client. I'll call you back." She turned to Sally with a wide, plastic-looking smile on her face and pushed open the door. Sally could hear soft Christmas music playing in the background as the woman said, "I'm so glad you could come in. Last-minute cancellations are part of the job, but I hate to have my chair sitting empty during the busy season."

"Thanks," Sally said, smiling. "I'm glad, too. My hair's a mess. Are you Sheila?" She pointed to the name in bubbled letters on the door.

"That's me," Sheila smiled. "And I know that someone named Sally called for this appointment a little while ago, so that must be you. You've come to the right place. We'll get you fixed up before lunchtime."

Sally stepped into the salon through the door Sheila was holding for her. A variety of mirrors and chairs greeted her. She watched Sheila's heels clack across the floor past a row of sinks.

"Take a seat anywhere you'd like. What are we doing today?" Sheila walked to the tall cabinet in the corner and opened it, rummaging through the pastes and pomades inside.

Sally ducked her head and slid into the black vinyl seat, staring at herself in the mirror. "Oh, I don't know. I need it cut for sure, and my roots are terrible right now."

"Well, that's easy enough to fix. We can touch up your roots and give you a nice new cut. How short do you think you want it?" Sheila stood behind her, pulling at Sally's curls, straightening them out to get a sense of their length, and moving her fingers up the strands to show Sally a few options. "Do you want me to grab you a look book?"

"Yes, thank you," Sally replied. "That would be very helpful. I don't want another old lady haircut."

A minute later, Sheila returned with a recently-published magazine full of fresh, fashionable hairstyles and handed it to Sally. She retreated to the work counter and got her bowl and brush ready to mix developer.

Sally frowned. There were a million hairstyles in this magazine, and she felt a bit overwhelmed. But as she flipped through the glossy pages, she found a full page of hairstyles for women who were "mature, but young at heart." *Perfect*, she thought. She decided on stacked bob. It was long enough to tuck behind her ear if she wanted and had some wispy pieces that came forward to frame the face. She committed the picture to memory to make sure she didn't forget once Sheila came back.

The smell of hair color permeated the small salon. Sheila returned, continuing to stir the hair color with her brush in a red plastic bowl. "Do we have a winner?" she asked.

"What do you think of this? I want to be able to make it look festive, so... if you have a better idea, I trust you."

Sheila leaned over, carefully studying the photo. "Festive, huh? I know exactly what we should do, especially with your curls. It will look fantastic. Trust me?"

Sally nodded. Sheila draped a purple cape around Sally's shoulders and snapped it under her hairline. Picking up her bowl of color, she gave the concoction one more stir and then set it down. Grabbing a yellow comb from her station and holding it in one hand, the color brush in the other, she set to work parting sections of curls and coloring Sally's roots. After a rinse and shampoo, Sheila trimmed her hair, which was as exciting as it was terrifying for a salon-goer as anxious as Sally. Still, it turned out better than she'd thought it would, and she smiled as Sheila set the blow dryer on low and fluffed out her curls.

"I'm going to add a little festive flair to the ends."

"Flair?" Sally's palms were sweating. What did that even mean?

"Don't you worry," Sheila said, pulling a clean plastic bowl and brush out of her station's drawer. "What brings you to McKenzie Bridge, Sally?"

Sally wondered if Sheila was trying to distract her from her very reasonable question about flair. "My best friend and I are visiting Mike Cunningham. Do you know him?"

Sheila paused and looked at Sally in the mirror, snorting slightly. "You can't fart in this town without everybody knowing. So when a handsome new police chief shows up in town, everybody takes notice."

Sally's cheeks flushed red. She couldn't argue about Mike being handsome. She grasped for something interesting to say in response and came up short. Luckily, Sheila kept talking.

"There just aren't enough eligible men in this town. Although, I managed to find a great guy."

"Oh?" Sally asked.

"We've been together for over a year now. You probably heard a little bit of my phone call, depending on how long you were waiting outside, but I'm just waiting for him to make it official." She held her left hand in the air and wiggled her fingers.

"What's he like?" Sally asked, happy to have the focus off of her.

65

"He's adorable. He's so caring. He has this aunt who is getting on in years and, you know, losing it a little bit. We worry about her. But even with all of that going on, he has been so attentive."

"That's nice," Sally said, her smile growing a little tense and rigid as she watched Sheila starting to mix more color. She frowned slightly. Weren't her roots done already? And why did she have the nagging feeling that she had already met this aunt?

Sheila spun her chair around, and Sally couldn't see what she was doing. Her eyes settled on a bowl of apricots on a small decorative table.

"Would you like one?" Sheila asked "I can grab one for you. The only thing is that I'd need to get the pit back. I use them for my garden when there's not, you know, a huge snow dump on the way."

"Oh, sure," Sally said. If she was eating a piece of fruit, Sheila wouldn't expect her to talk at all. She accepted the apricot, nibbling at it slowly as she felt the dye-laden brush moving along the lower parts of her hair. What was happening back there?

"My friends say that a year isn't long enough to get engaged," Sheila said, painting color on in thick layers. "But that's a pretty long time. It feels long enough. We're really in love, and I even take care of his aunt a little bit when she needs extra help. Have you heard about the recipe for Engagement Chicken?"

"Engagement Chicken?" Sally asked between apricot nibbles. The fruit was so tiny, she'd already reached the pit on one side, in spite of her intentionally small bites.

"It's a chicken roast that's so incredibly delicious it's supposed to make a man propose on the spot. It's got, um…"

the brush paused mid-stroke as Sheila tried to remember the ingredients. "You stuff some garlic and lemons inside, and also Spanish onions, and you use some dry white wine."

"Oh, that's it?" Sally chuckled, struck by how young Sheila seemed. "I've made that chicken a hundred times, and never got a proposal out of it."

"Are you married?" Sheila asked curiously. "I forgot to look for a ring before I put your apron on."

"I'm widowed," Sally replied. "My husband Harold died about a year and a half ago."

"Oh, I'm sorry," Sheila said, placing a hand briefly on Sally's shoulder.

"Don't be sorry. We had some beautiful times." Sally tried to make them sound better than they were, feeling bad about bringing down a girl just hoping for her boyfriend to propose. "If you're in love and think he's the one, just try to be patient. I'm sure he'll pop the question when he's ready."

"Yeah." Sheila sounded noticeably brighter. "Oh, wow, Sally, not to spoil anything before it's ready, but you're going to love your hair flair." Foil crinkled as Sheila wrapped the ends of Sally's hair. "Let's get you under the dryer to get it to process faster."

"What's your boyfriend's name?" Sally asked, the foil on her head crinkling as she shuffled toward the dryers.

"Trevor. Why do you ask?" Sheila said, blinking.

"No reason," Sally said, furrowing her brow. She thought back to what Kelly had said about him being a real piece of work.

When Sally returned to the chair, Sheila insisted on finishing her hair with Sally's back turned to the mirror. When she finally spun her around to the mirror, Sally's mouth dropped open in shock.

"You could be a bit nicer about it," Sally moaned back in the hotel room. "At least stop laughing so much."

Pearl gulped like a dying fish for air, wheezing and gasping in a fit of hysterical laughter. "Can't. You look like you fell asleep up against a freshly painted sleigh."

"I do not!" Sally looked sadly at the mirror, running her fingers through curls dyed red and green at the ends.

"What did you ask for?" Pearl chortled. "The Peppermint Patty Perm?"

"That doesn't make any sense. Peppermint Patty was a little tomboy who never fussed with her hair at all."

"Huh. Thought it was a Christmas thing," mused Pearl.

"If you must know, I asked for something 'festive,'" said Sally miserably.

Pearl snorted. "There's your problem right there. And then of course, you didn't stay and make her fix it."

"I could never. She already had so much on her mind, and she was really sweet, all things considered." Sally supposed she'd have to be, if her boyfriend Trevor was as bad as Kelly had made him sound. Then again, there was always the chance that Trevor was just as nice as Sheila said and Kelly just didn't know him as well.

"Sounds like you paid her to wreck your hair while she treated you like a free therapist. You should have just stayed here with me and watched *Mysterious Mountain Murders* instead of lettin' your hair become an innocent victim."

"Oh, shoot," Sally said, pinching the bridge of her nose "Mike. We're seeing Mike later at the parade."

"Aw, honey, your hair ain't so bad. It's festive, like you

68

wanted. I was kiddin' about it lookin' like a murder victim," Pearl said. "You love Christmas so much that, heck, you'll probably start lovin' your hair once you get used to it."

"I'm going to buy a big knit cap with a pom pom on it in the meantime," Sally sighed. "There are some cute ones in the gift shop."

"There's lookin' on the bright side. Shoppin' always makes things better."

As Sally turned to leave, Pearl cleared her throat. "It's a small world, by the way. I popped out earlier to go see if I could find some cabernet-"

"Pearl!" Sally interjected, "It's not even noon."

"And I'm on vacation. Anyway, guess who's stayin' next to us?"

"Who?" Sally asked, genuinely mystified.

"That family, the one whose little girl was wavin' at us in the woods. Guess that's why they keep poppin' up in places."

"Small world," Sally agreed quietly, thinking of the arguing they'd heard on their first night.

11

I Love a Parade

"What time's this thing kickin' off?" Pearl asked, wrapping her chunky peacock blue scarf tighter around her neck. She held the staple gun up to the strand of lights she was attaching to the edge of the trailer and pushed until she heard the *ka-chunk*.

"Six. Make sure you don't catch the wires," Mike reminded her. He was pushing the generator down to the back of the trailer, where an intimidating maze of cords was waiting to power the lights.

"I ain't stupid enough to do that. I had a cousin once who *was* stupid and got himself electrocuted. He kinda deserved it on account he was fixin' to rig up a hot tub in the back of his truck and parade around town naked as a jaybird. Last thing I wanna do is fry my insides and miss the parade. We gotta win a trophy after all this hammerin' and hawin' away."

Sally pulled a strand of red tinsel out of the plastic bag after tugging her new reindeer-covered knit cap down around her ears. "I'm just glad we found more tinsel at the discount store. I thought they would've been completely cleaned out this close to the parade."

"Thank the stars. We better all get movin'. The parade's startin' in two hours, and we can't have half-decorated candy canes." Pearl continued her stapling.

Sally raised her eyebrows, impressed with Pearl's new gusto. Was Pearl finally starting to feel some Christmas spirit? She stepped cautiously over the cords and weaved through the finished tinsel and lighted candy cane forest to the one candy cane that was missing red stripes. She pulled the tape out of her pocket and ripped off a piece with her teeth, attaching the strand of tinsel to the bottom and weaving it diagonally around the white PVC pipe. "After this, we need to make sure the lights inside the gingerbread house turn on and the tree spins," she said, consulting the list she'd made and all but memorized. Years of keeping track of the kids' and Harold's appointments on top of her own had made her incredibly good at keeping track of itineraries.

"Right," Pearl said. "By the way, I gotta say it was a stroke of genius to use that old record player for the turnin' tree."

Mike smiled. "It was Gavin's idea. He might have gotten a late start on this one, but he's been building floats like these for years."

Pearl stepped back to take in the entire display. "That's some fine float-finishin' if I do say so myself."

Sally stood on the trailer, adding the last of the lights to the gingerbread house. "Do you think it looks good?"

"Better than vanilla ice cream on pie," Pearl confirmed, flashing her a mittened thumb-up.

Sally beamed. She had always wanted to build a Christmas light parade float, and Pearl was being so encouraging it was hard not to feel like things were looking up. She lifted her arms and turned her torso to stretch her lower back.

"You ladies sure earned your cookies today," Gavin said, walking in with a fresh tin of sugar cookies. "My wife has been baking all day, and I think we have too many, even with the kids ready to descend like locusts as soon as they get the green light."

At 5:15, the sun had dipped behind the mountains, taking the last of the day's warmth with it. Sally slid into the truck and across the seat next to Mike, ensuring their bodies didn't touch. She was all too aware of the thin strip of space between them filled with its own electricity. Pearl took the window seat so she could wave at the crowds, and Sally wondered if she had shaken off her humbug attitude for her sake. Either that or Pearl was growing more comfortable in McKenzie Bridge.

They eased into traffic, drove two blocks down to the high school staging area, and pulled into the lot, stopping at the entrance for directions on where to park. Christmas lights and grand, glowing displays twinkled and flashed all around them. Some floats still had last-minute additions, tweaks, and repairs being performed by heavily bundled-up crews. One float was utterly dark, an older man yanking on the cord to a generator and swearing up a storm while his wife hushed him, glancing around apologetically at the kids milling about. There were scout troops, dance teams, and the local high school marching band. Mike eased the truck and trailer into a space behind a tractor and hay wagon with a gazebo lit up in white.

"What does a dang gazebo have to do with Christmas?" Pearl asked. "Was their theme 'Things That Take Up Space in a Public Park?'"

"Oh look, I think it's a town square. There are children at the front of it. I bet they're going to sing," Sally said, enchanted. "Let's get out so we can double-check everything on the float."

Pearl opened the door and grabbed the handle to climb down on the running board and the pavement. Sally slid over and followed her. When she rounded the back of the float, Mike was already on the trailer, working to fire up the generator. His breath billowed in front of him as he pulled the chain. Sally crossed her fingers inside her mitten, hoping he'd have better luck with their generator than the profane older man on the darkened float.

It was a one-man job, at any rate. Accepting that she couldn't help out with it, Sally was content to stand at the back of the trailer and watch the other floats for a little while. She had never seen so many lights in one place. A calliope of different Christmas songs overlapped from speakers on various floats, and the band was warming up with disembodied musical phrases and scales. It was perfect.

A blue glow caught her attention, and she walked up a few floats to see what she could only assume was supposed to be a theme involving life and Christmas on another planet. There were strange alien-like characters outlined in blue lights and a version of a Christmas tree that was a giant round ball covered in red glitter and lit from the inside. It was pretty avant-garde compared to the rest of the parade's more traditional offerings. While she considered the possible meaning, multiple families made their way over. Children leaned forward in strollers and pointed. A little girl with dark brown curls poking out from a knit cap giggled and clapped from her perch on her dad's shoulders. Sally turned to a harried-looking young mother and asked, "What is this?"

The young woman shifted her drooling baby to her other hip, blew the hair out of her face, and said, "Not sure what it has to do with Christmas. But *Out of This World* is the only show my kids want to watch. All day, every day."

"Ahh. I remember those days." Sally said. A twinge of melancholy blurred her eyes with tears as she thought about her three children, crowded around the television watching *Sesame Street.* Sally gave them a wave and headed back to find Pearl.

"There you are," Pearl said, reaching up and bopping the puff ball on Sally's hat with her mitten. "We're about ready to rumble! I think everyone in town's made it out to this shindig."

"Mom, Dad!" a high, clear voice called out. The little girl in the red beret they'd seen at the reindeer pen and in the forest was pulling her parents along, holding both their hands and swinging their arms as she walked briskly between them. She looked to be nine or ten years old. Her dark hair was pin-straight, falling down the back of her navy blue coat nearly to her waist."We have to hurry. Otherwise, we won't see *all* of them before they start moving!"

Her mother spoke with a light Japanese accent."Noël, we will see all the floats. That's the point of a parade. You don't have to go looking for them. You stand there, and they go right past you."

"Oh, come on," sighed the father. Pearl and Sally's brows raised in unison. They recognized these voices. They were the ones they had heard arguing through the wall in their hotel room. "Kiyomi, just let her have this. She's put up with a lot, no thanks to you. Can't you just-"

"Just *what*, Patrick? By the time we stomp all over the place looking at the floats just sitting here, there won't be a point in watching the parade at all."

"That's not true, Mom!" Noël insisted, rubbing her hands

together. "It's a completely different thing to see them still and see them moving! This is like getting to go backstage. I want to see both," she added, blinking her large, almond-shaped eyes and peering up through her lashes.

Patrick, her father, seemed to deflate slightly as if his daughter was literally melting him with a look. "Kiyomi, it's good that she wants to see how this stuff is all put together. It could nurture an interest in a STEM field," he offered. Noël smiled up at her mother, nodding.

Kiyomi's smooth brow knitted in irritation. "It's not about that. It's about how she always knows she can butter you up when she wants something, and then the two of you gang up on me. I should have stayed at the hotel."

Patrick opened his mouth to retort, but Noël cut him off by lunging toward her mother, clinging to her arm. "Mom, it would mean so much to me if you watched the light parade with us. I'm so glad we're here. I love you more than anyone."

Patrick looked mildly hurt, but there was a larger crisis the show of affection was averting. It certainly seemed to work. Kiyomi's severity softened, and she rested an elegant, gloved hand on top of Noël's beret. "You're such a good girl. You deserve this vacation. We'll look at all the floats for you."

"We all deserve this vacation," Noël insisted, reaching for her father's hand and squeezing it. "You and Dad work so hard, but you don't have to think about that right now, because Christmas is coming and it's going to be great."

"We agree, then? We'll see all the rest of the floats, for Noël?" Patrick asked, glancing at Kiyomi, who dutifully nodded.

"If we could just see one more, I'd be happy," Noël replied quickly. She skipped over to the police station's float, bypassing the glowing planet in favor of it. Sally couldn't help feeling a little proud of being chosen from among all the other floats.

"Your float is pretty!" the little girl exclaimed, grinning. She had a dimple on her left cheek. "It must have taken so much time to make!"

"Thanks, sweetheart," Pearl said. "Took a couple of days. Reckon it'll be worth it because we're gonna win."

"I think you definitely can," Noël said, cupping her mouth with one hand and leaning in conspiratorially.

"With my staplin' skills? I'm countin' on it. I risked my life for this float. I coulda gotten fried like a Sunday omelet on those wires, but it ain't old Pearl's day."

"Pearl." The little girl started giggling, delighted. "Is that your real name?"

Pearl nodded. "Real as rain, straight from my mama."

"I like it." The girl jauntily offered her little red mitten. "I'm Noël Ishida-Kaczmarek."

Sally watched from a distance. She hadn't seen Pearl interact this much with a child, not even Amelia. It was enchanting to watch.

"Big name for a little girl," Pearl chuckled, reaching out to shake Noël's hand.

"I'll grow into it. It's got part of both of my parents in it, just like me," Noël said, glowing proudly.

"Those your folks over there?" Pearl asked, nodding towards Kiyomi and Patrick, not giving away how much she'd overheard before the little girl approached their parade float.

"Yup. We're on Christmas vacation. It's our first one in forever. They took time off work and everything, and that never happens."

"Noël." Her father beckoned her over, offering Sally and Pearl a subdued wave to acknowledge them.

76

"Coming! Merry Christmas," Noël said, raising her iPhone to snap a quick picture before running back to her parents.

Sally and Pearl watched her grasp her parents' hands like lifelines, holding tightly, nuzzling a bit too fiercely into their sides one after another.

"Oh, my stars," Pearl said softly. "What a sweet little lamb."

Sally smiled at her friend. It wasn't like Pearl to be so sweet. Maybe this town was having an effect on her after all.

12

Head-Scratcher

Sally had never been in a Christmas parade. Her heart soared as she rode next to Mike while Pearl leaned out the window waving at the crowds. As they inched down the parade route, it was a delicate dance to keep pace with the marching band in front of them. Sally kept watch via the rear view mirror and made sure the lights were on and the tree was spinning. The entire route was crowded with watchers of all ages, bundled up and smiling despite the cold. Little children's eyes glimmered with excitement and the anticipation of seeing Santa, who was the grand finale of the parade.

Parents corralled children who yearned to reach out and touch the passing floats. Adults sang along as the marching band, wearing red Santa hats, played a rotation of popular Christmas songs.

The parade route went up Main Street and ended at the McKenzie Bridge Christian Church parking lot. After pulling in, they parked and walked back the three blocks to the town square, where the awards would be announced and handed out.

The mayor, a tall man with a bushy white beard and long black wool coat, stood on a small stage in front of the town Christmas tree. While the judges were crowded together deliberating, the mayor thanked the parade committee and told jokes to kill time. Mike stood to the side of the crowd with Sally and Pearl. Sally had her favorite floats in mind and hoped the judges would agree.

"If we don't win, I'm gonna have a come to Jesus meetin' with those judges."

Mike and Sally shared a look and didn't respond to her comment.

Finally, one of the judges, wearing a sash to identify him, approached the mayor with a piece of paper. He leaned over the stage and examined the contents with intense scrutiny. He straightened and said in a booming voice, "Ladies and gentlemen, this is the moment you've been waiting for. The prize for the best new float goes to 'Out of This World.'" While the crowd applauded, there was a commotion on the side of the stage.

"Uh-oh," Mike said, sighing heavily. "I'll be right back." He took off in the direction of the conflict, leaving Sally and Pearl standing by themselves.

Mrs. Birdie Grassley stomped briskly across the stage, her heavy, dark attire and slender bird-bones at odds with one another. "You can't give the prize to them. I simply won't allow it," she said, loudly enough for the mayor's microphone to pick it up.

The mayor let the microphone fall away from his mouth, but not far enough to avoid being heard by everyone. "Mrs. Grassley, what are you doing?"

"I will not have my Christmas festivities spoiled by this

display of... well. I don't know what that *thing* is. But it doesn't have anything to do with Christmas."

The winning float was a bit of a head-scratcher. Sally only knew what it was because of the young mother she had talked to earlier. As much as Birdie seemed to be overreacting and over-dramatic, Sally couldn't help but agree. What did a futuristic space scene have to do with Christmas? Judging from how the crowd cheered when the winner was announced, she and Birdie were in the minority.

A young man in a tan wool coat and a plaid cashmere scarf bounded up the stairs to try and corral her. "Aunt Birdie, please be reasonable. Don't make a scene." He spoke like these were words he'd repeated many times over the years. The microphones on stage continued to boom the conversation out across the crowd.

"Trevor Grassley, *you* be reasonable. This is a travesty. I can't be the only one who thinks that thing should have been disqualified for being off-theme."

"Come on, Auntie. Stand by the heater and calm down. The committee needs to give out the trophies now."

Birdie's eyes blazed into her nephew as the crowd held their breath. The mayor stepped forward to salvage the situation and said, "Let's have a warm round of applause for the founders of our Christmas Festival, McKenzie Bridge's own dear Birdie Grassley, as well as the late Dr. Bob Grassley." He clapped enthusiastically as Trevor led Birdie off the side of the stage by the crook of her arm, as though she was much older and highly infirm to the point of being unable to find her own way.

The audience, grateful for the break in tension, gladly joined in the clapping, although it seemed more scattered and subdued than the "warm round of applause" the Mayor had requested.

"She is a busybody if I ever saw one," Pearl whispered to Sally, who nodded. As much as she couldn't understand the winning float, she knew that times and traditions had changed, and she had seen how happy it made the kids in the crowd. It was a shame that Birdie had to try and ruin the trophy presentation. Didn't she realize that insisting on such a rigid definition of "Christmas" made her sound like she had no Christmas spirit at all? If she and her husband had founded the festival, shouldn't she be happy with how it was growing and thriving and spreading joy, even if it didn't fit her vision?

Mike appeared by their side before the clapping had stopped. "What a mess. Sorry you had to see that, ladies. Birdie's protective of this parade, and as she's gotten older, she's lost all tolerance for 'creative differences.'"

"It's just a dang float. Hell, I wanted to win, and I'm already over it. Did she forget her medication or somethin'?" Pearl asked.

"She's just used to being in charge. She was moved into an honorary position on the committee this year, but I don't think anyone told her what honorary means." Mike shook his head and frowned.

It was sad. Sally was embarrassed for the mayor and Birdie. It was hard to get older and be pushed out of things you loved. But she certainly could be handling it a lot better than she was.

"At least she has family," Sally said. "That young man up there calling her 'Auntie' seems to care about her. Trevor, right? She's lucky that she has him looking out for her. So many older people aren't as lucky." She thought she'd seen a glimpse, at least, of the caring young man that Sheila had described.

"She ain't a crone yet," Pearl pointed out. "She's with it enough to take care of the way she looks. And paranoid don't mean senile. The way he talked to her seemed patronizin' if you want my opinion, and I know you always do."

"I know what you mean," Mike said, looking unhappy. "But everyone who's been dealing with Birdie regularly lately knows that she needs a firm hand. It's a hard balance between 'firm' and 'kind,' especially when she thinks everything from her ego to her health is constantly under attack."

"Just sayin' that if my nephew talked me to that way, he'd get a smackin'."

"You're not Birdie," Sally said, mulling something over in her mind. "You don't need taking care of."

Something clicked for Sally. "I wonder..."

"Hm? What do you wonder?" Mike asked.

"Oh, nothing. I got my hair done this morning in the spa upstairs," Sally said, tugging down her knitted hat again. "I think I met Trevor's girlfriend, Sheila."

"You got your hair done?" Mike asked, brows raising. "Why are you wearing a hat, then?"

"It's cold out," Sally said defensively, holding onto it more tightly.

"Can I see?" Mike grinned. "Just for a second?"

"I-" Sally's protest was cut off shortly by Pearl snatching the hat off her head from behind, revealing the red and green dyed ends.

Mike bit his lip to keep a broad grin from spreading over his face. "I like it. I think even Birdie would have to agree that your hair is definitely in the spirit of Christmas."

"Too bad it's too late to put it on the float," Sally groaned, patting down her mussed curls.

82

Pearl handed back her hat. "Let the ends poke out, why don't you? It'll look cute as heck with those little reindeer."

"It does," Mike said as Sally put her hat back on. She was blushing, but even Pearl didn't call her out. They were all out in the cold, and everyone at the parade had cheeks like cherries by this point.

13

How Rude

December 19th

Sally and Pearl sat across from Mike in a booth, sharing breakfast at his favorite diner downtown. They had ordered their meals and were enjoying watching the view out the window when the door flew open. Trevor Grassley, dressed in khaki pants and a striped sweater under his wool coat, stormed in, pushing the hair out of his face. "We have a big problem," he said, heading right towards Mike, Sally, and Pearl.

The three of them looked up from their coffee cups. "What's the problem, Trevor?" Mike asked, frowning.

Trevor took off his scarf, using it to mop the sweat from his neck and forehead. "The problem," he bit out, "is that we have a live televised baking show that is supposed to happen in six hours. We're short a team of contestants. That storm hasn't even hit us yet, but they took one look at the forecast and bailed. You have to keep the roads open." He muttered something about how out-of-towners didn't know how to drive in the snow.

"What kind of bakin' contest?" Pearl asked, perking up in

her seat, exchanging a quick, conspiratorial look with Sally, who bit back her own grin.

Trevor glanced at her, frowning in irritation. His jaw muscle flexed, and he said, "It's a professional baking contest. It's the cornerstone of the week's activities." He ran a hand over his hair, irreparably mussed from the wind and the sweat he'd worked up. "It's televised live in Portland -the biggest media market in Oregon. My aunt is already worked up over last night's parade, and if this thing falls through...."

"Can't you just hold the competition with one less team?" Mike asked, keeping his voice even. It seemed that his strategies for dealing with Birdie and her nephew weren't that different. In a few years, Trevor might develop a local reputation for histrionics just as legendary as Birdie's, although Kelly's impression alone suggested that he was off to a fine start.

Trevor pursed his lips and hissed, "No, we can't hold the contest with one less team. The sets have been designed, and stations are being set up as we speak. I don't have the manpower to redesign the set this late in the game. Aunt Birdie is a judge and expects it to be perfect, and there will be no living with her if something else goes wrong. We need another team."

Sally raised her hand. "Trevor, we could do it. We could step in if it'd help out."

Trevor pulled his chin back into his neck and looked down at them. "You're telling me that you're professional bakers," he said flatly, with no small amount of skepticism.

"Well, no," Sally admitted, "but we do like to bake." Sally lifted her shoulders, tipping her head towards Pearl and smiling. "We're even used to sharing a kitchen."

"This is the Christmas Capital of the Northwest," Trevor said with forced patience. "We obviously have people all over town who like to bake. But this is a professional-level baking contest, and we need the best representation of baked goods McKenzie Bridge has to offer."

"What makes it professional? Y'all makin' weddin' cakes and big piles o' cream puffs covered in chocolate?" Pearl asked.

"Those have both appeared on the show, of course," Trevor said haughtily. "The theme this year happens to be 'Tasty Traditions.' We're walking it back to a simple and classic sugar cookie, but that doesn't mean that the standards for our bakers are any less high."

Sally pointed to Pearl. "She has a practically famous recipe. It's delicious."

Pearl shook her head. "Oh no, I ain't sharin' my recipe with this fool. He don't think we're good enough to be in his bakin' contest? Fine, he can find somebody else. Maybe this diner has a professional baker hidin' in back, just ready to pop out and save his skin."

Trevor folded his arms. "You have a famous sugar cookie recipe?" he asked, raising one eyebrow.

"I don't know how famous it is, but it's the best one in the entire state of Michigan, mark my words."

Trevor twirled his finger around in the air. "And you could pull together the ingredients and make them today if you had a chance?"

Pearl narrowed her eyes. "I could if I wanted to. Seems like a cookin' show should buy the ingredients for the contestants, but maybe I just got higher standards or somethin'." Mike snorted, trying to hide it by taking a quick sip of his coffee.

The man sighed, clenched his jaw, then licked his lips and composed himself. He seemed to visibly swallow his pride before asking, in a sickly sweet voice, "Would the two of you like to be a part of our professional baking contest this evening? It would be such an honor to have you."

Sally smiled and nodded. Pearl said, "Since you done asked so nicely, I reckon we would be delighted."

Trevor's shoulders relaxed. "Good. Great. Thank you. We're all going to meet at the high school gym at three. I'm sure Chief Cunningham can help you with any ingredients you need to gather. I'll email him a list of prohibited items; otherwise, whatever you can find in McKenzie Bridge is fair game."

He turned to leave and then spun around. "Oh, also. Hair and makeup are the responsibility of the contestants. Do try to get that done before you arrive on set."

Sally gaped. How rude. She just had her hair done and had thought it looked good. Even the red and green ends had started to grow on her now that she was used to seeing them in the mirror. Her hand absently went to her hair. It was too late to do anything about it now.

He glanced the women up and down. "One more little tiny thing. Hopefully, you have something else to wear. Something that's television-appropriate? Most teams wear matching aprons that are custom-made by a local seamstress, but obviously, there's no time for that now." With a swish of his coat, he tugged his scarf back on, turned, and strode out of the diner.

"I said I'd bake for him, and I'll stand by my word, but I can't say I like that soggy little fop of a man," Pearl said. Sally agreed although she kept it to herself. He was a snob, and she'd always felt a certain kind of aggravation toward people who thought they were better than others.

"Who *is* that soggy little fop of a man outside of bein' Birdie's nephew, anyway? Some fancy-pants hipster who wishes

87

he lived in a big city instead of a little tourist town in the mountains?" Pearl asked.

Mike chuckled. "He grew up here, and while he could leave for a big city at any time, I think he likes the comfort of being small-town royalty and old money. He has that status as long as he's associated with Birdie. If he left, he'd have no one and be no one, and I don't think he could bear that."

"Small-town royalty, my butt. Got no respect for nepotism," Pearl said. "At the bakin' contest, I ain't lickin' his boots or no one else's, just buttercream frostin' off spoons." She held up her coffee cup as if to salute.

"Wouldn't expect anything else from you, Pearl," Mike chuckled. Sally joined in, smiling affectionately at her best friend. She smoothed the ends of her colored hair and started to make a mental to-do list of everything they had to manage before 3:00 PM.

14

Live Bait and Imitation Vanilla

Sally and Pearl wandered past the live bait cooler to the next aisle in the cramped Harry's Country Store. Sally curiously surveyed the charming, eclectic variety of food and other supplies. There was an entire aisle dedicated to t-shirts and other souvenirs, including something called "Thunder Eggs." They looked like fossilized dinosaur eggs, but Sally was pretty sure they were just rocks.

Pearl frowned at the spice section, rifling through the packets and plastic bottles. "All they got is imitation vanilla. I need the real stuff."

"No one will know the difference. I've used imitation my entire life," Sally said, reaching for a large plastic bottle and checking the price.

"Exactly," Pearl said, "and you can tell." She swiped the bottle away from Sally, putting it back on the shelf, holding it between her pinched fingers as if she was trying to minimize contact with something so distasteful.

"Oh, stop it," Sally chuckled. "The number of my cookies and cakes you gobble up says otherwise."

Pearl swatted her arm, then pursed her lips. "Might as well skip the whole thing if we gotta use this garbage." She begrudgingly grabbed a smaller bottle of imitation vanilla extract off the shelf and dropped it into their red plastic shopping basket. "If they don't got real butter, I'm gonna kick a mule."

"Kick a mule?" Sally raised an eyebrow, biting back a smile.

"Used to say 'kick a dog.' That ain't politically correct anymore."

Sally's mouth dropped open. "You actually used to say you would kick a dog?"

"Ain't like I was gonna do it. It's like sayin' 'skin the cat.' Nobody skins cats, at least not that I know of."

"Just don't say you'll kick any animals," Sally suggested. "It could scare a kid if one overheard you and doesn't know how things 'used to be.'"

"Heck, if I wanted to scare a kid these days, I'd just say I'd kick a blue boo-bob from Goofball Galaxy."

"Is that what that show is called?" Sally laughed.

"Nah, but it should be. That float wasn't half as good as ours."

Down the next aisle, they passed camping supplies and dust-covered first aid kits on their way to the coolers in the back of the store.

Pearl skirted around a stack of canoe paddles leaning against the shelves. "You'd think they could spring for more than one store for general goods and sundries in this town, and maybe divide all this stuff up. They got four stores that sell nutcrackers and can't make space for real vanilla. What's this world comin' to?"

"Oh, I don't know. I think it's kind of cute. It's just like a

Walmart, only a lot smaller."

"Careful how loud you say that. Trevor might hear you and be mad all day because you compared somethin' in The Christmas Capital of the Northwest to Wally World. Could hurt our chances in the contest."

They gathered the rest of their ingredients, including, to their great relief, real butter. Afterward, Sally and Pearl headed out to Mike's pickup truck, which he'd given them for the afternoon to use while he was on duty in a patrol car. They drove back to the police station to store their supplies in the back room's refrigerator after a quick greeting to Gavin, who was on his computer.

"Maybe we should think about getting aprons or something else that matches. Trevor suggested it, but I think that's pretty normal for most team competitions, even baking shows," Sally said, neatly arranging the ingredients on an empty shelf below the officers' lunches and sodas.

"What have you got in mind? I ain't wearin' tinsel, mind. It'll get in the cookies, and that's just unsanitary."

"Right. I was thinking maybe matching shirts and aprons. There was that little shop with handmade linens. It might not be the same seamstress everyone else uses, but I'm sure I saw aprons in the window when we drove through town. Let's start there."

After dropping off the supplies, they took Mike's pickup truck downtown to the linen shop. They pushed open the door and were hit with the scent of cinnamon and lemon. Hand-painted signs were hung on the walls near the ceiling. The wood floors were scuffed with age and creaked as they walked. The store was a maze of hand-painted furniture, Christmas figurines, ornaments, and clothing lining the back wall. When they got further into the store, there was a display of hand-poured candles and an assortment of textiles, table runners, hot pads, and handmade aprons. The aprons hung on hooks and were a riot of color and patterns. Some had ruffles, pockets, and even sequins, which Sally thought was impractical for baking. How would a person even wash it if it got flour or dough on it?

Pearl stopped and picked up a candle labeled *Mom's Apple Pie* and sniffed. "This smells exactly like my grandma's kitchen used to."

"Did she bake pies from scratch?"

"Is there any other way? Her pie was so good that, if you put it on top of your head, your tongue would beat your brains out tryin' to get to it."

Sally chuckled. "That would be a sight." She held up an apron, red with white polka dots on the bottom, and a green top with straps with a dense poinsettia print. "What do you think of this?"

Pearl reached out to examine the fabric and stitching. "It ain't bad, but there's only one."

Sally twisted her mouth and turned back to the selection. The upside to a selection of handmade aprons was the guarantee that they would all be unique, but there was a downside, too. After pulling out several patterns, she chose a similar apron with green and white polka dots on the bottom, a red top, and plaid straps. She turned and held them both up. "These are great together, aren't they? Not too matchy, but coordinated?"

Pearl narrowed her eyes, and Sally's heart dropped. Then a smile broke across Pearl's face. "Always said you had better taste than Jackie Collins. Who cares if all the others got custom matchin' aprons? We ain't the same, and we're better for it, and we're too desperate to say boo, anyway."

Sally shook the aprons in front of her and bounced on her toes. "Oh Pearl, we're going to be on TV, and not because we were shot at this time."

"Calm your boobies. We gotta focus if we wanna win. And you know I wanna win."

"Me too. It's just that this is going to be so much fun that I can't help being excited about it. And how hard do we really need to focus when I've seen you bake those cookies perfectly with an entire bottle of wine in you? It will be an injustice if they don't win."

"You bet your sweet butt it will be. Let's get these aprons and get outta here." She turned to head to the register.

"Wait, what are we going to wear under them?" Sally asked, remembering how self-conscious she'd been at Trevor's snide implications.

"Don't know. You pick somethin' out. I'm gonna go look at those ornaments."

Sally paused, unsure if she'd heard correctly. "Ornaments?"

Pearl raised her eyebrows. "You look about as confused as a fart in a fan factory."

"If, for some reason, you are finding some Christmas spirit, I'm not going to ask any questions. But I'm glad."

Pearl tipped her head to the side. "Now lookie here, buyin' some chintzy tchotchke made by some poor kid in China ain't exactly the same as you babblin' and twirlin' on about Christmas like some manic elf."

"Not yet," Sally said, smiling.

Pearl huffed and headed to look at the ornaments. Sally turned to the wall of clothing. Long sleeves would be ideal, and solid color so they didn't clash with the patterns on the aprons.

Maybe a white button-down? Hadn't she read somewhere never to wear white? Was that still a thing? Chocolate splatters would show up on white, but flour wouldn't. She weighed the pros and cons, stepping to one end of the upper rack, and started sliding the hangers to get a look at anything that had potential.

After searching through the entire top row and finding nothing that worked, she turned her attention to the bottom row. She sighed and started digging. Halfway down, she stood up to stretch her back and caught sight of the mannequin she had passed earlier. Paired with some dark jeans was a crisp white button-down shirt with 3/4 inch sleeves. Sally eyed the top. She walked over and slid the cool cotton fabric between her fingers. It was lovely. The sleeves were cuffed and would stay out of the way of baking. The darts in the top would ensure it wasn't too puffy under the apron. Her eyes trailed down to the tag hanging at the end of the sleeve. She reached out, flipped it over, and sucked in a breath. This top was more expensive than any clothing item she had ever bought outside of formal dresses. She swallowed hard and turned back to the racks. Maybe there was a clearance section. Perhaps something they brought from home would work out after all. She bit her lip and considered.

A middle-aged woman in a chunky green sweater and hoop earrings stepped out from behind the sales counter and approached. "Isn't that white top just fantastic?"

Sally nodded. So many expensive things were. The cotton even looked wrinkle-resistant.

"Would you like to try it on? There's a curtained area in the back for changing."

"I think it's a little out of my budget," Sally admitted,

tugging at the hem of her coat.

The woman paused and then brightened. "Say, we have a mailing list. I've never seen you in here before, so I would bet you're not on it."

Sally shook her head. "We're just visiting, and it's our first time here."

The woman winked. "That doesn't matter. If you sign up for our mailing list, I can get you 25% off."

Sally did the math in her head. It was still a lot of money. "I actually need two. Can I get them both at a discount?"

The woman nodded. "Oh, of course. The discount would apply to your entire purchase, including the aprons."

Sally thought about it. If the aprons were 25% off, too, it was a sizable discount and wouldn't add up to much more than they'd planned on spending anyway. Her heart swelled. They were going to be on television and manage to look great while they were at it.

"Thank goodness for mailing lists," she said, smiling warmly at the store's owner. "It's a deal."

15

Calling All Cookies

The competition was set up in the McKenzie Bridge High School gym. Workstations from the science classroom had been wheeled in, and the shelves below them held various mixing and measuring bowls. Ovens were carted in on dollies by men from the local appliance store. The ranges were set next to shelving units to store the bakers' ingredients. Behind the stations were yards of black fabric draped over PVC piping to create a backdrop, and overhead, a banner read *Channel 5 Christmas Bake-Off.*

Sally stood inside the door to the gym, holding the shopping bags full of their still-cold ingredients and watching the bustling activity on set. Pearl had stopped off at the bathroom, and there was no way Sally was going to walk out to the stage by herself. Even though they were signed up as a team, she considered her role to be strictly that of an assistant since she was only decorating.

"What are you waitin' for? Let's get out there and mix up this batter," Pearl said, emerging from the ladies' room and wiping her wet hands on her pants.

Sally watched her, eyebrows raised. "Did they run out of paper towels?"

"Had none, and I ain't using those hand blowers. Far as I can figure, they get that air from inside the germy bathroom, heat it to get it hoppin' and blow it out again. I ain't plannin' on serving up E. coli today."

"I certainly hope not," Sally said. That would undoubtedly ruin Christmas.

"Let's get our tushes out there."

They skirted around the cameras being set up, carefully stepping over the cords snaking across the floor.

Brenda Adams, the bleached blonde reporter and newscaster from Portland, had changed into a red and green reindeer sweater and was adjusting the fluffy Santa hat on her head in the mirror hanging on the gym wall. Richard Garrison was standing between them and the baking station with Pearl's name on it. His unnaturally dark hair was perfectly coifed. A rumpled stage hand in a headset was trying to hand him a headband with a pair of fake moose antlers glued to it, but Richard ignored him as he pressed powder onto the fine lines on his forehead. As Sally and Pearl passed him, he turned to Sally and winked at her. She stumbled over a cord and flailed her arms to find her balance, all while carrying bags.

"Oh, my stars. You're as nervous as a long-tailed cat in a roomful of rocking chairs," Pearl commented grabbing the bags out of her hands.

Sally smoothed her hair. "I am not. I just tripped. You're the one who should be nervous. This is all riding on you!"

Pearl plunked her plastic grocery bag on the cart they were assigned. "And just why should I be nervous?"

At the table next to them was a man and a woman wearing

matching red sweaters and white aprons with red-stitched snowflakes. They were busy dumping their ingredients into high-quality glass containers they seemed to have brought themselves. The man caught Sally staring at him and pushed his glasses up onto his nose, his black hair cropped close to his head. He flashed a bright smile and stepped over with a hand outstretched. He tipped his head to the side and said in a nasal voice, "You must be the substitutes. I'm Paul, and this is Valerie."

"Nice to meet you. Is this your first time?" Sally asked.

Paul dipped his head coyly. "I don't mean to brag, but we won last year." He gestured to his partner Valerie. While Paul seemed to be in his early forties, Valerie had to be at least ten years older, short and round with pale skin. Her blonde bob was slicked back in a black velvet headband. Valerie nodded in their direction but offered no smile and kept her hands firmly on the mixing bowl.

Sally shook Paul's hand and introduced herself and Pearl.

Meanwhile, two identical boisterous women with teased red hair and matching jewel-colored jackets in an abstract design entered. One was pulling a collapsible canvas wagon full of supplies. "I told them I needed my lucky mixer. I can't use some second-rate model from the discount store," one said crossly.

"Tillie, don't be rude. You should be concerned about the quality of the ovens, not the mixers. These aren't even convection," said her partner, surveying the ovens and frowning.

Paul leaned in and said to Sally and Pearl, "That would be Tillie and Millie. They're twins, if you couldn't tell already, and they came in from Portland. They have been on at least two other reality television shows. They're as dramatic as the

98

Kardashians, at least if the Kardashians happened to live in the sticks. Their specialty is fruitcake. Birdie despises fruitcake, which is probably why she chose the theme this year and made sure it was something else."

Sally stifled a laugh with the back of her hand. "Birdie is involved in everything, isn't she?"

"Well, it has to do with Christmas in McKenzie Bridge, so of course she has a role," Paul chuckled. He gestured over to a fourth set of contestants by the furthest station. "Now, those two. They are a couple of Barbie dolls dipped in powdered sugar."

Sally leaned to look past Paul to the two women. She couldn't tell if they were sisters or a mother and daughter. Both of them were trim, smooth-skinned, and perfectly dressed. Sally patted her hair and pushed down her insecurities that threatened to sour her stomach.

"I never trust women who look that good. Always up to somethin', "Pearl said, folding her arms across her chest.

Paul leaned in. "The worst part is that they are amazing people. Debbie, on the right, is a foster mother and volunteers at the church. Denise, her sister, is a pediatrician who runs a monthly free clinic for the homeless in Eugene."

"That is so nice," Sally said, her insecurity bleeding over into genuine admiration. Looking past their obvious beauty, she noticed other things about the duo. Debbie pulled out a compact and covered the circles under her eyes with fresh powder. Denise pulled a hospital pager from her apron pocket and glanced down with furrowed brows. Then she excused herself and walked into the hallway.

"Oh good, you're finally here." It was Trevor, looking as prim and miffed as ever. He was wearing a dark green plaid suit

99

that pulled at the buttons. Shiny wing-tipped shoes, utterly impractical for the weather, completed the outfit. "You both need some blush, at least. Otherwise, you are going to look like a pair of doughy-cheeked ghosts. Doe-y eyes, yes. Doughy cheeks, never." He skittered away with a promise to return with whatever he could find on such short notice.

"He's so stuck up, he'd drown in a rainstorm," Pearl said with a shake of her head.

Sally had to agree. Opening her purse, she fished out her compact and flipped it open to peer at her reflection. She didn't think she looked doughy. Yes, she was looking her age, but so what? She turned her face from side to side and examined her appearance, conceding that maybe she could use a little more blush. She clapped the compact closed. Once they set up, she could head to the restroom and adjust her makeup. She wouldn't give Trevor the satisfaction of rubbing the wrong shade of blush all over her cheeks because he couldn't trust her to do it herself.

While Trevor's visit with them had been brief and insulting, he positively gushed over the other teams. He fawned over the red-headed twins that Paul had compared to backwoods Kardashians. Sally pursed her lips and dragged her attention back to Pearl, who was busy unpacking their ingredients. "Wonder if altitude is an issue, now I think of it."

"What?" Sally wasn't sure she had heard correctly.

Pearl pursed her lips. "Altitude. Ain't never baked in the mountains. Might change things."

Sally froze. It had never even occurred to her that altitude could be an issue. She scanned the room. Maybe they could ask one of the other contestants.

"Oh no. I know what you're thinking. We ain't askin' any of

these yahoos about it. They'll lie, and we'll end up with hockey pucks for cookies."

Sally frowned. While she wanted to assume they were honorable, Pearl might be right. Why would the other contestants want to help them? She checked her phone, confirming there was no cell service. Then she had an idea. "Hang on. I'll be right back." Sally headed to the administrative offices of the high school. Maybe someone would be working and could give her the Wi-Fi password.

Her shoes clicked on the tile floor of the darkened hallway. It was eerie in the empty high school. Somewhere a door slammed. She jumped and then laughed at herself. Good grief. Was she afraid to walk alone in a school?

Following a line of plaques on the wall, she finally arrived at the administrative offices. They were dark. *Shoot.* Then a door across the hall opened, and a man backed out of it, hauling a wheeled trash can behind him. "Excuse me," Sally called out.

This time he was the one to jump. "Oh, you scared me. Thought everyone would be in the gym."

"I didn't mean to startle you. Can you please give me the password to the Wi-Fi?" she asked.

"Sure. Anything else I can help you with?"

Sally had pulled out her phone and was ready for the password. But maybe he would know the answers to her questions. "You don't happen to bake, do you?"

"Bake?" He asked, gripping the trashcan and furrowing his brows.

"Yes. We aren't from here, and I need to know if the altitude will affect our recipe for the bake-off."

Understanding washed over him, and he nodded once. "I see. Well, far as I know, you only have to worry about altitude over 3500 feet." He put one hand in the air, palm down. "McKenzie Bridge, that's only about 1200 feet." He put his other hand considerably lower than the first. "You shouldn't have anything to worry about." He dropped his hands back onto the can and smiled.

Sally's shoulders relaxed.

"Oh, and the password is 'Santaforever!' One word, upper-case 'S',' with an exclamation point at the end."

Sally entered the password into her phone. Immediately a reassuring set of stacked, curved lines lit up in the top corner of her phone's screen. "Thank you."

He pretended to tip his nonexistent hat in response and then headed down the hallway, whistling.

Sally headed back to the gym, happy to report the good news to Pearl that they wouldn't have to alter their recipe.

Pearl wasn't convinced. "You better double-check that information."

"Why? He was nice, and he lives here."

"For all you know, he could be related to one of these other yahoos and be throwin' you off the road to victory."

"Oh, fine." Sally opened her browser and spent a few minutes clicking through search results. Of course, the man had been right. With a satisfied smile, she showed her phone to Pearl.

"Guess men who can cook and bake are just poppin' out of the woodwork in this town," Pearl said. "Could get used to that if I trusted any of 'em to do it as well as I can."

16

Sabotage

While the four teams finished setting up behind their stations, the production team adjusted the set's lighting. Trevor gave them his version of a pep talk. "Now, just remember, this is going to be broadcast to the largest media market in Oregon. I need you all to be the superstars that you..." he looked at Sally and Pearl. "...that you could be. Dig deep, people."

Sally shifted on her heels, beads of sweat breaking out on her skin from the blazing lights. Beside her, Pearl scoffed and lifted her coffee cup to her lips. "Well, ain't that an inspiration."

Sally smiled. It was ridiculous. She'd always wondered what it would be like to be on a cooking show and even dreamed of it, but it seemed so improbable that they ended up here. She glanced at the side door as a shaft of light cut across the gym. Mike entered, smiling at her and flashing her a thumbs-up sign. She returned the smile, her face flushing. Even Trevor couldn't possibly say that she needed more blush.

"And now, our celebrity judges." Trevor dramatically gestured to the side of the gym where three people stood in shadow. "Ladies and gentlemen, please welcome to our judges' table

Mr. Jake Dannon, star of the stage and screen." A smattering of applause filled the room. "My aunt, Mrs. Birdie Grassley, local sponsor of this event and founder of the Mckenzie Bridge Christmas Committee." Birdie wore a black turtleneck sweater dress that looked like soft cashmere. Black-heeled boots clicked across the floor as she made her way to the judges' table. She had her jittery little dog tucked under her arm and snuggled close, and he peered anxiously through one of the heavy gold bangles on her wrists. Paul let out an audible groan, and Sally turned to see that none of the contestants seemed happy Birdie was back as a judge. That woman didn't seem to know how to make friends. "And last but not least," Trevor announced, "Congresswoman Dené Buyers." A woman with a sharp chin-length bob and a fuzzy white vest over a thin red sweater waved to the crowd as she took her seat next to Birdie.

Sally leaned over and whispered to Pearl, "I need to pee."

"You always gotta pee at the most inappropriate times. When we get home, you are gonna see a doctor about that teacup-sized bladder."

"It's just my nerves."

"You're gonna have to hold it till the commercial."

Sally tried to ignore her bladder and turned her attention toward where Trevor was giving the judges their instructions. She glanced down at the contestants' instructions on laminated paper. They would begin their baking process at 4:00 PM for the early broadcast, and they would need to be finished for judging at 6:00. In between, the station would be doing live shots to show the contestants' progress.

Sally looked over at her friend. Pearl was cool as a cucumber as she mixed the ingredients from memory. Sally tried to make herself useful by following behind Pearl with a damp cloth to mop up the mess.

As they worked, Sally stole glances at the other contestants, trying to figure out what kinds of sugar cookies they were making. Paul and his partner were mixing chocolate frosting for the tower he was building with cardboard tubes. It looked like their finished batch was going to be pretty complex in presentation.

"I don't think the wonder twins have stopped smilin' since they got here."
Pearl pointed to where Millie and Tillie were mixing ingredients and beaming for the cameras. "Ain't their faces tired from all that grinnin'? They ain't gonna win a bakin' contest on personality. They gotta deliver the goods."

"Give me something to do. I feel silly just standing here," Sally said, restlessly shifting from foot to foot.

"Could you check to make sure that oven is heatin' up? These cookies are gonna be ready to go in pretty soon, here."

Sally turned to the oven and realized the display screen was dark. When she pulled it open, it was stone cold. What in the world? She pressed the buttons, trying to get it to turn on with no result. She reached around to where the cord was connected and saw that it ran underneath the draping they had put up for the backdrop.

She turned to Pearl to tell her but thought better of it. The last thing she needed was for Pearl to say something on television that would be offensive or get them in trouble.
She ducked around, cut through an opening in the draping, and followed the cord across the gym floor. All the stoves had been attached to extension cords and taped down to prevent tripping. Extension cords had been taped together to ensure they did not come unplugged. But as Sally walked closer, she

saw the problem immediately. Someone had cut through the tape and unplugged their oven. It looked like they had done the same thing to Paul, too. How rude and underhanded. She looked around but was alone as the crew was out running the show. She plugged their oven back in, as well as Paul's. With a huff, she stood up and headed back to the station to preheat the oven.

When she stepped back through the curtain, Pearl looked up from where she was cutting out little angels from the dough and hissed, "Where have you been?"

"Someone unplugged our oven," Sally reported, crossing her arms over her chest. She still couldn't believe the nerve. "Paul and Valerie's, too."

"What?" Pearl's mouth dropped open. "You think it was on purpose?"

Sally nodded gravely. Then she whispered, "I just don't know who would try to sabotage us like that."

Pearl and Sally both looked at the other contestants. Paul's partner was quizzically looking at their oven and double-checking the preheating temperature she had punched in.

The blonde women at the end were rolling out their dough, sprinkling it in powdered sugar.

When their eyes scanned the "wonder twins," Millie caught her attention and smirked. Sally elbowed Pearl and pointed with her chin toward Millie and Tillie. When Pearl looked over, they both had self-satisfied smiles plastered on their faces. Pearl stepped back from the counter and slipped her apron off. "Aw, hell. We are about to have a come to Jesus meetin'."

Sally grabbed her arm. "Don't. We can't fight on live television."

"Are you kiddin' me? That's the best place to fight."

"No," Sally said firmly, through gritted teeth. "It's Christmas, and Mike is the police chief, and we are his guests." Sally tried to keep her voice calm and level, but the same thing was happening that did when she was nervous on the phone: raising an octave higher than usual.

"Oh, for Pete's sake. Those two herpes deserve to hear a piece of my mind."

Sally frowned, puzzled. "Do you mean 'harpies?'" she asked slowly.

"Nah. Herpes," Pearl confirmed confidently.

Sally tried to slow her breathing. She usually found Pearl's absurd mix-ups amusing, but panic danced around the edge of her vision. It was growing impossible to ignore.

"You fixin' to have a panic attack on live TV instead of a fight?"

Sally shook her head once, swallowing hard. She said in an even tone, "The best revenge is just winning anyway, even if they tried to pull a dirty trick on us, so let's concentrate on that. Get those cookies baked so I can decorate them."

"Fine, but any more shenanigans, and they're gonna be at the wrong end of my rolling pin." With a final disapproving head-shake, Pearl seemed to let it go for the moment and returned to cutting out the angels.

Wow. Sally inhaled through her nose and exhaled out her mouth, quickly washing her hands. She returned to help Pearl by laying the little angels on the cookie tray, careful not to smudge their edges. Pearl's lines were astonishingly precise for not having a cookie cutter, a testament to just how many times she had done this before.

"Remember, when you can shake that tray and the cookies move, they're done. Just don't overcook them."

"I know," Sally said, her heart rate dropping. This was the part of the process she felt confident about. "You may have to help me with that because I still need to mix the pearlescent frosting."

Pearl smiled and bumped Sally with her hip. "We do make a pretty good team. Us against the herpes."

Sally chuckled and agreed. Things were going fine, and they had a real chance to win. Pearl had the perfect recipe for cookies, and Sally, naturally artistic, had channeled her painting talent into elaborately decorating cookies and cakes for years.

"All right, teams." Trevor's voice cut through the murmurs and clanking of pans. "It's currently five o'clock. That means you have exactly one hour to finish your entries and place them on the judges' table. Now is a great time to take a quick break if you need to. We won't be doing any more live shots for 15 minutes at least."

17

Winner Winner Chicken Dinner

Sally leaned over the work table, her tongue between her teeth, the piping bag steady in her hands. These lines had to be perfect. She had spent the last thirty minutes practicing and perfecting her plan for the final six angel cookies. Of those, they were going to pick the prettiest finished one to present to the judges. On the back shelf sat a tray of practice cookies to give the production crew after the show, along with some extra that Pearl had stretched the dough to make.

"Do we need so many?" Sally had asked, wondering if they'd even have time to bake the necessary ones.

"Reckon so," Pearl said. "You never know who might need a cookie."

The first batch of angel-shaped cookies was fluffy and perfect, waiting for Sally's artistic touch. She had made pearlescent icing for the body of the cookies, which she piped slowly along the end before working her way toward the center, allowing the frosting to spread into a smooth base. Once that was done, she selected the gold icing for the first round of details. Just as she was about to start, a commotion broke out across the set.

"What did you do?" It was Millie, hands on her hips, standing next to her sister and looking down at their tray of cookies, wide-eyed.

"I don't know. *Someone* must have mixed up our ingredients," Tillie said, glaring stormily at her sister.

Millie's face turned crimson. "Are you insinuating that I mixed up powdered sugar and flour?"

"I'm not insinuating anything. But it sure looks like we have no powdered sugar for frosting and a whole container of flour that should have gone in the dough." She dipped her finger in the glass container and popped it in her mouth. "How did you manage to mess up this badly?"

Millie burst into tears. The entire gym was silent except for the escalating drama between the sisters, who started to trade angry accusations. Sally scanned the room and noticed the producer giving a cameraman a sign to keep rolling. Sally's heart ached for Millie. It was an awful mistake she'd made once in her mother's kitchen. They'd been able to laugh about it then, but they'd had plenty more ingredients, and there wasn't a camera crew breathing down their necks or the pressure of a competition.

Pearl leaned over and whispered, "What a mess. Glad you know what the heck you're doin."

Sally smiled and put her arm around Pearl's shoulders. Now that they were nearly done and the cameras were wholly focused on the twins, it gave them a second to relax.

"They mighta done it on purpose to get more screen time, you know," Pearl said.

Tillie was in a rage. She berated Millie, her voice rising by the minute. While Sally watched, Millie took the jar of flour and retaliated by dumping it right over Tillie's head. There was a collective gasp on set.

"Oh, my stars," Pearl said, blinking. "Their bakin' might not win this thing, but they're stealin' the show right out from under us."

Sally glanced over at the judges' table. The Congresswoman's hand was over her mouth, trying to hide a smile. The stage-and-screen star was sitting back, openly laughing. Birdie, in the middle, had her head in her hands as her little dog barked shrilly at the chaos.

Sally glanced at Pearl. "I'm going over there. Birdie looks like she's going to have a meltdown over this. We're almost done, anyway."

"You gotta decorate these other cookies!" Pearl insisted, pulling the last extra batch out of the oven.

"We don't even need those. We've baked an insane amount of cookies."

"These are important cookies. I'm tellin' ya!" Pearl said, her voice rising.

"We're not going to upstage the harpies by getting into an even bigger fight," Sally sighed, taking off her apron. "Trevor's busy. I'm going to go check on Birdie." Noticing that Birdie didn't seem to have a bottle of water in front of her, she grabbed an unopened one from their station and crossed over to the judges' table.

"Suit yourself, but I'm tellin' you, she ain't gonna appreciate it," Pearl shrugged, grabbing the piping bag and starting in on frosting her final mystery batch of cookies.

Birdie looked up at her as Sally approached. Her expertly-applied makeup appeared smudged, as though she'd been crying behind her hands. "Yes? Can I help you?" She asked stiffly. Her little dog stopped barking but growled quietly. Birdie calmed him down with a few firm strokes along the back of his sweater, and he licked her hand.

"I noticed that no one brought you more water," Sally faltered, holding out the bottle. "We're pretty much done, so I thought that-"

"You thought what? That it might be a good time to poison me?" Birdie accused, smudged eyes narrowing.

"No," Sally said, bewildered by how one woman could be so intensely paranoid. "It's still sealed, see? They left these bottles at all the stations for the contestants. This one hasn't even been opened."

Birdie's eyes were still narrowed, but she reached out and accepted the bottle. She cracked it open and took a sip.

"It's so awful that people are fighting so close to Christmas," Sally said. The other judges were still focused on the spectacle, but Birdie looked right at her as though truly perceiving her for the first time.

"It's a disgrace," Birdie answered, her lip quivering. "This year, it's just one after another. The light parade was more than I thought I could take, and now two trashy reality stars are ruining the baking show. What my husband would have said."

"Your husband?" Sally asked.

"Yes, my Bob. He had such a sweet tooth. I was never any baker, artist, or much else, but I could always organize an event," Birdie said, taking another sip of water. "It felt like a way I could take care of him, and now everything is ruined."

Sally couldn't help herself. She reached out to pat Birdie's shoulder. The woman flinched as though she'd been hit, but relaxed once she saw Sally's gentle smile.

"It's not ruined. You've done a wonderful job, Birdie, at least I think so."

"Well, thank you, I suppose," Birdie said brusquely. "You'd better get back to your station and ensure everything's done, because the competition ends at 6:00 sharp."

Sally nodded, turning and heading back to the station where Pearl was finishing some funny-looking angels. "You should have waited for me," Sally groaned. "You're so impatient with decorating!"

"Was worried you'd be over there for too long. How'd she take it, anyway?" Pearl asked.

"She's having a rough time, but I think she appreciated it," Sally shrugged. "She's just sad and lonely, Pearl. You'd think that you-" she cut herself off, freezing.

"You'd think that I what, now?" Pearl asked, staring hard at her poor frosting job.

"Nothing. I'm sorry," Sally added, face flushing.

"Never mind. It's all water under the bridge," Pearl muttered. "Just proof that you can be old and sad and not turn out like that, if anythin'. Well? Are we gonna win this thing?"

"Yes," Sally said, relieved that they could move on before her slip-up made things truly uncomfortable, even if it still hung between them. The three of them were all widows, but only one had suffered the tragedy of losing Pearl's young children.

Sally made a mental note to make sure that she was extra sweet to Pearl for the rest of the year. She filled another piping bag with frosting, reaching for one of Pearl's extra cookies so she could help out.

"Shoot. You really are better at this than I am," Pearl joked, watching Sally lay down her precise and pretty lines. "Ain't gotta be perfect to taste just as good, though, can promise that much."

Finally, the clock struck six. "Hands on the table, everyone!" Trevor cried shrilly. Except for the twins, it did seem like everyone had been done for a while, and they were fairly relaxed as they did what they were told.

The redheaded twins exchanged miserable looks as they placed their hands on the station's work surface.

Trevor addressed them with all the affected dignity of any true master of ceremonies. "You've done the finest possible work you can, but the hour of judgment is upon us."

"Oh, heck, he's more dramatic than those herpes girls," Pearl whispered to Sally, rolling her eyes.

"Please place your finest sugar cookie on the plate provided and present it to the judges," Trevor instructed, retreating to the judges' table. Paul and Valerie plucked a cookie from their elaborate stand, placing it carefully on the plate. Millie and Tillie tried to unstick a strange and misshapen cookie from the cooling rack where it seemed to have fused. The picture-perfect humanitarian blondes laid three cookies on the plate, arranged in tiers like a fluffy miniature wedding cake. Sally and Pearl picked out their prettiest angel, and Sally carefully centered it before carrying it over to the judges' table.

Trevor meticulously cut each cookie into three roughly equal portions. Sally sighed to see their beautiful work broken up like that, but she supposed it would be a lot to expect the judges to each eat four entire cookies before dinner.

They tasted Millie and Tillie's cookie first. Sally suspected it was to get that part out of the way quickly. The stage-and-screen star and the Congresswoman smiled diplomatically through their grimaces, but Birdie spat her bite of cookie out into her napkin.

Next was Paul and Valerie's cookie. The judges mumbled about how pretty the presentation on the stand was but took points off for the criteria being a *simple* sugar cookie. Birdie commented that the dough was bland and undersalted, and Valerie hung her head.

Debbie and Denise smiled at each other, and the judges seemed to enjoy their cookies, but Birdie was quick to comment, "The rules said to present one cookie. This is clearly three cookies."

"Auntie-" Trevor started, murmuring a string of words about it being a technicality she could surely overlook, but she was having none of it, pushing the plate away.

The three judges' brows raised in surprise when they tasted Sally and Pearl's cookie. "Unexpected," commented the Congresswoman, nodding in approval and taking another delicate bite. "It's like there's another dimension to it."

"This tastes familiar, but I can't put my finger on it," admitted the stage-and-screen star, chewing slowly with a knit in his brow.

Birdie chewed silently, staring hard at the tabletop.

"Probably is familiar," Pearl said, "if you've ever been to a Taco Tuesday." Sally chuckled. Pearl wasn't going to say it out loud, of course, but the secret ingredient was a cup of sour cream in the dough.

Trevor cleared his throat. "Now that the tasting portion of the competition is complete, I must ask all the contestants to leave the gym so that the judges may deliberate. As a reminder, the winning team will be interviewed by our news team right after they are crowned victors, so don't go anywhere."

Sally and Pearl filed out with the rest of the contestants. The general mood was subdued confusion as each team murmured uncertainly among themselves. One of the twins started weeping, and with the cameras not trained on them, the other offered a surprisingly gentle hug. The humanitarian blonde bakers quietly discussed their odds. Valerie's face was stone, but Paul approached Pearl and Sally with a tentative smile.

"Something was wrong with our oven during the contest. Then, strangely, just after Sally left, it started working again. I don't suppose you'd know anything about that."

"It looked like two ovens came unplugged somehow," Sally said. "I went to check because ours wasn't working, and it looked like yours was out, too."

"You helped out last year's winners," Paul said, sounding surprised.

"Well, it was the decent thing to do," Sally said.

"Damn decent," Paul commented. "However this thing turns out, I owe you one."

After a few minutes, Trevor poked his head outside the gym door. "Please form a single-file line in an orderly fashion and assemble before the judges' table."

"So much fanfare for a small-town bakin' show," grumbled Pearl.

"A small-town *professional* baking show," Sally corrected, and they both snorted behind their hands.

When Sally caught sight of Birdie's face, she knew they'd won. Biting back a smile, she waited for the announcement to confirm it. While Pearl punched the air in triumph, Sally tried to think of something to say to express her gratitude to the most uptight and picky woman in McKenzie Bridge, but it seemed that there was no need because she was sending Trevor on a quick errand. When he returned, it was with another one of Pearl and Sally's winning angel cookies, and Birdie settled back in her chair, taking a big bite. Meanwhile, Sally and Pearl accepted their prizes, a pair of gift certificates to the spa at Holiday Farms and a golden trophy in the shape of a snowman wearing a baking hat.

18

Never a Dull Moment

Brenda looked directly into the camera with a bright smile. "Welcome back to McKenzie Bridge, where we are interviewing this year's winners of the Channel 5 Christmas bake-off." She crossed her legs and leaned forward, manicured hands clasped over her knee. "Sally, a little elf told us that you and Pearl aren't *just* award-winning bakers."

Sally looked at Pearl, who shrugged. What in the world were they talking about? Sally's mouth went dry, and she tugged on the hem of her shirt. Was that her microphone crackling with the movement of the crisp white cotton she was wearing?

Richard's mouth dropped open, his brows raising nearly to his inky-black hairline. "Why, yes. That's true." He pointed at Sally and Pearl. "It's never a dull moment for the two of you adventurous ladies. You two helped the local police chief bust an international drug ring about a year ago. Can you tell us about that?"

Sally froze, the heat of the portable lights blazing.

"Pretty much sums it up there, Richard," Pearl offered.

Richard was undeterred. "Oh, don't be coy. We want to hear

all about it. There must be something the original reports didn't cover that you can share."

"Short version is that we went down to Mexico for a vacation and got tangled up with some crazy lady named Dottie. She ended up murderin' somebody and gettin' busted for drug-mulin'. Shoulda known she'd be up to no good, being a former pageant queen and all."

A muscle fluttered in Brenda's jaw. She blinked her dazzlingly made-up eyes and replied in a steely voice hidden behind a smile, "do you have something against pageant queens? I personally have found them to be delightful." She tucked a piece of bleached blonde hair behind her ear and waited for Pearl's reply.

"Look, if you wanna get fixed up and parade yourself around in a bathin' suit, then go right ahead. Ain't no skin off my back. But if you're still talkin' about it 40 years later, you're gonna end up on my suspect list."

Richard Garrison smacked his knee, his laughter measured and made-for-TV. "Fair enough." Then he leaned forward conspiratorially. "Tell me, do you know where Dottie is now?"

Pearl scoffed and said, "How should I know? Probably locked up somewhere, tellin' someone how pretty her pageant tiara was."

Sally's voice creaked when she spoke. "She's being held at a medium-security prison after being sentenced to 30 years."

Pearl whipped her head towards Sally. "How in blazes do you know that?"

Sally stared, wide-eyed. She hated being put on the spot.

Luckily Pearl seemed to remember, snapping her fingers and saying, "Oh right, I remember. You're watchin' the trial on Court TV or somethin'."

"Getting back to the beauty pageant thing, what about that made you suspect her?" Brenda shifted in her seat.

Good grief. Sally didn't think Brenda would last very long in the media business if she melted down whenever somebody talked about a beauty pageant. She wondered if the pretty young newscaster had a few titles of her own to feel defensive over.

Pearl narrowed her eyes at Brenda, and Sally sensed disaster coming. She laid her hand on Pearl's knee and said to Brenda, "I love beauty pageants. I was in one when I was younger. As for Dottie, it wasn't her beauty pageant history that made her suspicious as much as her general disconnect from reality. We didn't suspect her at first, but as evidence kept pointing in her direction."

That seemed to appease Brenda, who relaxed her shoulders and nodded in agreement. Sally let out a breath, relieved they were back on track and even more relieved that she'd managed to get all those words out on live TV without fumbling them terribly.

"However you figured it out, you two are heroes in my book," Richard boomed and then spread his arms out. A spattering of applause broke out from onlookers. Sally felt her face flush and looked at her boots, waiting for the feeling to pass.

"We're so glad you're here, and congratulations on your victory today, ladies. Back to you in Portland, Dave," Brenda said after being given a hand signal by one of the stagehands to wrap it up.

Pearl let her elbows rest on either side of the chair and just nodded, flashing a quick smile. Sally looked up from her lashes, smiled, and then gave the camera an awkward wave, unsure of what she was supposed to be doing.

"And we're out," called the stage hand. The cameraman immediately turned off the cameras and headed to the table set up with coffee and doughnuts. The stagehand approached and helped Sally and Pearl untangle their microphones from inside their clothing. Having done this many times before, Brenda and Richard were able to remove and wrap theirs up without assistance.

"I need to visit the little girls' room," Brenda said before giving Sally and Pearl quick handshakes and heading into the station's trailer.

Richard clapped his hands together. "Well, that was delightful. Make sure you two ladies stay out of trouble up here. Although, I think you'll have difficulty finding it in McKenzie Bridge, at least as long as you stay on Birdie's good side." He chuckled darkly.

Sally gave a slight nod. The last thing she wanted was trouble. She thoroughly enjoyed their quaint, picture-perfect Christmas experience, now complete with winning a baking contest. Nothing was going to wreck it, and even Birdie was starting to seem less scary.

Pearl gave Richard a hearty handshake and said, "This one's been grinnin' like a possum eatin' a sweet tater ever since we got here." Pearl hitched her thumb at Sally. "Only danger she's facin' is an overdose of Christmas spirit."

Richard clutched her hand and leaned in. "Don't worry. We haven't had an overdose of Christmas spirit in about three years." He winked at her before dropping her hands, giving them a wave, and heading over to where sawhorses had been set up as a perimeter, lined with adoring fans. Pearl rolled her eyes as Richard began to take selfies and literally kissed a baby.

Sally's eyes scanned the crowd, and she smiled when she saw

him. Mike stood to the side, his arms crossed, beaming back at her. She grabbed Pearl's arm, pulling her giddily towards where Mike was waiting.

"How are the superstars?" he asked when they got within earshot.

"I think Brenda ran to the bathroom to un-knot her panties. I thought she was gonna put me on trial for bein' anti-pageant," Pearl said. "Ain't like I'm ashamed of thinkin' there are better ways for gals to get scholarships."

"Even if that's true, antagonizing Brenda was hardly called for," Sally sighed. "I *was* in a pageant as a girl, and it was a nice experience."

"I think you two did great," Mike said.

"Thanks," Sally said. "I don't think I'm cut out for live television."

"Nobody's cut out for live television unless they can smile while they pee down my back and tell me it's rainin'."

"I thought that was politicians?" Mike asked.

"Mike, bein' in law enforcement and all, I thought you'd know that ain't limited to politicians. Somebody's always willin' to dish out bull crap they want folks to believe is gold."

"Oh, stop, Pearl. It was nice of them to interview us. It's nice of them to be here in town at all. They could be at home with their families, but they're here with us instead. That's a big sacrifice, especially this time of year."

Pearl waved her off. "Next thing you'll be tellin' me they deserve a medal or somethin'."

Mike draped his arm around Pearl's shoulders. "I'm starving. I've got to stop by the station for a second, but then we can head home. If the two of you are ready to return my truck, I'll drive us back to my place, and we can enjoy dinner together."

Sally frowned. She had wanted to try out the cute little café in town. But if Mike already had something planned for dinner, she didn't want to put him out. Pearl noticed her expression and said, "I think Sally here had her heart set on the Reindeer Café. Think we could do that tonight instead?"

Sally smiled and gave Pearl a grateful look. "I went online and checked out the menu earlier. It looks like they have burgers named after each reindeer pulling Santa's sleigh. It sounds so fun."

Mike ran a hand through his hair. "I guess so. But I'd be doing a terrible job serving and protecting if I didn't offer a warning. You're taking your life in your hands by eating there."

"It's not good?" Sally asked. There hadn't been many reviews, but the website looked nice.

"Let's just say I wouldn't order anything that could give you food poisoning if it's a little undercooked."

"If it's that bad, we probably should figure out somewhere else," Sally said sadly.

Pearl nodded in agreement.

Mike relented. "Tell you what, let's see who's cooking. If Joray is cooking, we'll go there. But I'd recommend going somewhere else if anyone else is behind the grill."

"Fair is fair," Pearl shrugged. "I'll take those odds if you can vouch for at least one good cook."

As they wove through the crowd, snow gently fell, and Sally's heart swelled with gratitude. Bell-ringers with red kettles and festive hats were quick with a smile. Sally fished around in her pocket and pulled out a five-dollar bill. She folded it up and shoved it inside the little slot, accepting a candy cane as a thank-you for the donation. The smells of cinnamon and freshly baked pie seem to permeate the streets. Maybe they pumped the scent through the streets as they did at Disneyland. Sally wasn't sure, but either way, she loved it.

McKenzie Bridge seemed to represent everything she loved about Christmas. The small-town spirit, the cheeriness that hummed in the air and swirled around everyone walking in the streets. Even groups of people were caroling at different spots throughout the town so that just when one of them faded out of earshot, another could be heard singing another song.

If only her kids were there. She would love to introduce sweet little Amelia to all this Christmas magic. Instead, her poor granddaughter would have to look up at a skyline with palm trees but no hope of snow. Lauren's in-laws probably didn't even have a chimney. How was she going to explain that to Amelia when she was older?

Finally, Sally could see the Reindeer Café sign hanging out over the sidewalk, fashioned to look like a fancy green scroll. A brown reindeer was painted next to it. A crowd packed inside was steaming up the windows, so it wasn't easy to see much through them.

"Hang out here for a second. I'll go in and assess the situation," Mike said, opening the glass door. Jingle bells tied to the top of it announced his arrival. For a brief moment, Sally could see inside. People were pressed against the wall at the small vestibule, waiting for a table. That wasn't a great sign.

Sally looked longingly at the cozy lit interior. She thought she could see Richard at one of the tables, joined by a man in a brown farmer jacket, but the door closed too quickly for her to be sure. She was a little miffed, because she didn't think they'd left the contest that far apart. Either Richard had reservations, or he was being given preferential star treatment.

Mike came out a couple of minutes later and said, "Well, the good news is that Joray is cooking. The bad news is there's about an hour wait."

"I'm so hungry I'd eat with the devil himself if he had an open chair." Pearl crossed her arms, shivering and stuffing her hands against her sides.

"Pearl. You shouldn't say such things," Sally scolded.

"All I'm sayin' is I can't wait an hour. Although it's probably nice and cozy where the devil's eatin', too, if you catch my drift."

"I get it," Mike said. "None of us wants to wait an hour, and we certainly don't want Pearl running off to have dinner with the devil when we can fix cold and hungry just as well. Why don't we grab my truck and head back to the house? I've got some steaks that are begging to be seared tonight. I can have food on the table in less time than it will take us to get a seat here, scout's honor."

"Sounds like a solid plan. My coffee is kickin', so I'd appreciate it if we stopped off at the station first, and right quick," Pearl said.

Sally was mortified. Did Pearl really just talk about having to go poop in front of Mike? She just shook her head at her friend.

Mike ignored the comment. He extended an arm in motion for Pearl to lead the way back to the high school's parking lot.

When they reached the station, Pearl headed straight for the bathroom. Sally lowered herself into Gavin's office chair and pulled out her phone, which had automatically connected to the Wi-Fi. A text message from Lauren popped up.

19

All is Right With the World

```
Hey mom, big news. Call me when you can.
```

Sally read the message twice. What in the world? She scrolled up and clicked on Lauren's number. The phone rang twice before she picked it up. "Hey, Mom." Sally could hear muffled loudspeaker noises in the background.

"Hi, sweetie," Sally said, brow furrowing. "I just got on the Wi-Fi and saw your message. Is everything alright?"

"Yes. At least no one's badly injured or dead, but unfortunately, Brad's dad has kidney stones. He thought he could pass them, but he's in the hospital now."

"Oh, dear. Is he going to be alright?"

"Mom, it's kidney stones," Lauren chuckled. "It's painful but not that serious. They have to either get them through his system or break them up with a laser, but there's no way to know exactly how that will go, or how long it might take.

They're not in any shape for hosting visitors, in any case, so Brad and I have decided that we're going to come out and see you instead, if you don't mind."

"What?"

" We changed our flights and cashed in more of our credit card miles. Our flight doesn't leave till tomorrow, but we should be there in plenty of time to enjoy Christmas."

Sally's eyes filled with tears as she looked at the softly falling snow. She was going to share this perfect Christmas experience with her granddaughter, after all. "Oh, Lauren, This is the best present you could ever give me." Her lip trembled as she spoke, and her voice wavered.

"Don't get all weepy on me yet. I've got more news."

Sally laughed and wiped her nose with the back of her hand. "Don't pay any attention to your silly sentimental mom. Go on."

"Joel, Tom, and Henry are coming too."

Sally almost dropped the phone. "You're kidding."

"Yup. And they had a last-minute cancellation at your hotel that opened up two rooms, so we booked them. We can all stay there at the resort with you, although Windsong is still a huge 'maybe.'"

Sally could hardly breathe. She was sure she'd been this happy at other points in her life, but she couldn't remember them at this beautiful moment. "I can't believe it. I'm in shock."

"Don't keel over before we get there. The last-minute flights were not cheap."

Sally tried to feel guilty but couldn't find it in herself. She was seeing stars.

"Oh, hey, Mom, I've got to go. Brad wants to go shopping

for a snowblower."

"You've made me the happiest person in the world, Lauren. Please text me your flight information and stay in touch."

"I will. See you soon!"

Sally set her phone down and wiped her eyes with the back of her hand, sniffling softly.

"That was either extremely good or terribly bad news," Mike said, going to the coffee machine in the office and pouring himself a stale cup. "Excellent news, I hope?"

Sally nodded, eyes brimming. "My kids are coming for Christmas."

Mike smiled and lifted his cup. "Guess there's a little more Christmas magic in this town than I thought, and that is saying something."

Sally couldn't stop smiling. Although they planned to exchange gifts after the new year, she would have to get them a little something to open on Christmas morning. Oh, this was going to be perfect.

Pearl emerged from the bathroom and flipped the light off as she walked out, closing the door behind her. "It's probably best if y'all steer clear of that room until the spring thaw. It ain't pretty."

Mike laughed. Pearl noticed Sally's teary eyes. "Well, shoot, I know I turned the fan on in there. Did Santa go and put you on his naughty list or somethin'?"

Sally shook her head and laughed. "Lauren just called. My kids are coming for Christmas. They're coming here, all of them."

Pearl stared, then rocked back on her heels and smiled. "Well, don't that just beat all. That's some downright Christmas magic if I ever heard it."

"That's what I said," Mike exclaimed.

Pearl crossed over to Sally and pulled her up from the chair. "I'm happy for you, kiddo. After we get some of those steaks in us at Mike's place, we gotta figure out what we're gonna do about Christmas dinner with all these folks comin'."

"Don't worry about that. I got an extra ham when they were on sale. There should be plenty to go around." Mike set his cup in the little sink next to the coffee pot and pulled his knit cap out of his pocket before slipping it on his head. "Not meaning to intrude on your family dinner, of course," he added slightly awkwardly.

Sally was so happy that she didn't even think before she spoke. "Please, intrude! You're practically family after all we've been through, Mike."

Pearl's brows shot up, but Mike only grinned. "Thank you, Sally. I'm sure I don't have to tell you that means a whole lot."

Puffs of breath clouded in front of Sally and Pearl as they waited for Mike to lock up the station. The sun had given way to a starless night. The soft, falling snow muffled the sounds of the downtown activities. All they could hear was their boots crunching and shuffling in the unplowed parking lot.

"Seems to be gettin' deeper, don't you think?" Pearl asked, nudging some of the gathering snow aside with her boot.

"I'll never complain about snow for Christmas," Sally said, catching some flakes on the end of her mitten.

"Yeah, well I'll hold you to that," Pearl said dryly.

Sally pulled open the passenger door to Mike's truck and slid across the seat. She smiled at Mike, who smiled right back at her with a toothy grin as he started the truck and adjusted his mirrors.

Her kids were coming. It was Christmas. She was in

McKenzie Bridge. She was sitting between her best friend and Mike. Her breath caught. She still wasn't sure who Mike was to her, but she was glad to be here with him. At that moment, all was right with the world and would continue to be, all through a delicious steak dinner that Mike cooked to medium-rare perfection.

That night back at the hotel, Sally brushed her hair, dreaming excitedly of when her family would join them for Christmas.

"That gift shop has a good chilled wine selection," Pearl said. "Gonna go while they're still open. I'll be back in a jiffy."

Almost as soon as she left the room, however, she returned.

"What–" Sally started.

"Shh!" Pearl hissed. She reached for the plate of extra cookies they'd baked at the competition, including her somewhat messily decorated angels, hurrying back out to the hallway.

Sally crept toward the door Pearl had left ajar, listening in confusion. Her eyes widened at the sound she heard. Was someone weeping out there?

"Had a feelin' earlier someone might need a cookie," Pearl said. Sally watched through the gap at the door's hinges as Pearl knelt next to Noël, sitting curled up in her pajamas, hugging her knees close and hiding her face in her arms. She sniffled, raising her head and looking up at Pearl.

"Are those angels?" she asked. "I love angels." Her voice wavered and choked as she started to sob, burying her face back in her arms. Her curtain of dark hair fell forward over her shoulders.

"Shh, shh. You're okay now. What's the matter?" Pearl asked, crouching to sit on the floor across from the girl. She set the plate of cookies between them.

Noël glanced up, reaching forward. She took one of the

cookies and bit into it as if it might put a plug in her tears. "It's my parents. I love them more than anything. I thought this vacation would remind them how much they loved each other, but-" Another sob wracked her little body. Pearl stroked Noël's hair back away from her tears.

"Your folks are only human. So were mine. They're helpless about lettin' us down sometimes," Pearl fumbled. "But they love you like the moon and stars. Anyone with workin' eyes can see that."

"I don't need them to love me," Noël cried softly. "I need them to love each other."

"Why are you out here? Are they scarin' you?" Pearl asked softly.

"I don't want my mom to see me cry. I'm in girl scouts because she wants me to be a strong woman," said Noël.

"Heck. You're a woman, and that means bein' strong. Even when no one has a right to ask it of us, or we shouldn't need to be, we women weather through. We come out tougher for it."

"Even when it hurts?" Noël whispered, taking another bite of her cookie.

"Especially when it hurts. My mama's the strongest woman I ever knew, and she cried. She cried lots because she was survivin'," Pearl said softly. "You got the soul of a survivor, too. I can tell."

"Thank you," Noël sniffled. "But this trip was supposed to fix things. I thought that if we had the perfect Christmas, I would be able to fix everything."

"Now, you listen to old Pearl. Your folks may have their complications, but you ain't one of them. Ain't nothin' you're doin' wrong or could do wrong."

"What can I do right, though?" Noël asked fiercely. "How

131

can I make this Christmas perfect when they can't stop arguing?"

Pearl was quiet for a long moment. "What do you think of my cookies here? These are award-winners, mind. Is the frostin' on this one perfect?"

"I like it," Noël said kindly.

"Heck! You didn't answer the question," Pearl chortled. "Tryin' to spare my feelins' like the sweat pea you are." Noël giggled through her tears. "This cookie ain't perfect. Her mouth is all messed up, and the harp looks like she's been in some kinda accident. But she's special, tastes like heaven, and she's for you. This Christmas can be special, too, even if there ain't no such thing as perfect."

The door to the next room cracked open, and Noël's exhausted-looking father, Patrick, peered out. "Sorry," he mumbled. "Was she bothering you?"

"Of course not. I was on my way over anyway to bring your family some cookies. I was on a bakin' show with my best friend Sally earlier, and would you believe we won? Had some extra, and wanted to spread some Christmas cheer and such."

"Oh," Patrick said as Pearl straightened and pushed the plate of cookies into his hands. "Thank you. That's very kind of you."

"Thank you, Pearl," Noël said, taking Patrick's hand and wiping her face on her sleeve. "You're right about them tasting like heaven."

Sally scurried back away from the hinges when she heard a door shutting and Pearl grunting as she stood up. She did her best to be utterly silent as she returned to her evening routine, trying to look as though she'd never paused.

"Were you eavesdroppin'?" Pearl asked suspiciously as she

shut their door and planted her hands on her hips.

"No! Of course not," Sally said.

"You weren't born a good liar, and you ain't one now," Pearl said flatly.

"I think you said some kind things to that little girl," Sally offered. "Not to mention inspiring. You could have turned this trip around for her."

"I say that's bleak as all get out, if so," Pearl replied, hunting through her toiletry bag for her toothbrush. "Poor little kid shouldn't need a pep talk when her folks are a room over bein' selfish. They should be the ones makin' her feel better, not some old coot in McKenzie Bridge."

"They could be doing their best," Sally said. "You don't know if they are."

"Yes, I do," Pearl said. "Their best ain't good enough, and that's the bone I got to pick."

20

Out of Luck

December 20th

Sally rubbed her eyes and swung her feet over the side of the bed, socks brushing the carpet. *What in the world?* She leaned over, switched on the bedside lamp, and then surveyed the carpet. Wet. The whole floor was wet.

"Pearl, wake up," she hissed.

"Why?" Pearl pulled a pillow over her head and groaned.

"I think our room is flooded."

Pearl rolled over and cracked one eye open. "What're you talkin' about?"

Sally lifted her feet and wiggled her toes, "My socks are soaked."

"You pee in the bed?"

Sally scoffed, "No. Our room is flooded." A knock punctuated her sentence. Sally slid off the bed and slopped to the door, pulling it open.

An older man in knee-high rain boots greeted her, his eyes rimmed with exhaustion. "Sorry to bother you, but we've had a flood and need to evacuate the premises."

"Oh my stars," Pearl said, throwing her blanket off. "Are we talkin' a flash-flood or just a soppy carpet? I can put up with one of those better than the other."

"It's a mess. Clogged pipes. Right now, it's just water, but if we don't get it fixed, we'll be up to our eyeballs in sewage."

Sally looked at her feet, suddenly nauseous. Sewage? Their lovely room was going to be covered in poop? With wide eyes, she turned to Pearl, who was reaching down to grab her shoes.

"We need you to pack your things and come to the restaurant."

"But where are we going to stay?" Sally asked, her voice squeaking. The other hotels in town were booked. They couldn't just sleep in the street.

"Well, we're working on that. But for now, we need to clear out the rooms and get that flooding under control." The man just backed away, mumbling to himself, leaving them standing on soggy carpet.

"What are we going to do?" Sally cried. "This is a disaster."

"If this don't beat all," Pearl said, tiptoeing her way to the bathroom and slamming the door.

Sally looked around their room. Then she remembered that the kids were supposed to be flying in. They couldn't possibly all sleep in the restaurant downstairs. What kind of Christmas would that be? She had told them they were coming out for the perfect Christmas, and now they were ankle-deep in water that would soon be sewage.

Dressed in snow boots and dragging their roller bags behind them, Sally and Pearl trudged down to the restaurant and were met by a room full of bleary-eyed employees and guests. Salon workers, including Sheila, were clearing out some of their essentials from upstairs. Children slept on their parents' laps. The staff was bustling about with carafes, chasing empty coffee cups, and delivering hastily scrambled eggs.

Pearl offered a little wave to Noël, held by her father. She seemed on the edge of sleepiness but still managed to wave back before nuzzling her face into Patrick's neck.

Sally couldn't summon her usual optimism. A young woman with a nose ring, hair pulled back, and a faded concert t-shirt approached their table. Her tired eyes flitted to Sally's red and green-tipped hair and she nodded in approval. "Nice color. What can I get you?"

Sally and Pearl just ordered coffee since the kitchen wasn't outfitted to do much under the current circumstances. When the waitress moved to another table, Sally rested her head on her hand and looked out the window. The rising sun was starting to cast promise over the day.

The front door opened and a man in a flannel shirt, muck boots, and a utility jacket strode inside, a blast of cold air following him through the door. A middle-aged woman with bright red hair rushed up to him and kissed his cheek. He stood with his hands on his hips, the weight of the situation keeping him from smiling at his wife. He slung one arm around the woman's shoulder, tucking her into his side. Then held up his other hand. "Folks, can I have your attention?"

The room went silent. Pearl slid out of the booth and swung around to sit beside Sally so she could see better.

"We apologize for the inconvenience."

Murmuring started.

"My wife Carol and I know that this is not what you expected when you booked your stay at Holiday Farms. We pride ourselves on customer service."

"When can we go back to our rooms?" someone asked.

The owner cleared his throat. "Not for a day or two, at least. Again, we do apologize for the inconvenience."

The room erupted.

The owner used both hands to calm the room. "We have options for you."

His wife, Carol, stepped forward. She wiped her brow, dark circles under her eyes. "Craig and I have been working all night to figure this out. We have several private summer cabins that their owners have donated for use during this time. We understand if you would rather depart early, and we will refund your money."

"How will we get to the cabins?"

"Who assigns where we stay?"

"We're still working out the details. I need to mention to all of you that they're forecasting a possible major snowstorm between now and Christmas, so if you plan to be home for Christmas, you may want to leave sooner rather than later."

Sally picked at the paper napkin under her coffee cup, shredding it anxiously into pieces. They could stay with Mike, of course. She was sure that his offer still stood, now more than ever. But what about the kids? They wouldn't all fit, even in that lovely big lodge. And was she ready to stay in such close quarters with him? Her heart fluttered thinking about it. She had never stayed under the roof of a man besides her father and Harold.

She slipped her phone out of her bag and sent him a text telling him what was happening.

```
I'll be there in ten minutes.
```

Sally let out a breath and relaxed. She handed the phone to Pearl, who read Mike's text and nodded. They had a way out of the chaos erupting in the restaurant. When Mike walked through the front door, Sally's heart flipped. He was her knight in shining armor, or rather, uniform. He scanned the room, and when their eyes met, they both smiled. She gently elbowed Pearl, and they both slid out of the booth.

"Thank God. Seein' you just dills my pickle," Pearl said.

Sally and Pearl pulled their luggage to the door, where Mike insisted on taking over. His breath billowed as he heaved the cases into the truck's bed. "I have plenty of room back home. Happy to have you."

The passenger door creaked as Sally pulled it open. "I don't know what we would do without you."

"I do," Pearl said, pushing Sally over and climbing in beside her. "We'd be swimming in shit for Christmas."

Sally laughed, grateful for the heater's warmth and being out of the conflict-ridden restaurant.

"Hang on," Pearl said, hopping back out of the truck. "Gotta go check on somethin'. Be right back."

Mike pulled the door shut and rubbed his hands together as they waited for Pearl to return, cupping them in front of the heater. "We'll get you settled at my house, and then we can come back into town unless the two of you could do with some more shut-eye."

"I've always been an early bird," Sally said. "Now that we're awake, we might as well stay this way and try to enjoy what we can of our vacation." Her voice sounded flat and dull when she said it despite her best efforts. All she could think about was her children on a plane, flying out to find that when it rained for their mom, it poured. Or, rather, it snowed.

"Thanks for waitin'," Pearl said breathlessly, opening the passenger's side door and climbing in. The warm truck quickly melted the snowflakes clinging to her coat.

"What did you need?" Sally asked. She had thought Pearl would get more coffee for the road, but she didn't seem to have a to-go cup in her hands.

"Wanted to check on that kid and her family, make sure they got somewhere to go. It looks like they're endin' up at one of the cabins, though her ma ain't thrilled about the likely doublin' up with other guests it's gonna have to be. They seemed to be on the fence about goin' home, but they've settled on stayin' for now. Still tryin' to get a McKenzie Bridge Christmas out of this shebang. I'm tellin' you, Sally, if they can pull a halfway decent Christmas outta this, you've got no excuse for complainin' about yours."

Sally tried to count her blessings as Mike pulled out of the parking lot, past groups of people trudging to their cars or waiting for the van to take them to the alternative cabins. It helped to remind herself that, technically, she was getting the McKenzie Bridge Christmas she was promised, even if an inconvenience was thrown in along the way. She was better off than so many people. Her mistake was letting herself hope for the impossible when it seemed like it just might be within her grasp.

"Hope you wanted snow for Christmas," Mike said, turning on his windshield wipers as the flakes started to come down more heavily.

"They were saying at the hotel that a big storm might be coming. The newscasters and Trevor mentioned it, too. Have you heard anything about it?" Sally asked.

Mike nodded grimly. "The forecast looks messy. Even more reason to enjoy walking around downtown McKenzie Bridge before it hits."

Sally turned to look at him. Then, realizing how close they were sitting, she turned to face forward. She hadn't had the chance to brush her teeth this morning, and her breath smelled like coffee. "I always love a white Christmas, but there was snow already." The entire town had been blanketed in two inches when they'd arrived, and as far as Sally was concerned, as long as the snow covered the grass, it was a perfect amount.

"Not real snow. For McKenzie Bridge, this is just a little dusting. When we say 'a big storm is coming,' we mean we're going to get dumped on in feet, not inches. It was supposed to hit north of us, but it shifted overnight. That can happen in the mountains. Now it's headed straight for McKenzie Bridge."

"All your wishin' for a snowy Christmas done jinxed it, Sally. Good thing we got a nice cabin and a fire to keep us warm," Pearl said. Then she sat forward and looked at Mike, "You got enough wine? My rule is a bottle for every six inches of snow."

Mike shook his head. "You've got your priorities straight. We can pick up a couple of bottles today in town."

"A couple for you? Sounds good, but I'm gonna need more than that," Pearl said. Sally elbowed her playfully before her expression turned serious.

"I hope those folks will be comfortable in the mountain cabins," she said quietly.

"They've got a girl scout with them. She don't mind a bit of adventure," Pearl said. "Probably knows how to build a signal fire and everything if somethin' goes wrong."

21

Hoover House

Pearl and Sally settled into Mike's guest room, complete with crisp hotel bedding and fluffy white towels. The window faced the river and mountains beyond. "You must have learned your hospitality when you were growin' up down South," Pearl said, walking out into the living room with a pair of fuzzy slippers on her feet. Mike was sitting in his leather recliner, laptop balanced on the tops of his thighs.

Sally walked out of the kitchen where she had been making a cup of coffee. Her brows were knitted in worry. "What are we going to do about the kids? What if the hotel isn't opened by then?"

Mike tapped his fingers on his keyboard. "I've got an idea." Mike pulled out his phone and punched in a message. The reply was almost instant, and a smile broke across his face.

Sally dropped down onto the couch next to Pearl. She needed some good news.

"A fishing buddy of mine owns the Hoover House. He was supposed to come up for Christmas but is taking his new wife to Fiji instead."

"Hoover House?"

"President Herbert Hoover used to visit up here to go fly-fishing. It sleeps 12, so there's plenty of room for everyone."

"And it's nice inside?" Sally asked, beaming.

"Oh my stars, Don't look a gift horse in the mouth," Pearl said, looking up from the game she was playing on her phone.

"Oh, I don't know. It sounds expensive." She couldn't agree to something like this without talking to Lauren first.

Mike held up a hand. "I'm going to stop you right there. There isn't going to be a charge, no expenses to worry about. I told my friend what happened at the hotel, and like those other folks donating space in their homes, he is happy to help accommodate in the spirit of the season."

"See?" Pearl said. "He solved that faster than a one-legged man in a butt-kickin' competition."

Mike ran a hand over his chin. "Speaking of your family, is there any word on their flights?"

"She said their plane was leaving today, but I haven't had reception at all up here," Sally admitted. "It's only when I'm connected to the Wi-Fi. That was true even at the high school during the baking contest."

She checked her messages, but there was nothing from Lauren. Hopefully, their plane got off the ground alright.

"Can we turn on the news and see if there have been any plane crashes?" she asked nervously. Pearl rolled her eyes.

"There ain't been no plane crashes. You're just worryin' because it's what you do when you're not in control of your immediate situation," Pearl said. "You keep thinkin' I don't know who my best friend is, and it's gettin' on my nerves. Let's see if there's any true crime on Mike's cable."

Mike obliged by tossing over the smart remote. "There's

Netflix, you know. Hulu, too."

"I just want to see the news," Sally sighed. "We're not going to watch true crime all day, Pearl. There's still so much in this adorable little Christmas village to explore, and I want to do it before the snow gets much worse."

"It's a tourist town. Things are designed so that you can see 'em all in about a weekend," Pearl grumbled, flipping the station to the local news. "Oh, looks like Mike gets the Portland station."

"Of course. They broadcast it locally as well as in Portland," Mike said. "It's just part of the Christmas festivities around here to have some colorful newscasters camped out in the cold all week, and also on our TV screens at home."

Brenda and Richard were seated side-by-side in their arm-chairs. Brenda wore a long festive sweater dress over a pair of tights, and she was pulling it down slightly over her knees. She looked like she was freezing as the snowflakes in the air fluttered down even more densely than they had when leaving the resort.

"So, as I said, folks... batten down the hatches. Rudolph's nose might be glowing, but this snow shows no signs of slowing!"

"It's just as Brenda says," Richard chimed in, seeming a little put out that she had to say it so adorably and upstage him. "Here in McKenzie Bridge, we aren't just going to get a white Christmas. We're looking at the distinct possibility of a white-*out* Christmas. Stay safe and warm, folks, and remember that these mountain roads come out swinging when that old north wind rolls through. Unless strictly necessary or for emergency purposes, travel should be avoided, although there might be time to run to Barry's Butcher Shop for a last-minute Christmas ham, 20% off from now until the new year!"

"Richard," Brenda scolded. "I don't think our sponsors want people out driving once the roads get bad. What a great time for some Christmas movies or a family board game night instead, folks!"

"Well, that's just great," Sally said glumly, taking the remote and flipping to the weather channel. She stared bleakly at the frothy colored blotches all over the state of Oregon. "They're saying two feet of snow will fall between now and Christmas, at least. Flights are probably canceled out this way."

"It's like I said," Pearl said. "You done jinxed it.

It took a few minutes longer for them to return to town. Sally and Pearl enjoyed a light breakfast of toast and coffee while they waited for Mike to lash chains around his truck tires. When they were finally set and approaching town, Mike's phone began to ring. He pulled over to the curb and answered it.

Sally and Pearl listened in on the one-sided conversation and watched Mike's face turn from happy and relaxed to tense and worried. "I'll be there in ten minutes." He snapped the phone shut, staring straight ahead through the snow that fell on his windshield between wiper swipes.

"Everything okay?" Sally asked.

"I've just been told that Mrs. Grassley was attacked."

Pearl shook her head. "Birdie Grassley? Is she sure it ain't a plastic Santa or a particularly threatenin' lampshade?"

"Let's not jump to conclusions. I have more questions than answers, but they are bringing her to the station. Someone, at least, thought that there might be a legitimate reason to be concerned."

"Oh dear, how awful," Sally said. "I hope she's alright."

"I wouldn't worry too much. She always seems to be," Mike said, sounding annoyed. "I don't have time to run you home. Can you hang out at the station while we sort this out?"

"Sure," Sally said. "We've spent so much time there on this trip, it might as well be a second home."

"I ain't settin' up a daisy vase and a pair of homey lace curtains in a jail cell," Pearl said flatly.

They pulled into the small paved lot, parking in the spot with a sign above it marked *Police Chief.*

The tidy but aged station was growing familiar to them by this point, though they'd typically been there after-hours when they'd visited. Towards the back, this area was new to them. Wide planked wood floors were faded in spots. One wall was exposed brick, and the other was covered with bulletin boards. Two metal desks sat side-by-side on the left. On the right were two small empty cells. An office was at the back of the building, and a bathroom was on the other side.

"Think I just stepped back into Mayberry. Is Sheriff Andy Griffith hiding back here somewhere?" Pearl joked.

"It's not fancy. But this little town doesn't have the tax base to build something new and flashy. We are trying to get the city council to update. So far, the best they have done is get us new laptops."

Pearl pulled her coat off and hung it on the coat rack on the wall. Sally followed suit. Mike skipped the rack and went straight to turn on the coffee machine. "It's going to be a long day." He leaned on the cabinet and waited for it to heat up. "I've got to meet with Birdie, but the two of you are free to look around."

"I've never seen the inside of a jail cell," Sally said. "I'm a little curious about it."

"Be my guest," Mike laughed as Sally and Pearl slid off to sit on one of the benches behind bars.

"Admit it, you just want to listen in on the conversation between Birdie and Mike, and you know that we can hear it from here. You didn't come all this way to worry about Birdie Grassley's histrionics, Sally."

It was true, but Sally still couldn't help thinking of how sad and alone Birdie had looked at the baking contest. While she'd laughed the first few times about her status as the town worrier, she started to feel bad about her initial judgments.

If that yappy little dog could love Birdie, surely there was something good about her buried beneath the surface.

"I will, if you admit wanting to listen in on a good mystery just as much," Sally shot back.

"I'll call that one a draw," Pearl grumbled.

Sally's phone buzzed with a text from Lauren.

```
Our flight was canceled. We are booked to fly out
tomorrow instead. I will keep you posted.
```

Sally leaned back and sighed, showing the screen to Pearl. Pearl patted her knee but didn't say anything. A sense of dread settled in Sally's stomach. Maybe she shouldn't buy presents until she was sure they would get here. She might jinx things again.

Then the door to the station burst open, an angry Birdie Grassley bringing a storm of her own.

22

Grandma Got Run Over by a Reindeer

"Doc's on her way over," Mike said, setting his cell phone down on the desk before leaning across it, making eye contact with Birdie. "Why don't you tell me what you remember about the accident?"

"This was no accident," Birdie said, her tone forcibly calm. "Someone tried to kill me. And worse, they tried to kill poor Maximillian." Birdie sat in Mike's chair, holding an ice pack to the side of her head. Her Pomeranian, for once completely unperturbed, was on the ground eating kibble out of a pop-up food bowl.

Mike kept his face neutral. "Tried to kill you? Could you elaborate a bit more on that?"

"Yes. I distinctly heard from behind me the words, 'Get her.' And then those animals were knocking me down and walking right over my head. I had to shield Maximillian with my own body."

Mike glanced down at the dog, who seemed none the worse for wear. "I wasn't aware that reindeer could attack on command."

"Of course you weren't," Birdie spat. "You aren't from around here, but isn't it obvious? If they can pull a sleigh on command, doesn't it stand to reason that they could attack someone on command?"

Mike raised an eyebrow and leaned back.

Across the small office and just within earshot, Sally and Pearl huddled together in the open cell. It was the only place to retreat in the small office while still being able to hear what was said inside of it relatively well. Sally wondered if Mike would have let them if he knew just *how* well they could hear.

"This is just too sad for words," Sally whispered.

"I don't reckon. Ain't there already a whole song about it? Didn't they make a movie too?" Pearl blew into her coffee mug, steam running away from the cup.

"Oh, Pearl, stop joking around."

"I ain't jokin', just statin' facts."

The room was hit with a blast of cold air as a pretty blonde in a calf-length parka pushed open the door, a blast of cold air on her heels. "Hey, Doc," Mike said, stepping forward to shake her hand.

Sally's brows raised. The doctor was Denise, one of the humanitarian blondes from the baking show. "Heard we had a run-in with wildlife," she said, letting go of Mike's hand and turning to Birdie. "What were you doing in the woods?" She slipped her pack off her shoulder, setting it on the desk. Undoing the zipper, she pulled out a pen light and a stethoscope. She flashed the penlight in Birdie's eyes.

"Don't make it sound like I was out in the woods. I was downtown, and I was attacked."

Denise leaned back, looking at Mike and then back to Birdie. "I'm sorry. I want to make sure I heard correctly, Mrs. Grassley.

Did you say that you were attacked?"

Birdie nodded vigorously. "Why else would I be here? Someone tried to kill me just days before Christmas." She turned to Mike indignantly. "Why on earth are you just sitting here? Shouldn't you be out there trying to find the intended killer?"

Denise furrowed her brows and looked at Mike again.

Trevor burst through the door, pulling a woman behind him. Trotting to keep up on her high-heeled boots was his girlfriend, Sheila. "You're not going to believe this," he said breathlessly, seeming to anticipate the unique status of sharing terrible news. It was only when he saw Birdie that he stopped and surveyed the scene, biting his lip. He pulled his hat off and held it against his chest. "Sorry. I thought I was the first one to report it." He let go of Sheila's hand and rushed to comfort Birdie by gently massaging her shoulders, dropping his hat on the desk.

He addressed Mike. "I guess you already must know, but a reindeer crashed through the front window of the coffee shop when it was full of people. Destroyed the dessert cases and knocked over tables. It's a mess down there."

Mike put his hands on his hips. "Was anybody hurt?"

Trevor shook his head. "Just those special Christmas cupcakes Sheila makes." Trevor pretended to wipe a tear from his eye. "It won't be the same without one of those on Christmas eve." Sheila puffed up a little bit inside her Burberry coat, proud that her boyfriend was acknowledging her.

"That last thing you need is a cupcake," Birdie said, pursing her lips. "You're not playing Lacrosse in high school anymore, and age has a way of catching up to a person."

Trevor thumbed his belt loops and pulled up his pants around his skinny waistline. "I see you're starting to feel like yourself again, Aunt Birdie," he said tersely.

Mike walked over to the jail cell, addressing Sally and Pearl. "Ladies, this could take a while. If you want, feel free to head downtown for a bit. They're running the last big pre-Christmas sales today, and it would be a shame to miss them."

"Really?" Sally sat up from where she lounged against the cell's back wall, torn.

Pearl whispered, "Don't you think we should stay? This whole thing stinks more than a locker room after a chili cook-off."

"What do you mean?"

"Oh, never mind. I'm sure Mike'll fill us in later. Let's make a run for it. I got a hankerin' for some pie." She slid off the bench and then turned to pull Sally to her feet.

"Do you want to take my truck?" Mike asked, glancing over his shoulder at the pair.

Sally shook her head. "It is so pretty outside. I'd rather walk." She needed some air to clear her head.

"If we don't come back, look for two ice cubes on the side of the road," Pearl called back.

Sally lifted her coat off the hook by the door and slid it on. "Oh, stop it. You aren't going to freeze to death walking three blocks."

"Do you girls mind if I join you?" Sheila asked. "I love a good sale, and these shoes are way more comfortable than they look." She shifted her Gucci handbag on her shoulder and smiled at Sally. "Trevor's got his auntie handled, and Chief Cunningham can probably sort out what happened with the reindeer, but I don't want to be here for 'a while'. I could use some retail therapy."

Pearl looked about ready to growl, but Sally smiled at the younger woman. "If you think you can keep up with a couple of old pros like us, of course you're welcome to join."

"Your hair looks great, by the way," Sheila gushed to Sally as she fell into step beside her with Pearl on the other side. "It really suits you."

"It's grown on me," Sally admitted, smiling as they headed for the snowy streets.

23

Noël

Light snow began to fall as they walked towards downtown. Long shadows stretched across the valley from the western mountains, and shop lights started to flicker on, promising warmth and festive activities inside.

"Hey, kiddo, sorry your kin might not make it out." Pearl offered.

Sally lifted her chin, "They'll make it. I have faith."

Pearl gave her a sideways grin. "Alrighty then. We should walk by the coffee shop. I wanna see the wreckage."

Sally linked arms with Pearl as they stepped off the curb to cross the street. "I still can't believe a reindeer almost killed Mrs. Grassley."

"I ain't convinced. Santa probably sent him to attack that Grinch."

"She's just being dramatic," Sheila chimed in, trotting to keep up on her heels. "Trevor spends a lot of time worrying and checking in on her, but she really just likes the attention."

"Oh?" Sally asked. "She seemed truly scared, and that reindeer caused some real damage, it sounds like."

"It could have been a bird hitting the window and she would have reacted the exact same way," Sheila assured, rolling her eyes.

"At least it didn't flood her house with poop," Pearl grumbled, increasingly unhappy about their talkative tag-along.

"Oh, shoot. You two were staying at Holiday Farms, weren't you? That's awful luck. I had to cancel so many appointments before Christmas, and that's when people give the best tips," Sheila said sadly. "Are you staying at one of the cabins? I heard that people were relocating."

"With the police chief, actually," Sally said, and Sheila grinned.

"Oh, the *handsome* police chief," Sheila said slyly. "You go, girl!"

Sally blushed, and Pearl nudged her as if that could turn off the heat in her cheeks.

The salted roads in town were turning the beautiful snow into gray slush. Even so, the trees up the mountain were snow-coated, and Christmas carols were pumping from the speakers on the corners. Kids crowded around the window of the old-fashioned toy store, watching the model train circle the multi-level track built to resemble the town and surrounding mountains. Sally clapped her mittened hands together. "Oh, it's just like a movie," she sighed. They rounded the corner onto Main Street, which was bustling with last-minute shoppers and tourists who had risked the snow to drive up for a day immersed in Christmas magic.

"Where should we start? Pie?" Pearl winked.

"Let's stop by that cute gift shop," Sally suggested. "I want to get an ornament for Mike's tree."

"Marking your territory, huh?" Sheila giggled. Sally cringed inwardly. Was it really so obvious that there might be something between her and Mike, even to a relative stranger? She reminded herself that Sheila seemed fairly obsessed with love at the moment. She also admittedly struggled to understand what the girl saw in Trevor after meeting the man.

Pearl leaned back to look at Sally, whose face was flushed. "Ain't you glowin'. You're happier than ol' Blue layin' on the porch chewin' on a big ol' catfish head."

Sally nodded, relieved to have an excuse. "I am. It's been a perfect trip. Well, minus the hotel flooding, and grandma getting run over by a reindeer." She covered her mouth with the back of her hand to stifle a giggle. Sheila, on the other hand, giggled openly.

Every trip had a few hiccups. The biggest one so far had been the disaster with the hotel, and Sally was still uncertain about what might be done when the kids arrived, if they even could fly in with the incoming awful weather. Her brows furrowed, and she focused on breathing through her nose.

Pearl patted her hand. "Let's hope nothin' else goes wrong."

Pulling open the door of the Prancer's Point ornament shop, they were hit with the smell of cinnamon and wintergreen. People navigated the crowded displays, overflowing to accommodate the last-minute rush. They pushed inside and let the door close behind them.

Sheila drifted away from them to look at Christmas garlands. Sally made a beeline for the tall, thin tree in the corner covered with handmade ornaments. She lifted a rustic-looking snowman off the branch and turned the tag over to read it. "Pearl, these are made by children at an orphanage in Cambodia. Isn't this too cute?"

"That some fancy way to say child labor?"

Sally clicked her tongue and shook her head. "Do you have to be so cynical about everything?"

Pearl pulled her chin into her neck and considered. "Yes. And I ain't gonna apologize for it. You got sunshine comin' outta your butt, so we balance each other."

Sally chuckled. "Fair enough." She slipped the ornament ribbon back onto the branch and surveyed the other ornaments. She wanted to find something that would remind Mike of her and Pearl. But she didn't want it to be romantic, so anything with hearts was out.

While she balanced on tip-toes to read the inscription on an ornament hung towards the top of the tree, a ruckus broke out on the other side of the store.

"What in tarnation?" Pearl said. Shoppers were moving away from the sound of rising voices.

Patrick and Kiyomi were at it again. The two were standing next to a manger display, and Kiyomi's arms were crossed over the front of her Louis Vuitton scarf. She glared stormily off over her shoulder.

"I don't know why you're so mad," Patrick said, running a hand over his hair.

"You have the emotional intelligence of a goat," Kiyomi said, ice coating every word.

"I just thought it would be a good idea."

Kiyomi's head snapped back towards him, "You were wrong. It's a ridiculous idea."

"Where's their little lamb?" Pearl asked, frowning. "Aw, heck. You know she can't stand to see them fightin'."

"She must be around somewhere," Sally said, glancing around the ornament shop. There was Sheila, by the garlands, and various other people milling around, but before Sally even

156

spotted her, Pearl was striding over in the direction of a red beret by a gorgeously lit display of angel ornaments.

Sally followed at a slight distance, listening without intruding.

"Pearl." Noël smiled up at her. "It's good to see you!"

"Always good to see you," Pearl replied, "though probably better when I got some award-winnin' cookies to give you. Hope you and your folks liked 'em."

Noël nodded so vigorously that her red hat shifted on her head.

"These are some real pretty ornaments you found. You got a favorite?"

"This one," Noël sighed, pointing at a pretty blonde angel with snowy skin and long, delicate hands poised over a harp. "She's so pretty."

"Reckon so," Pearl said. "Maybe she's your guardian angel."

"What?" Noël giggled. "You can't buy a guardian angel."

"Sure can. I see a price tag," Pearl said, but Noël just shook her head, continuing to laugh.

"Real angels are different. You don't always notice them, but they're around. They take care of you," Noël said, hugging her elbows. Her father's voice grew momentarily louder, and she ducked her head down between her shoulders.

"Angels'll do that," Pearl replied after a moment. "And you know what, even if the real ones go unseen a whole lot, the fake ones are still nice to look at. We got different favorites, though." She plucked one from the display, with long dark hair and a serene expression. "Don't you think she's pretty, too?"

"I guess so," Noël said, her smile growing a little more shy before fading. "She looks like my mom."

"And like you," Pearl offered. "Your ma's a pretty lady and you take after her."

"I'm mad at my mom," Noël said suddenly. "My dad just tries to make her happy, but nothing is ever good enough. They think I don't know, but..." she bit her lip, leaning in to tell Pearl something that Sally couldn't quite catch.

"Well, darn," Pearl said, loud enough that Sally *could* hear. "That's real tough, kiddo."

"She had no right, and she still treats Dad like it's his fault, even though she's the one who-"

"Tell you what," Pearl said, pulling down a few angel ornaments with brisk determination. "It sounds like you need a whole fleet of guardian angels. Can old Pearl give you a Christmas present?"

Noël's eyes were wide, but she nodded, watching Pearl pull down angels of all hair and skin colors with all different kinds of instruments in their hands.

"They'll keep you safe if you keep them safe. We'll make sure we get a nice box or somethin' at checkout. You look at them whenever you're feelin' like the world is a little bit too much, okay?"

"My parents can pay you back," Noël offered, cradling the little angel figurines in her hands. "They have money."

"So do I, and I spend it how I please," Pearl answered, pulling down another three for good measure. Sally watched as Pearl went with Noël to purchase about ten of the angel ornaments, all of which were individually wrapped in tissue paper and laid in a segmented box.

At this point, Noël's parents seemed to notice what was going on, and strode over to the cash register in embarrassment, but Sally caught their attention, approaching and clearing her throat.

"Your daughter is such a trooper," she said, catching the two of them off guard.

"Oh?" Patrick asked guardedly.

"She's taken everything in such stride. The hotel flood," Sally quickly clarified before it could seem like she was referring to her parents' constant fights. "She's something special."

"Well," Kiyomi said stiffly, "She's very tough, but no one in our family needs charity."

"What about gifts?" Pearl asked, returning with Noël at her side. "Don't mean to overstep, of course."

"It is overstepping, respectfully," Kiyomi said tersely, taking the box, which Noël clung to. "Noël has enough things."

Patrick fumbled in his wallet for money to repay Pearl, but she waved it away.

"Where I come from gifts are gifts! They're just trinkets. Ain't no debt attached."

"And maybe you have a friend with a windowless van waiting around the side of the building," Kiyomi challenged. Pearl clenched her fists, and Sally rushed to grab her elbow.

"Ain't no debt attached," Pearl gritted out, her voice supremely controlled. "Just wanted to spread some Christmas cheer after that pipe got clogged. It messed up all our plans, and your girl done kept smilin'."

"Thank you, Miss Pearl," Noël said softly, clutching the box with her eyes stretched wide. Patrick tried to push a $100 bill at Pearl, but she waved it away.

"Gifts are gifts," Pearl said, simply and flatly. "Merry Christmas to y'all."

24

That Didn't End Well

Sally was relieved to walk through the door of Mike's house. She was ready to relax, and Mike insisted on taking care of dinner. Sally was thrilled with everything from the wine to the seafood, expertly seasoned and cooked. She couldn't help but think how nice it was to have a host who was both handsome and a great home chef.

Then, the stomach cramps set in. Pearl was the first to rocket out of bed and run down the hall to the bathroom, followed shortly by Sally, who rocketed in the opposite direction to the downstairs toilet.

As she clung to the porcelain, she thought she could hear Pearl and Mike in similar situations, though she tried to block out the sounds. She'd heard Harold sick many times over the years and Pearl sick a few, but even as she threw up her seafood, she was in a disembodied state of denial. This couldn't be happening, not in McKenzie Bridge, not just before Christmas.

When she finally managed to half-crawl back to their room, Pearl was sprawled face-down on the mattress.

"Ain't never eatin' oysters again," Pearl moaned. "Talk to

me about somethin' pretty that smells nice, somethin' pastoral or some such."

"Um," Sally started, faltering. "There's this meadow. And there's a little spring. Fresh, clean, and babbling."

"Brooks babble," Pearl grunted into her pillow.

"Don't be snarky. This spring babbles too," Sally said, equally unwell and perhaps more irritable. "And little flowers are dotting the hillside, and there are cows-"

"Cows!" Pearl heaved over the side of the bed, splashing vomit down the side.

"Mike's bedspread!" Sally said, scrambling for the waste-basket in the corner and cradling it in her lap as she coughed and spat feebly.

"Why'd you have to tell me about cows?" Pearl asked hoarsely, panting. "They stink. All I can think about are them nasty pies underfoot in those green fields. Couldn't you have done a pasture with no cows?"

"There isn't any such thing!" Sally shot back. "Pastures are for grazing! Not for easing nausea!"

"I'm goin' back to bed," Pearl said.

"Clean up the vomit, at least," Sally said, but Pearl was already snoring.

Sally sighed. She went to the bathroom, found a bucket, a scrub brush, and some cleaning supplies, and ensured there was no trace of Pearl's messy mishap or her own wastebasket upheaval. It took a lot of disinfectant and scrubbing while feeling worse than hungover, but finally, Sally managed to finish the job. She deposited everything in the shower and then fell into bed herself, hoping that Mike was okay but afraid to disturb him in case he'd gone the way of Pearl and passed out. The only upside was that her family missed getting sick with them. Thank goodness for flight delays.

It was well after noon when Sally woke up, and it was still before either Pearl or Mike. She slipped on her bathrobe and slippers, feeling uneasy about the midday winter sun, obscured by clouds but nevertheless glaring through the windows as she made toast. On another day, she might have tried to get a griddle and some french toast going, but today they would all be lucky to keep some dry, crusty bread down. They were losing precious time, and she hardly wanted to be sick when her kids rolled into town, however, or whenever that might be.

"Good morning," Mike said, his eyes alarmingly bloodshot as he slumped out to take a seat at the kitchen island. "Or rather, afternoon."

"Heck of a night," Sally commented neutrally.

"I owe you and Pearl an apology. I think I'm going to get the health inspector down to Harry's. Their refrigerators aren't turned up high enough."

"It's ironic," Sally chuckled hoarsely as she set a slice of toast on a plate and set it in front of Mike. "We're getting buried in snow, and the refrigerators can't keep oysters at a temperature that won't make people sick."

"Well, there's no way I screwed up," Mike said, holding his hands up to ward off the accusation. "I'd never do that. I'm a pro at food prep."

"And yet..." Sally led, putting another two pieces of toast in the slats.

"I might have screwed up a little," Mike admitted. "I thought serving oysters would be a real smooth move."

"In a perfect world, it would have been," Sally said.

"You must think it's pretty dumb," said Mike. "Never again, and that's a sacred promise."

"No more oysters, maybe," Sally agreed with a laugh lighter than she felt, "but you could keep trying smooth moves. Most of yours are pretty good."

"That means a lot, coming from you," Mike said, smiling over his dry toast before taking a careful, nibbling bite.

Sally bit her lip. "I should go check on Pearl," she said.

Back in their room, Pearl was awake, and the TV was on. In a rare break from form, it wasn't a true crime show but instead the local news.

"More snow?" Sally asked weakly, handing a plate of toast to Pearl.

"Tons more snow," Pearl confirmed, staring grimly at the screen.

"Maybe the flights will make it," Sally said. "It's possible. Airplanes fly above the clouds, so they're also above the snow, right?"

"Sally, darlin', I adore you for cleanin' up my puke, but I don't think any of it works like that."

"They need to make it out here," Sally said quietly but fiercely. "I need my kids with me. They said they were coming."

"And sometimes we can't control when our kids are with us, or how. And they can't, neither," Pearl said. "They'd be here with you if they could be, I know it, but ain't none of them pilots, or stupid enough to fly in this weather even if they were. You should be grateful if they're grounded."

Sally furrowed her brow. "I've got to call Lauren. I need to hear her voice, at least."

"Even if it's bad news?" Pearl asked, taking micro-bites out of the corner of her dry toast.

"It won't be bad news," Sally said, pressing her thumb

against her daughter's picture on the phone and waiting for the ring and the answer.

"Hi, Mom." Lauren sounded exhausted on the other end of the line.

"Honey," Sally said brightly. "What's going on? Are you in town yet? Mike has a truck, so he can come and get you. I'm sure we can rent a car seat for Amelia at the airport."

"Mom." Lauren sighed heavily. "I'm so sorry, Mom. I've been putting off calling you because I feel so bad, but we're not en route. The weather's too bad for planes to take off, and it's even worse where we'd all be landing. We're stuck in Minneapolis until it clears up, and that could take a while."

"I don't understand," Sally said numbly. "You said you were coming."

"I would come, Mom. All of us would. We're trying, but this is where we are. This is how it is."

"Do they have an estimate for when the plane might leave?" Sally felt like her voice and body were in different places, and neither of them could feel or process what was happening.

"Mom." Lauren's voice grew short, patient with a frustrated edge. "I don't think we're going to make it. The airport is a mess. We'll keep trying, but it doesn't look good."

Sally pursed her lips, the phone against her ear.

"Mom?" Lauren asked.

With a great effort, Sally bit back the protests and frustration she wanted to voice. "I understand," she said. "I know you can't help it. Well, sorry, sweetie. I love you. Bye."

She hung up, burying her head in her hands. Pearl, still smelling faintly of vomit, reached over to hug her, but Sally couldn't bring herself to push the other woman off. Instead, she clung back, and the tears started to flow fast and hard.

They spent the rest of the day in pajamas, watching Christmas movies and curled up on the couch. Sally's heart was heavy, exacerbated by the lack of food and sleep. Around dinner time, Mike announced he was heading into town to check on things with Gavin and to bring back soup from the diner.

"God bless that man," Pearl said.

"Maybe we should go with him?" Sally suggested, although her heart wasn't in it.

"You try to move me off this couch, and I'll jerk a knot in your tail."

Sally laughed and let it go.

25

Timber

December 22nd

After a long hot shower and thoroughly brushing her teeth, Sally felt human again and ready to tackle the day. She had a full agenda planned for them, starting with an event she had been looking forward to for weeks. After a quick breakfast and cup of coffee, Mike drove them down to the elementary school.

"What are you up to today?" Sally asked him.

"Gavin and I have a budget meeting this morning. I have a report due to the City Council by the end of the year, and with Birdie breathing down my neck, I need to make sure it is top notch."

Pearl shook her head, "That woman could make a pastor mad enough to kick in stained glass windows."

"Let's just hope today is a nice boring day. I will meet up with you for lunch," Mike said, stopping in front of the school. "Have fun. Don't do anything wild at the quilt show." He smirked.

Sally and Pearl wandered down the rows of quilts hung on

display in the elementary school gym. Sally's mother used to quilt, but Sally had never had the patience for it. As she read the tags, she saw that the quilts had come from all over the country. Intricate designs of nativity scenes, winter wonderlands, and other traditional Christmas patterns made it hard to pick her favorite. It was the largest quilting show of its kind in the United States, and both Sally and Pearl were impressed.

"Look at this!" Sally said, racing over to a beautiful nativity quilt pattern. "Look how they've captured the night sky perfectly. I imagine this is exactly what it was like the night Jesus was born."

Pearl leaned in to admire the stitching. "That's all fine and dandy, but you know that the historians say he wasn't even born in wintertime."

"Pearl Dawson. I don't know where your Christmas spirit has gone, but you better dredge it up."

Pearl turned to find Sally staring at her, eyes blazing. "You got your granny panties all in a wad over this?"

"It's not just this. I love this time of year, and every time I turn around, you're being critical and dismissive."

Pearl tucked her chin into her neck. "Oh, my. Fancy words, you must be real mad."

"Of course I'm mad. You know how important this is to me. And I don't need you pointing out anything else negative. Not now, not after everything has fallen apart and my kids are delayed in Minneapolis, of all godforsaken places."

"Fine. I'll keep my mouth shut unless I got somethin' to say that's sweet as candy or as nice as Jesus."

Sally let out a breath. "Good. Why do you have such a hard time with Christmas anyway? Is it because of-"

Before Sally could finish her question, there was an enormous crash outside, followed by screams and honking cars in the town square.

"What in the world?" Pearl asked as they ran towards the exit to see what was going on.

Pushing through a side exit, Sally and Pearl found themselves standing at the tip of the 30-foot tall Christmas tree that, minutes before, had been standing in the middle of the town square. Now it was lying on its side, blocking the street. Horrified people were standing around nervously, chatting about how they had barely escaped getting hit by the tree.

"Anyone hurt?" Sally asked no one in particular. A few people glanced her way and shook their heads but then returned to talking among themselves. Sally and Pearl followed the tip of the fallen tree into the town square, trying to get a better look. By the time they reached the halfway point, sirens were screaming from the direction of the police station, and they saw Mike jump out of his truck and run over to where the maintenance crew was crowded around the tipped tree stand.

Sally paused and watched. Mike stood with his hands on his hips, his head dipped down, listening to the animated crew leader recount what had happened before the accident. Then Mike looked up, nodded once, and started shouting directions. They needed to get the tree back up and divert traffic around to the other side of the square. Gavin ran up a second later and, upon receiving instructions from Mike, took off across the square to guide the cars safely around the affected area.

"Well, this is excitin'," Pearl said. "Bet that don't happen very often."

Sally nodded. As Pearl prattled on, Sally couldn't take her eyes off Mike. *What would it be like to be with a man like him?* She wondered. He would probably be a good husband. He was strong and kind and knew how to take charge of a disaster, even if he couldn't cook shellfish safely. She couldn't complete her thoughts because her stomach flipped like she was a teenager again. She giggled to herself, which drew a confused look from Pearl.

"You in shock or somethin'?" Pearl asked, peering closely at her.

Sally shook her head and then pulled Pearl away from the downed tree. The crew was busy on their radios. They would probably need a crane to get the tree back into position. It was a mess. "Let's get out of their way," Sally said, trying to gauge the overall direction the crowd seemed to be drifting.

"I agree. I wonder if they'll try to get that thing back up and sparklin', or just hack it up into pieces and haul it away."

Sally gaped at her. "They can't do that. It's not even Christmas yet, and there has to be a tree in the town square for Christmas."

Pearl raised an eyebrow but kept quiet. Sally figured she was probably trying to honor the vow she had just taken about not being negative.

"Come on, let's get ourselves a piece of pie. You can watch Mike and his sweet little tight butt prancin' around from the window." Pearl winked at Sally and grabbed her arm, pulling her across the street into the diner. They managed to grab a table by the window and watched as a crane showed up and slowly eased the tree back into the stand, anchoring it with cords and stakes in the ground. Mike waved at them from across the street as he directed traffic around the cleanup efforts and the crowd slowly dispersed. When the tree was finally back in its rightful position, a smattering of applause broke out inside the diner and on the street. Mike turned from his duties and smiled up at the tree for a moment, then went back to directing traffic.

Sally pulled out her phone and connected to the free Wi-Fi. She had a text from Lauren.

> Good news! We got a flight out of Minneapolis later today and are going to try and fly through Salt Lake City. I'll keep you posted. Love you Mom.

Sally tapped a quick acknowledgment and smiled. She knew something would work out. Sally and Pearl quickly paid their bill and wandered outside, only to see Birdie crossing the street in front of them. They followed her as she headed straight for Mike, with Maximillian under her arm wearing a dog-sized black Balenciaga sweater. "I have been attacked twice under your watch. Do you care to explain yourself, Chief Cunningham?"

"Hello, Birdie. I'm trying to direct this traffic, but what can I do for you?" Mike asked patiently.

"You can do your job, for starters."

Mike motioned around her. Cars eased by. "I thought I was doing my job."

Birdie stopped in front of him and poked his chest. "Are you even listening to me? Someone tried to kill me again today."

"How?" Mike asked, turning to let traffic through.

"What do you mean, how? That tree almost crushed me."

"Are you all right?" Mike paused before asking the question carefully.

"Of course I am. No thanks to you."

"This was just an accident. There's no proof or even evidence that somebody pushed that tree over on purpose, never mind that they were trying to target you specifically. It could have fallen on anyone. Thank goodness it didn't," he added quickly before that could be taken the wrong way.

"There's only no proof or evidence because you haven't bothered to look for them. I feel it in my bones. Somebody is out to get me."

"Listen, Birdie," Mike said, sighing heavily. "I care about your safety, and I want you to feel safe. I truly do. But I have over two feet of snow coming and a town full of tourists, not to mention the runaway reindeer damage we are still trying to clean up. When I get a minute to breathe, I promise we'll look into it."

"We never had this sort of chaos before you came here. Now your incompetence is going to get me killed."

Mike squared his shoulders and opened his mouth to speak. Gavin returned in time to put his hand on Mike's arm and say, "Now look here, Birdie, we are doing the best we can. Do you know of anyone who would want to hurt you?"

Birdie lifted her chin. "Of course I do. I've lived in this town for almost seventy years."

Mike squeezed his forehead with his hand, sighing. "Anyone in particular?" he asked patiently.

"Could be those neighbors of mine and their awful ice rink. Or maybe Malory from the flower shop. She never forgave me for my online review of her store. She deserved it. Her flower arrangements for poor Bob's funeral were tacky. The whole town was talking about it for months on end, and I had to endure the mortification."

Sally watched Mike closely. His face was shadowed with

stress and exasperation.

"Why am I even telling you this? You are the chief of police. Our tax dollars pay you to figure this out. And if you're not up to the task, I'm sure we can find someone who is. In the meantime, I'm going home."

Birdie walked away, shaking her head. Gavin turned to Mike. "Sorry about that, Mike. When she gets something stuck in her craw, it's hard to pry it out."

"That's one way to put it," Mike said.

"I didn't mean any disrespect. I know how she is, and I don't even blame her for it. I just wanted to head her off so we can deal with the rest of this mess." Gavin ran a hand through his hair.

Mike tipped his head back and blew out a breath. When he looked back at Gavin, he was all business. "Alright. We need to talk to the businesses about closing early. Hopefully, that will encourage the tourists to drive back home before the road down the mountain closes and the roads get worse."

Gavin winced. "None of these cars have chains on the tires. They will slide off into the river if the roads get slippery. I'm worried it's already to that point."

"I was thinking the same thing," said Mike. "It might already be too late. Have Kelly call the superintendent and see if we can get the high school gym reserved for a shelter."

"Got it, boss." Gavin went to his cruiser, speaking into his corded radio.

"What can we do to help?" Sally asked. She glanced around the picture-perfect town that already had broken tree branches lying across Main Street. The monster of a snow storm barreling down on them would doubtless guarantee even more damage.

"Well, the storm's set to start really burying us tonight. We'll get steadier snowfall and lots more of it, and it'll just keep up through Christmas Eve. Things are about to feel a lot more crowded in the Christmas Capital of the Northwest with these folks from out of town stuck here. Do you really want to spend your vacation helping out?"

"Yes, absolutely," Sally said, glancing at Pearl, who was nodding along.

"We could definitely use some extra hands to volunteer at the gym. Hand out coffee to the grown-ups and hot cocoa to the kids, maybe pitch in with kitchen duty, and make sure everyone has a warm change of clothes from the Salvation Army if they need it. Generally do your best to keep spirits high."

"Well, that's one thing Sally's just dandy at," Pearl said dryly.

"Not that you'd ever guess, based on your lack of a Christmas spirit," Sally laughed.

"You done better than you think, kid. Just 'cause I ain't singin' carols don't mean I ain't cheered to have you around."

"So you're glad you came? Even with the sewage and the snow?"

"It's my first Christmas in years I ain't spendin' alone. Reckon 'glad' is a good word for it."

"I'm glad you came, too," Sally smiled. "More now than ever."

26

A Dead Raccoon

Mike dropped Sally and Pearl off at the school to meet up with Kelly, who was in charge of organizing the shelter. Kelly stood outside, hugging a cup of coffee in her mittened hands and bouncing on her heels to stay a little warmer. "Hey, girls. Thanks for coming. We have a lot to do," she sighed. "We have about 75 people who will be here soon. I think that around 30 of them are kids."

"Just let us know what to do," Sally said, following her through the double doors. Inside the gym, volunteers set up cots donated by the National Guard. Across the gym, lunch tables were being set up by high school students. Kelly seemed to have things well in hand.

"We have bedding coming over from the hotel. They are still shut down. Some of the restaurants in town are helping with food and supplies."

She turned to Sally and Pearl. "Dinner's covered. Could you help us with some dessert?"

"What do you got in mind? I'm more of the supervisin' type," Pearl said.

Kelly clapped her on the back. "Why don't you start by making some brownies, or your famous cookies for the kids to decorate? You should have everything you need in the kitchen."

Pearl pulled her chin into her neck. "How many cookies we talkin'?"

Kelly chuckled, "As many as you want to make. I don't think 'too many' is possible when you've got kids far from home and hungry."

Sally looped her arm through Pearl's. "Come on, friend, let's get busy. The kids'll be here soon."

Not her kids, but someone's, and that would have to be enough for now. Sally's heart swelled to think there was a place for her to put her love after so many let-downs and disappointments.

As promised, the cafeteria kitchen had all the ingredients to make sugar cookies, even sour cream. Sally and Pearl borrowed aprons hanging on hooks near the door. Sally dragged a large mixing bowl off the shelf and found a spatula. She set them on the counter and started measuring out flour.

"Any word from Lauren?" Pearl asked with a sideways glance.

Sally frowned. "Not since the last text. They are still stuck in the airport, and they're going to try to fly through Salt Lake City next. The boys hope to drive down from Seattle if the roads open, though."

"That's somethin'," Pearl said.

Sally rolled her shoulders back. "Yes. Maybe they can still make it." She smiled sheepishly. "I have to admit that if Windsong couldn't make it, I wouldn't be heartbroken."

Pearl cracked an egg into the mixing bowl. "You got that

175

right."

Kelly's voice called out from the other side of the door to the gym. "Hey, you can't go back there–"

A moment later, the door burst open. Birdie burst in, hair disheveled, with one of the lenses in her glasses cracked. Her face was flushed red, and her mouth twisted into a scowl. She was breathless and wild-eyed, clutching Maxmillian, who was shaking.

"What happened to you?" Sally asked, abandoning the measuring cup and wiping her hands on her apron.

Birdie blew the hair out of her face. "What do you think happened? I got tangled in the tinsel with Santa?"

Pearl bobbed her head. "That'd do it."

Sally gave her a disapproving look, and Pearl shrugged.

"Are you alright?" Sally asked, pulling over a metal stool for Birdie, whose silence as she took it was probably the closest thing to gratitude that she could express.

"I'm pretty far from alright," Birdie sniffed. "I came here because the police won't listen. I'm hoping maybe you will." Her eyes lingered on Sally before she said somberly, "Someone tried to poison me." Birdie dropped a black trash bag on the floor of the kitchen.

"What?" Sally's eyes went wide. What in the world did she have in that trash bag? She both wanted to see very badly, and dreaded what the black plastic might be hiding.

"This morning, I opened my door to find a fruitcake on my porch. Fruitcakes are trashy. So I put it in the trash where it belonged. Good thing, too, because it would have killed me."

"Let me guess. It was poisoned." Pearl smirked.

"Pearl, let her tell the story," Sally said.

"Thank you, Sally. I was sitting in my front room, enjoying

a warm fire and reading to unwind after that tree almost killed me, when I heard something outside. This town has a terrible raccoon problem, and sure enough, when I opened the side door near my garbage cans, the awful creatures were making a meal of my garbage, dragging it all over the place. I grabbed my broom and ran out there, slipping on the ice and almost breaking my neck. I *did* break my glasses. Poor Maximilian was traumatized, barking up a storm. Once I got to my feet, I went after them. Those coons scattered, except one. That one stumbled a few feet like a drunken hooligan and then just fell right over. His body started shaking like one of those beds you put a nickel in to make it vibrate, and then his eyes rolled back in his head, and he died."

"How terrible," Sally said, covering her mouth with her hand.

Pearl took a breath through her nose. "Not sure how a dead raccoon proves someone tried to do you in."

Birdie pulled out a plastic sandwich bag. "I have the proof right here. After that raccoon stopped flopping around on my driveway, I ran back in, grabbed some gloves and a baggie, and dug in the trash for a sample. I know that's what killed him, and that it was supposed to kill me."

Sally and Pearl leaned in to look at the small piece of crushed fruit cake. "Don't that beat all," Pearl said.

"I need your help. You solved that murder in Mexico. I saw the story on the news. I'm not ready to meet my maker yet. Maximillian and I have a cruise booked for next year, and it's non-refundable."

Pearl stepped in front of her and pointed in her face. "If you want our help, you gotta stop bein' rude. We ain't from around here, but we're just as good as you are, and we ain't gonna hear

177

you implyin' otherwise and insultin' us."

Birdie scoffed. "I don't know what…"

Her words trailed off as Pearl slowly shook her head without breaking her icy gaze.

Birdie took a step backward and swallowed. "I'm sorry. It's frustrating not to be taken seriously when I'm in danger."

"It's frustrating even when you're not in danger," Sally said gently. "But what can we do, practically speaking?"

Birdie's eyes blazed anew. "You can make that police chief do his job, for a start. He won't listen to me. I bet my Birkin he'll listen to you."

Sally wasn't sure how to respond. Her mouth went dry. She didn't want to get involved with this.

"Oh, my stars. Come on, Sally, let's see if there is anythin' to this once and for all." Pearl turned to go before looking back at the black trash bag on the ground.

"If there's a dead raccoon in there, you'd best get it out of where food's gettin' prepared for folks in need. Ain't sanitary."

"We will help, but we promised to get these cookies done first," Sally said.

"Leave the fruitcake and put that raccoon out back. We'll go talk to Mike and come to your place after."

"That way, you can get cleaned up after your ordeal," Sally said, touching Birdie's arm.

Birdie considered, her mouth set in a grim line. "I'm not leaving my evidence here. But I'll head back. I need to feed Maximilian anyway. In all the confusion, he missed his second breakfast, and I had to leave him at home all alone." Her eyes flitted around the kitchen. "I will see you later." With a formal nod, she picked up the trash bag and strode out of the kitchen, a bit off-kilter, but with her chin held high.

Sally and Pearl both let out a breath and then laughed at the same time. After giving the area a good disinfecting, just in case, Sally and Pearl set out to finish their cookie project. When that was done, they headed over to the station.

"You have to listen to us, Mike," Sally said. "Someone is trying to murder Birdie. I know about her reputation, but I actually believe her."

Mike looked up from the papers on his desk. His face stayed blank as he considered how to respond. "I don't think this is anything besides an overactive imagination." He turned his attention back to the list he was making.

Something about how he dismissed her out of turn caused ire to rise in Sally. She leaned forward and put both hands on his desk. "I know you are stressed, Mike, but I don't appreciate you minimizing our concerns. I'm starting to see just how Birdie feels in this town."

Mike stared silently at the massive stack of paperwork on his desk before he sighed, setting his pen down and leaning back. "Fine. I trust you, Sally, and I'm sorry for minimizing your concerns. That wasn't my intention. What do you want to bring to my attention regarding Mrs. Grassley?"

"Birdie was poisoned. Well, not poisoned, but almost poisoned."

"Really? Like she was almost run over by a reindeer. And almost crushed by the town tree?"

"Exactly," Pearl said. "There's a real pattern formin' here, and we're on the case. Could use some backup, though."

"I have a conference call in ten minutes. Can we please talk about this later?"

"I think that Birdie needs us now," Sally said, surprised at

179

the powerful way her words came out. Mike raised his brows.

"Do you have any evidence for this?" he asked, sounding like he strongly doubted any could exist.

"A fruitcake," Pearl said.

Mike leaned back in his chair. "I might not be overly fond of the woman, but let's refrain from calling Mrs. Grassley names." Sally and Pearl exchanged exasperated glances. "There is so much to do in this town for people who are truly in need and actually in danger. I have to address all of that first. Birdie isn't more important than those displaced tourists, whatever she might believe."

"She isn't less important, either," Sally said. "Please, Mike, for me?"

He shook his head unhappily. "The truth is that in Mexico, about a dozen laws were broken on our end. It took a lot to clean that up. I can't afford to get mixed up in another incident like that in a town I'm supposed to keep clean and quiet. I'll give it some thought, and I swear to you that we will revisit this later, but please try to understand that my career and sanity both need a break from Birdie Grassley for a little while."

"Fine." Sally turned on her heel and stomped out of the office. Pearl followed behind, mumbling about men thinking they knew it all.

27

Fruitcake Controversy

Sally paced the hallway of the school, her long winter coat unzipped and hat in hand. She was too mad to enter the gym just yet. A tempest of emotion swirled inside of her. How could Mike be such a disappointment? She should never have come here. Even if it was just her and Pearl, they could have stayed home and had a lovely quiet Christmas with only the murder investigations on television to concern them.

Pearl leaned against the lockers, her arms folded. "You done throwin' a hissy fit?" She tipped her head and straightened. "We ain't gonna solve this crime with you wearin' down this floor with your pacin'."

Sally stopped and tipped her head back, closing her eyes. "What are we going to do?"

"We gotta come at this logically. Make a list. Ask questions. Find evidence." Pearl ticked the list off on her fingers. "Bust the perp."

Sally rolled her shoulders back and sniffed. She could do this. Maybe she was meant to be here so that she could help Birdie. No one else was going to. She and Pearl were perfectly capable of figuring this out. Her storm of emotion settled into calm confidence. Her eyes were clear as she said, "Let's do this."

Pearl clapped. "That's the spirit."

A few minutes later they sat before a notepad and plates of pizza that had been brought in for dinner.

"Birdie got nearly run over by a reindeer, toppled by a tree, and poisoned by a fruitcake. We should look into all of those, and any connections she might have to people who could be involved," Sally said, tapping her pen against the cafeteria table.

Pearl smacked her thigh. "Now you're soundin' like Sherlock Holmes."

Sally laughed half-heartedly. "I wish I felt that way. It's tough to even think of a place to start when so many people in this town dislike her so intensely."

Pearl jotted down three columns on the notepad and labeled them *reindeer, tree*, and *fruitcake*.

"Might want to start with the reindeer, since that happened first and all. What was that handler's name?"

"Steve, I think," Sally said, squinting as she dug back through her memory. "Oh! And you know what? When we stopped by that Reindeer Café with Mike after the interview, I think I saw him in there, sitting with that newscaster Richard Garrison. Remember how Richard made that strange comment about how there's not much difficulty in McKenzie bridge, except for where Birdie's concerned? What if they were planning something then?"

"Addin' Richard to the list just because he's a smarmy creep," Pearl chuckled. "Brenda don't seem suspicious to me, though."

"Brenda seems like an open book," Sally agreed. "It would

be a heck of a twist if she had anything at all to do with it, but I think we can rule her out until we're really scraping the bottom of the barrel."

"They woulda both been nearby when that tree came down in the town square," Pearl pointed out. "Even before it happened, since that's where their studio's set up. Who else woulda been by that tree, or involved with it?"

"Whoever put it up," Sally said. "We should also look into where the stand came from and if there was anything wrong with it. Write down 'chamber of commerce,' and 'tree stand.'"

Pearl's marker squeaked on the paper.

"Last thing's just the fruitcake, and I think I know darn well who's behind that one, as well as the motive. Dang herpes sisters woulda been salty about losin' after even playin' dirty didn't work, and stuck here after the roads closed down. Fruitcake might as well be their callin' card if Paul was tellin' the truth about it bein' their specialty and all."

"Would they be so direct?" Sally asked, watching with her brows furrowed as Pearl jotted down *Tillie* and *Millie*.

"Don't think I need to tell you that subtlety ain't exactly their forte," Pearl said dryly. "They're the primary suspects, if you're askin' me.

"Oh," said Sally suddenly. "Don't forget about Trevor. If he stands to inherit Birdie's money, he might be getting impatient."

"Good call." Pearl wrote it down and underlined it in the space beneath all three columns. "Gotta say, darlin', we got a good list to go by, here. With your investigation skills, you could give ol' Mike a run for his money." Pearl capped her marker, sitting back in satisfaction.

"Don't talk about Mike right now." Sally waved her off. "I'm mad at him. Harold always acted like the things I cared about didn't matter. The last thing I need is more of the same from Mike, whether or not we're just friends."

"Try not to take it so personally," Pearl said, patting Sally's shoulder. "He's got an awful lot on his plate, and he's tryin' to prove that he's the chief of police this town needs in a crisis as well as all the borin' cushy times he's mostly used to by now. He don't need you emasculatin' him on top of all that."

"You might be right. It's just a good thing Birdie has us," Sally said. "She probably doesn't have a lot of people in her corner, so she needs someone, doesn't she?"

"Reckon some of that's her fault, on account of mistakes she made," Pearl said, tightening her lips. "That bein' said, it's easy to see why she's a pill you swallow easier than most. You've got a good heart like that."

"Oh?" Sally asked. "What do you mean?"

"When you see someone lonely, you don't think it's their fault. Sometimes all a lonely person needs is knowin' that someone believes they don't truly deserve their loneliness."

"She doesn't deserve her loneliness any more than you do, Pearl," Sally said quietly. "I hope you know that."

"I ain't gonna pretend I don't know what your talkin' about. Heck, my brain knows you're right. But they were in my care, you know. That day I nodded off readin' in the garden."

Sally clasped her hands and bent her head out of respect, and to hide the deep pain she felt on behalf of her friend. Pearl always brushed it off like it was all in the past and no longer affected her, but Sally was a mother, too. She knew that couldn't be true.

"How are you doing now that Christmas is coming?" Sally asked. "How do you feel?"

"I dunno. Bit numb, probably. It's been so many years since it happened, and I always kinda just ignored the whole thing. Ain't ever wanted to let myself feel much this time of year, and sometimes it comes out in funny ways."

Sally furrowed her brow. "Like buying someone else's little girl a box full of angel ornaments?"

"I reckon so. Kinda weird I suppose," Pearl said, flushing surprisingly deeply for a woman who seemed incapable of blushing out of embarrassment. "Her parents probably think I'm off my rocker or fixin' to kidnap her. I just felt like I'd bubble over or explode or somethin' if I didn't help. They don't know what they've got with that girl. They don't appreciate it while they got it, and that rips me up inside."

"Lauren posted on Facebook after Harold died," Sally said. "Something about how grief is love with nowhere to go. Maybe your love is looking for somewhere to go again, Pearl. And for the record, I don't think that buying those angels was weird. I think it was kind and generous and appreciated."

Pearl sounded throaty when she spoke again, passing her sleeve over her eyes. "Let's start investigatin' the folks on this list before you get me all choked up with your dang Christmas swoonin'."

"Shoot. Excuse me," Sally apologized as her phone buzzed. It was a curt text from Mike asking for them to meet him at the station, stating he would be done in an hour and could drive them back to the cabin. Sally bit her lip as she showed it to Pearl.

"Oh, sweetie, I know you're tore up over this rift. It will right itself in time, I promise you." Pearl said, patting Sally's arm.

Sally hated having any strife between them. Her stomach roiled at the thought of the drive home and the uncomfortable evening together at his house. "I'd like to make things right before we go home. I know he didn't mean to be harsh."

"Course he didn't. What do you wanna do?"

Sally took a deep breath. "I have an idea."

28

Duty Calls

Mike hung up the office phone, a grave look on his face. "Gavin, I have to go over to Blue River. A couple of kids heading up to the hot springs have gone missing."

Sally stopped dead in the doorway of the police station, just in time to overhear Mike's words. She'd come to try to smooth things over with Mike, Pearl in tow. They'd even picked up a bunch of cooked cocktail shrimp as an inside joke. Now, it sounded like Mike was being called away to do his duty as police chief. Sally frowned. In her head, she thought she would apologize, and they'd share a good laugh before heading back to his place for wine and to relax by the fire before a busy day of investigating tomorrow.

Of course, that couldn't happen, Sally admonished herself. *Pearl and I should be at the high school gym helping the families who are stuck here, eating off paper plates and sleeping on cots instead of in their warm beds at home two days before Christmas.* Maybe she was making too big of a deal about all this. Mike was obviously under pressure. Here she was making demands and adding to his stress.

"Pearl, we've been a little selfish," Sally mumbled.

"A little *shellfish*, more like," Pearl joked, tapping the container of cocktail shrimp. Sally rolled her eyes.

"You are too much."

Mike caught her eye before looking away, seeming to look for anything else to focus on besides the women entering the police station. Sally swallowed. Was he still angry about before? The unresolved conflict made her skin crawl.

"Mike," she blurted out. "I know you're under a lot of pressure and just trying to help the people in the most need. I'm sorry if I didn't seem to get that before."

"Oh," Mike said, sounding surprised. "Honestly, Sally, I'd forgotten all about it. Don't worry."

Sally shifted on her feet, still holding the container of shrimp. Had he forgotten? How could he forget something she had worried about all day? She tried again. "I want to tell you that I know how hard you work. Pearl and I are going back to volunteer at the shelter this evening. You should eat before you head out into the cold to look for those missing people."

Mike squinted at the shrimp. "Is this revenge for those oysters? Because, while I admire a good joke, there could be lives on the line."

"Fully cooked, and they were so chilled they were practically frozen," Sally giggled, "and given the cold we walked through to get to the station, they're still that way." She held up the container.

"You girls shouldn't be walking around as the snow piles up," Mike said, setting the food on his desk, prying off the plastic lid, and nodding approvingly. "Are you up for staying at the shelter until I can drive back? It could take all night, depending on whether we need to organize a search party."

"I'm fine with that," Sally said, smiling. "If there's one thing I've learned from you today, it's that people in need take priority. Just come get us when you're done."

"I'm fine with it, too," Pearl said. "Ain't no skin off my nose. I've heard there are lots of little kids comin' in who will want some more of my famous award-winnin' cookies. Who am I to deprive them of heaven itself?"

Sally's spirit lifted as they fell into easy banter. Sally and Pearl sat in the chairs across from Mike's desk. Mike was all business as he gathered supplies, occasionally pausing to eat, and shared with them how he planned to organize the search party.

"This town is darn lucky to have you," Pearl said.

As Mike zipped up his jacket, he met Sally's eyes and ran a hand over his hair, "I've been thinking. I shouldn't have dismissed you so fast. When I get a second, let's talk more about Birdie. If anything comes up in the meantime, Gavin will be here. He'll probably be bored. Feel free to put him to work."

"Thank you," Sally said, looking up from under her eyelashes.

"I've got to get out there." Mike grabbed his gloves and hat off his desk.

Sally and Pearl stood as he moved towards the door. Mike hugged Pearl. She patted his back. "I'll say a prayer for you," she whispered, but Sally heard anyway and smiled.

When Mike stepped in front of Sally, he met her gaze. "Be careful. I don't want you getting hurt while I'm tromping through the mountain snow." He smiled, and she let herself get lost in his eyes for a moment.

Pearl cleared her throat and broke the spell. Sally pulled her eyes away from Mike and picked a piece of invisible lint from

189

the shoulder of his jacket. He leaned over and brushed his lips against her cheek. "I'll be back soon."

And then he was gone.

Sally's hand went to where his lips had been. The electricity between them hung in the air even after the door to the station closed.

She hoped he would be alright. She would settle for alright over perfect, she thought, with things as dire as they were getting.

"Come on, we gotta get back to the high school," Pearl said, taking her hand. "Mike will be fine. And in the mornin', we got an attempted murder to solve."

They stepped outside, and Sally pulled her coat tighter around her midsection as the wind blew cold snowflakes right into her face. "I really hoped the snow would wait a little longer to start coming down so hard and fast," she groaned.

"Ain't ideal, but there's a silver linin'. If no one can travel, it means that everyone is still in town... includin' those sisters who might have a bone to pick with the fruitcake-hatin' judge who spat out their cookie."

"I'm still trying to convince myself that their grudge could possibly go that far," Sally said, chuckling.

"Those bunnies are dumb enough to try it, I reckon, and too wrapped up in their own brand not to leave a callin' card. Can't wait to talk to them herpes girls again, and if this snow keeps pilin' up, we might just get a chance."

"Harpies," Sally reminded her with a chuckle.

"I said what I said, and I ain't takin' it back."

Millie and Tillie were in the kitchen, preparing dessert for the evening meal. They were deep in conversation about what reality show they should audition for next. When they noticed Sally and Pearl in the doorway, their conversation ended abruptly.

"What are you whisperin' about?" Pearl asked, walking to stand at the counter opposite them.

"Not that it's any of your business, but we are planning our next audition," Millie said. She squeezed a pastry bag of red frosting onto a row of cupcakes.

"With all this snow, might be stuck here forever," Pearl said, looking out the window at the storm.

Tillie scoffed, "That is not happening. We have chains and 4-wheel drive. Going to try and get out tonight or first thing tomorrow."

Sally and Pearl shared a look. They couldn't let the sisters leave without getting answers. What could she ask to get more information? They needed to know where the women were the morning the fruitcake was delivered.

"So, what have you been up to since the bake-off?" Sally asked, trying to sound casual.

Millie shrugged, "Shopped until the snow and roads got bad, then came here last night."

"You were here all day?" Pearl asked, narrowing her eyes.

Tillie looked up from her cupcakes. "What are you getting at?"

Millie touched her arm and, with a slight shake of her head, said, "I think what Tillie meant to ask is if there is something we missed or somewhere we should have been?"

Tillie pressed her lips together. Obviously, they were being cagey, Sally thought.

"We heard you like to bake fruitcakes," Pearl said.

Millie smiled, "That's true. We are famous for our secret

recipe."

Tillie nodded.

"And Birdie Grassley humiliated you on live television?" Pearl pressed, leaning her elbows on the counter.

Millie's smile disappeared, "That's true. That woman is awful."

"So you have reason to want to get back at her?" Pearl asked, tipping her head and raised her eyebrows.

Millie squared her shoulders and put her palms on the table. "If you have something to say, just say it."

Sally stepped forward and put a hand on Pearl's arm. "We are just looking into a situation with Birdie."

"What kind of situation?" asked Tillie, pausing her work.

Sally swallowed. "Well –"

"Where were you this mornin'? We need details." Pearl said impatiently.

"None of your business," Millie said.

Pearl straightened up and balled her hands into fists. "Now you listen here. We are lookin' into a bonafide crime, and right now, you're on our list of suspects."

"If you just tell us where you were this morning, we can move on to the rest of our list," Sally said.

Millie and Tillie paused, and then Tillie said, "What crime are you talking about?"

"Someone tried to poison Birdie with a fruitcake. And since that's your specialty and you have a motive, we thought we should ask you about it," Sally said, keeping her voice even.

Millie blew out a breath, "Fine." she pointed at Sally and Pearl and said through gritted teeth, "If you tell anyone what we are about to share, you will regret it."

Pearl pulled her chin into her neck but didn't say anything.

"We were dyeing our hair," Millie confessed, shifting on her feet.

"What?" Sally asked.

"Our hair. This red isn't natural. We dye it. But no one can know," Millie said.

Tillie nodded, "It's the only reason we got on those reality television shows. If we had our natural brown hair, they wouldn't have given us a second look."

"And now it's become our brand," said Millie with a flourish.

"Where did you get it dyed? Was Sheila involved?" Pearl asked.

"Gosh, no. She doesn't know. No one knows. We did it in the bathroom on the other side of the school."

"Can anyone vouch for you?" Sally asked.

The timer on the oven went off and Millie pulled on a potholder to retrieve a tray of cupcakes from inside. "What is with you two?"

"The boxes of dye should still be down in the bathroom trash can. You're welcome to go look for yourself," Tillie said, moving the cupcakes onto the cooling rack.

"Fine. We will check it out," Said Pearl, reaching out to take one of the frosted cupcakes.

Millie smacked her hand, and Pearl grunted.

"We told you what you wanted to know. Promise to keep our secret, and I'll give you a cupcake." Tillie said with a grin.

"Deal," Pearl said. She swiped a cupcake and took a huge bite, getting frosting on her cheeks and the tip of her nose.

29

Sleuths on the Loose

December 23

The next morning, after sleeping fitfully on cots in the high school gym, Sally and Pearl were determined to make the most of their time.

Lauren called to report that she and Henry, families in tow, were in Salt Lake City. Henry had threatened to litigate if someone didn't get them a flight. Joel and Tom were waiting for the roads to clear to drive down from Seattle. So far, everyone was stuck, but Sally still had hope it would work out. Until then, Sally and Pearl had some work to do.

Luckily they had been given a personal care kit and could freshen up before they headed out with Kelly's blessing.

"Are you sure you're set for volunteers?" Sally asked.

"Yes, you are free to enjoy the day. We can probably use you later, though."

"Deal," Pearl said.

Sally and Pearl didn't wait for Kelly to change her mind. They headed out into the storm, which had slowed down temporarily.

The town was deserted. Only the occasional vehicle ventured out, and most of the roads were unplowed.

"Ain't it funny how the reindeer was our first stop when we rolled into McKenzie Bridge, and now it's our first stop in the investigation for the attempted murder of the town fuss budget?" Pearl asked. "There's a kinda poetry to it. On Dancer, on Dasher, on... and on, and on, I guess."

"It's as good a place to start as any," Sally reasoned.

Steve, the reindeer's owner was easy enough to locate. He was the same man they'd seen that first day, although he wasn't selling carrots as the snow continued to pile up. He was busy pulling down heavy blankets for his animals and draping them over their backs, all the while avoiding the antlers and hooves of his deer. "He seems kind of on edge," Sally said, leaning close to whisper to Pearl.

"Wouldn't you be on edge if your reindeer were caught runnin' over grannies and we showed up to tempt fate? Bad for business if they did it again." Pearl joked. Sally elbowed her playfully in the side as the man approached them.

"Can I help you two ladies?" Steve had a plaid hat with flaps pulled down over his ears. His brown farmer's coat was unzipped, his belly hanging over his jeans. In spite of the cold, it seemed that he'd worked up a sweat getting the reindeer pen ready for the storm.

"How are they doing? Is everything alright?" Sally said, pursing her lips sympathetically. She wanted to speak first to make sure that Pearl didn't rush in and make them sound too suspicious. "We heard that a particularly frisky reindeer got loose and caused some havoc in town."

"That's one way of putting it," Steve groaned. "It's not true, at least not the way people say. I've got a good group here.

Santa himself couldn't ask for a better-behaved team."

"So, what happened?" Pearl prodded. "If these deer are so good, what made Rudolph jump the gate and run down an old lady?"

The reindeer owner shook his head, lighting his pipe and taking a deep pull before dropping the match in the snow. "I want to show you ladies something in my trailer if you'll follow me."

"Oh hell no," Pearl hissed to Sally. "The last time a man said that to me, he didn't exactly show me a candy cane, if you catch my drift."

"It should be okay with the two of us," Sally chuckled. "You can run and holler for help while he's tying me up if that puts your mind at ease."

"If I don't have a heart attack runnin' in this cold, anyway," Pearl grumbled.

Fortunately, Pearl's concerns seemed misplaced. Steve opened his trailer, and when he turned around, it was nothing untoward or obscene. It was a set of red harnesses that looked to have been cut.

"Clean through," he remarked, holding up a place where the leather had been sliced neatly with something very sharp. "Seems like someone came in a few nights back to cut the harnesses, and they must have spooked one of my more nervous boys something fierce. He took off running like he'd been whipped. I'm just glad no one was hurt, or they'd be coming for my license and my animals, and I couldn't take that, I don't think."

"I'm glad, too," Sally said. It was clear to her that the reindeer's owner loved them, and while he might have been biased, looking into their large gentle eyes, it was hard to

196

imagine them deliberately attacking an old lady.

"A person would have to be a right fool to think you had somethin' to do with it, with so much to risk by tryin'," Pearl said.

"Luckily, no one's accused me yet," the owner said. "Keep waiting for the ax to fall, but maybe that's just knowing that more snow is coming. It's a feeling of heavy dread., and we've all got it to some degree right now."

"Do you eat often at the Reindeer Café?" Sally asked, wanting to make sure she didn't leave that stone unturned. "The other day we tried to get in for dinner. It was too crowded, but we thought we saw you with that newscaster Richard Garrison."

"I was grabbing dinner with Richard. Why do you ask?"

Sally frowned. She didn't know if it was polite to say that the rugged outdoorsman and the coifed newscaster couldn't possibly have been more different. "I didn't know you were friends," she admitted, weighing whether this made Richard more suspicious.

Steve pulled on his pipe, seeming unsure if he should say anything. "We're friendly," he said neutrally. "We were meeting at the café that night because he wants to ask out Brenda and was hoping that we could arrange a sleigh ride with the reindeer to make it more romantic."

"He's old enough to be her father," Pearl said, suppressing a gag reflex.

"I know. I think that he'll be disappointed," Steve chuckled. "I gave him my rates and offered some options, because money is money, but it seems like the weather is on Brenda's side. My deer aren't going out in a blizzard no matter how much he wants to pay me. "

Steve gave Sally and Pearl some complimentary carrots, and after feeding the reindeer, they moved on to their second stop.

"We're makin' good time," Pearl panted, shuffling more quickly through the deepening snow to keep up with Sally. "Chamber of commerce is next, right?"

Sally nodded, the puffball on her hat bobbing back and forth. "Even if the runaway reindeer's cut harnesses are a dead end for now, we need to find out what we can about that tree."

The chamber of commerce was housed in a yellow renovated Victorian home-turned- business. The gingerbread trim was painted blue, and twinkle-lights ran along the roofline. Sally smiled at the festive wreath before pushing open the door.

"Can I help you?" the receptionist said, peering down her nose as Sally and Pearl tromped snow into the lobby. "We're closing soon."

"I hope so," Sally said breathlessly, trying to stomp as much snow as she could from her boots onto the large, heavy mat by the door. "We have an appointment to see the head of town maintenance. I think his name was Gene."

"Oh, right. You and the rest of the town," the receptionist joked darkly. "He's in his office. It's the room at the end of the hall with the light on. He's the only one still working, so you can't miss it. Try not to keep him too long, would you? Once he's through with your appointment, we can both go home."

Sally nodded, walking past the reception desk at a quick clip to get to the end of the hall with Pearl just a few steps behind her.

"Hello," said the man behind the desk. He looked like he might be fairly jolly on a better day, small, plump, and smartly dressed with a bowtie under his soft chin. The current stressful situation had him looking like he was melting into his chair. "You must be Sally and Pearl. How can I help you ladies today? I don't suppose it has anything to do with *the* tree." The way he said it, with emphasis, made it sound just like no one had talked to him about anything else since it had happened. "If you have some great hindsight revelation about how it could have gone better, please tell me now so we can get that out of the way."

"Oh, no, that's not why we're here," Sally said, her face falling. "You've been getting that much criticism for a freak accident?"

"Well, he's the one who rigged it up, ain't he?" Pearl asked. "Makes some kind of sense, however unfair it might seem for folks to pile on."

"If someone was going to be blamed, I'd be the logical one to gun for," Gene said glumly. "But I've been doing this for almost twenty years now. That's a lot of Christmas trees. I know what I'm doing when I put one up. The supports are in place, the stand is staked into the ground. After all those years practicing and perfecting my technique, it would take a hurricane to knock over a tree that I put up."

"So, why did this tree fall?" Sally asked, leaning forward.

"Why are you ladies so interested?"

"We're solvin' a mystery," Pearl said matter-of-factly. "Think you got done dirty by some foul play."

"Is that so?" Gene asked. "I guess it beats getting accused of being terrible at my job. People are even calling to fire me."

"We don't want that," Sally quickly assured him. "If anything, we want to prove that it wasn't your fault. Can you give us any information about the tree? Something we should know about how it was put up, or what might have happened to contribute to the fall?"

"Yeah," Gene said after a moment. "I guess it couldn't hurt. I'll tell you ladies what you want to know, and I hope it can help all of us out." He cleared his throat.

"The tree is no bigger than usual, no smaller than usual. It always comes from up the mountain, because those are the only trees in town that grow big enough for a town square display. I mounted it the way I mounted all the others, and it was strong, straight, and pretty. Now, the stand came from the Grassley family. The old one was giving up the ghost, and ironically, we were replacing it due to safety concerns. The Grassleys jumped right in to get us a new one. State-of-the-art, ordered straight from Berlin. The thing might have cost as much as my first car or more."

"So Birdie donated the tree stand?" Sally pressed, eyebrows raising. If Birdie had hand-picked the stand, she would expect it to be up to the same punishing standards the woman applied to everything else.

"Birdie has been involved in making McKenzie Bridge's Christmases beautiful for many decades," Gene said carefully. "When Dr. Bob Grassley was alive, he contributed as well. Now that Birdie is getting on in years and the responsibilities are getting a little more overwhelming as the festival continues to grow annually, I think her nephew Trevor is helping her allocate her funds. He's the one who signed the check for the tree stand on Birdie's behalf."

"So Trevor has access to Birdie's money," Pearl said thoughtfully. "He manages her finances or somethin'?"

"I probably shouldn't be telling you this, but I'm desperate. I want to keep my job." Gene fidgeted uncomfortably. "Birdie is older, and she's been more anxious and paranoid since her husband passed. But she's not incompetent or senile. A few years ago, Trevor tried to make a case claiming just that. He tried to establish a conservatorship and take over her finances. He failed because she's still a sharp lady, but it's clear that he doesn't want to wait for the inheritance."

"I knew he was a greasy little weasel," Pearl muttered.

"He's her nephew. Maybe he sees sides of her the rest of us don't get to," Gene admitted. "She does seem more on edge lately."

"Birdie is the reason we're here," Sally said. "She believes the tree falling was an attempt on her life."

"Like everything else?" Gene asked flatly. "I can't see how that could be possible. If anything, Birdie, or at least her family, contributed to the fall. I was told to come out and adjust it after we received a complaint from someone in the estate that the thing was crooked. I took a ruler at a right angle to the thing myself, so I know it wasn't crooked, but messing with something balanced will unbalance it every single time. I was out calling shots when it collapsed, and I'm glad no one was injured. That's a blessing from baby Jesus himself."

"Maybe," Sally mused. "Who complained about the tree? Was it Birdie?"

"I don't think it was, but I wouldn't rule it out. The caller ID said it was Trevor's phone, but it wasn't him. The voice sounded undeniably female. Hard to tell if it was old or young. It was almost like she was trying a fake accent or pitching her voice lower. It was a bit strange, but we pay attention to calls from Trevor's phone since he's doing so much on behalf of Birdie these days."

The two women thanked Gene for his time, expressed their well-wishes, and left the chamber, puzzled over the conversation they'd just had.

"Don't it sound like Trevor's got somethin' to do with it, after all?" Pearl asked, frowning. "It was his phone, and it sounds like he's been wantin' control over his aunt's money for a while. Even Mike said he wanted to be a big city boy. Maybe a big windfall is what he's waitin' for before he makes that a reality."

"It could be," Sally said, thinking back to the conversation she'd overheard in the salon about how he wouldn't propose until he *got the money.* "Let's consider him a suspect, maybe even our primary one."

"We gotta get our craft supplies and make a board," Pearl said. "So as we can update our notes with it."

"I think all the craft stores are closed,' Sally said sheepishly. Pearl snorted.

"Well, ain't that useless as all get out. Crime-solvin' from memory and notes like a couple of putzes. I'm starvin'. Let's lay out the evidence over some lunch and see if Mike or Gavin are hanging' around the station."

30

God Bless Gavin

After grabbing a quick bite of lunch, Sally and Pearl returned to find a car parked in front of the station.

"Oh good, Gavin's here," Sally said, pulling open the door. She wasn't ready to have this conversation with Mike again and risk him shooting them down. They needed answers. When she walked in, she found Gavin bent over the copy machine, punching buttons and mumbling under his breath.

"Gavin," she said, pulling at the hem of her sweater, "we need your help."

Gavin spun around. "Oh, hey there, ladies. Mike said you might be stopping by, or I'd tell you to take a number. Seems like everyone else in this town could use some help right now." He looped his thumbs through his belt loops and hitched his pants up. "What can I do for you?" He abandoned the copier with a curse under his breath and returned to his desk, where a stack of papers waited.

Sally kept her voice even. "We have an urgent situation. A raccoon was found dead and could be rabid. Or maybe it was poisoned. Either way, it is an issue of public safety."

"What's got you so worried about a dead raccoon? Do you have any reason to think that it was rabid or poisoned? Either way, problem solved."

"He's as lost as last year's Easter egg," Pearl said, shaking her head.

Sally stepped closer to his desk. "We need to find out if he was poisoned and if it was meant for Birdie Grassley," she said.

Gavin sighed. "Birdie Grassley thinks she's been poisoned every other day. The rest of them, she thinks trees and reindeer are trying to kill her."

"Alright, but Birdie might have a good reason to think someone's tried to poison her. Pearl agrees, and Mike's coming around to our point of view. Is that enough concern to warrant your attention?"

"Do you have some evidence?" Gavin sighed.

"A piece of the fruitcake we think is poisoned," Pearl said. "Probably a bit stale, but you know what they say about fruitcake."

Gavin shook his head in defeat. "Okay. It's your vacation and your time. I think we have some different testing processes included in one of the kits from Homeland Security. There's a downed power line across town I have to deal with, but I can probably dig one out for you real quick. It'll rule out or confirm some more common and deadly poisons, and a chunk of fruitcake should be enough."

"You want the raccoon, too?" Pearl asked. "I think Birdie's got it in deep freeze. I might not like the lady, but she knows how to cover her bases."

Gavin blew out a breath. "Bring me whatever you've got. Come back in an hour if you can manage it, and be careful in that snow."

Fortunately, Birdie's house wasn't far, and though Sally and Pearl had never been there, it was no secret in the town of McKenzie Bridge which house was Birdie Grassley's. Not only was it the most prominent house in town, but it was also the most opulent and graced with a homemade ice rink next door.

"Tough to miss," commented Pearl. "We'd best approach carefully. She might be on high alert since that fruitcake got left here by a skulker in the dark."

"Now you sound like you're in some movie," Sally chuckled. "If she's that paranoid, she'll have surveillance cameras, and she'll be able to see that it's us."

"That's good thinkin'," admitted Pearl. "The things you can get with that kind of money us regular folk just plum forget about sometimes."

"You watch as much true crime as I do," Sally pointed out.

"I know it!"

Sally raised a gloved finger to her lips to quiet Pearl as she stepped onto the porch and rang the bell. Her suspicions about the surveillance cameras were likely true because the door flew open too quickly for Birdie to be anywhere else but right by the door.

"It's you!" she said. "What have you found out?"

"We don't have all the pieces put together yet, but we have made progress," Sally said. "We don't think the reindeer owner is behind it, and the man who put up the tree didn't seem guilty to us."

"Do you have any suspects?" Birdie asked in a hushed voice.

"You bet your sweet bippie we do," Pearl answered, but Sally kicked her boot with her own. She didn't know how Birdie would take it to hear that her nephew was their number one suspect for the time being.

"We have some leads," Sally said instead. Birdie nodded, seeming heartened by the news.

"Well, I suppose that's better than nothing. Are you just here to tell me this?"

"We're gonna need that fruitcake and that raccoon for testin'."

Birdie seemed reluctant. "It's all the proof I have in the world. If I give it to you, I'll have nothing else to present as evidence that someone's out to get me except for my word, and no one thinks that's good, anyway."

"Maybe," Sally said, biting her lip. "But as much as I want to leave you with that security, Birdie, you put your trust in us when you let us investigate your case. You need to put your trust in us by giving us your evidence, too, or we might not be able to do it as quickly as you need."

"And if you're life's on the line, that's right quick," Pearl pointed out.

Birdie seemed to remember herself and stepped backward. "Come inside from the cold," she mumbled, opening the door a little wider. "I'll fetch them. Did you walk here? You should warm up by the fire for a few minutes."

Sally and Pearl's brows raised in unison, surprised at the hospitality but certainly in no place to reject it. They slipped out of their snow boots and followed Birdie across her spacious tile foyer and into a gorgeously-decorated parlor.

"You have a beautiful home," Sally commented, lowering herself into the velvet seat of an antique chair.

"I do," Birdie answered, with the neutrality of one who had no actual control over the circumstances of the house coming to her. "It's been in my family for generations, you know. Built before the town was even properly founded. We've been here from the very start."

Sally's eyes scanned the room. Some portraits looked ancient, giving way to more casual photographs from the last century. She noticed that the family tree seemed to dwindle and end with Birdie, a sizeable smiling man who must have been the late Dr. Bob Grassley, and Birdie's dour-looking nephew, Trevor.

"You must be very proud of it," Sally said.

"I suppose, but not in the way I am of the festivals, parades, and contests I founded," Birdie replied shortly. "I always wanted to be known for what *I* did instead of who I was descended from. Not that it matters when a great line blinks out, anyway."

"What do you mean?" Pearl asked. "You can't be the last of 'em."

"Children weren't in the cards for Bob and me. When I die, everything will go to Trevor, but he's allergic to hard work if you haven't noticed. I worry about what he'll do with it all."

"He seems devoted to you," Sally said, fishing gently for information on that front. What they'd observed about Birdie and Trevor's relationship was, to put it shortly, a little concerning at times. "He also seems devoted to the things you've worked hard to build."

"He likes being related to me," Birdie said. "And those things barely resemble what they were when I built them, anyway. I imagine he'll scrub away the last traces of tradition to try to bring a younger, hipper crowd into McKenzie Bridge if he doesn't just sell it all and leave with his girlfriend."

Sally thought back to the snippets of conversation she'd heard before getting her hair done, how Sheila had said something about wanting a salon of her own in sunny Los Angeles.

"Do you trust Trevor?" Pearl asked bluntly. "As your team of investigators, we gotta know. You don't think he coulda thought up somethin' like this, do you?"

"I don't trust my nephew as far as I could kick him," Birdie said sourly. "He lost the last shreds of that when he tried to make the case that I was unstable and needed someone to manage my life and finances. I might be a little particular about the way I like things done, but I'm not mentally incompetent. I humiliated him by being sharp as always, and ever since then, he's been about as nice as little Maximillian after the vet snipped him."

"But you let him do things to help you out," Sally said, thinking about the baking contest and how Trevor had fussed over his aunt, as well as the check for the Christmas tree stand.

"He's tried to get back in my good graces, but he's got a long way to go before I trust him again, and I'm not sure I'll live that long."

"Do you think Trevor would ever get impatient about that inheritance by... you know, offin' you?" Pearl asked, drawing a finger across her neck.

Sally swallowed, keeping her eyes straight ahead, not looking at Pearl. It tended to be either high risk or high reward in situations like these.

"Oh, no," Birdie said immediately. "You women listen carefully to me. My instincts are good. My instincts are *damn* good. My nephew is a sniveling little weasel of a man, but he doesn't have the stomach for murder."

"What about his girlfriend?" Sally asked. "How well do you know her?"

"She's nice enough, I suppose, but there's nothing between her ears," Birdie snorted. "All those fumes and chemicals at the salon have killed off her brain cells, if she ever had any, to begin with."

Sally thought that was a bit harsh. Sheila was just a young woman with dreams and in love. That shouldn't merit being called stupid.

"What about the contestants at the bakin' contest?" Pearl asked. "We had been thinkin' about that those red-headed sisters who have been on reality TV before might be behind it on account of fruitcake sort of being their thing."

"It's 'their thing' because it's trashy, just like them," Birdie sniffed. "But I remember their fruitcake. I choked down a real bite for a fair competition. I can tell whoever baked this one used more nuts and fruits than butter and sugar. It practically fell apart. I detest them, but their fruitcakes hold together."

Pearl pursed her lips. Sally could tell she wasn't convinced.

"I think we can rule them out," Sally asked.

"No idea. But I trust you two will figure it out. Let me get you that evidence." Birdie retreated to the kitchen and returned a minute later.

Sally and Pearl left Birdie's house with a small plastic baggie and a large black trash bag in tow. Pearl had volunteered to carry the latter, which was a relief to Sally. The frozen, dead weight of the raccoon was unpleasant to think about, even when it was just swinging at Pearl's side.

"We're back," Pearl announced as they entered the station. Gavin seemed surprised they'd returned at all, with the sky darkening and the snow growing heavier by the minute, but he gamely took the fruitcake and the raccoon back to a room they hadn't seen before. It had metal tables and several empty cages along the walls. Sally figured it was probably for animal control, yet another thing the police station likely couldn't outsource due to the budget of the small tourist town.

Gavin squinted, doing his best to collect samples from both the frozen raccoon and the slightly-squished fruitcake. "Let's hope these things are sensitive," he groaned as he set out two testing strips and hovered a dropper above each, carefully squeezing a few drops of each sample into the holes marked "Place Sample Here."

Sally watched, feeling slightly dazed. It always seemed so much more dramatic in the crime shows, with boiling Bunsen burners and beakers and little pipettes with skulls and crossbones on them. This seemed very anticlimactic by comparison.

"Okay, so..." Gavin squinted at the instructions with the kits, reading them off. "'Allow the liquid to travel into and through the detector. Look for a blue/green color to form if cyanide is present, as seen below.'"

All three of them leaned in. Gavin was the most surprised when the test strips turned immediately blue.

"I'll be damned," he said, massaging his brow. "The old bat was right. This *is* poison." He put both hands on the table and looked down. "I need to talk to Mike about this. We're shorthanded as it is, and we have too much ground to cover in a town full of people who can't stand her."

"Don't worry, we're on it," Pearl said. "Got some gut feelins', and mine are usually right."

"Just be careful," Gavin said. "I don't want anyone to get hurt. If anything happens to you, Mike will throw me off the mountain or drown me in the Cougar Reservoir."

"Easy there, sport. We ain't lookin' to get you in trouble." Pearl said.

"We'll keep it between us," Sally said, grabbing Pearl's arm and steering her towards the lobby. "Thanks, Gavin!"

They used their smartphones on the police station's Wi-Fi for a quick and dirty research session on cyanide's properties, uses, and history.

"Huh. Didn't know you could use apple seeds or apricot pits to make it," Pearl remarked. "That means that even with their dinky grocery store, someone in McKenzie Bridge could manage to do it, I reckon."

Sally frowned. "You know... there was a whole bowl of apricots in the salon when I got my hair done. I ate one, and Sheila said that she saved the pits for her garden."

"I believe they're for pushin' up daisies, alright," Pearl said dryly. "Don't prove nothin' for sure. But worth lookin' at. Do you reckon the salon's up and runnin' again after that pipe clogged and flooded the downstairs?"

"I'm not sure, but all the shampoos and hairsprays are probably enough to cover the smell of sewage," Sally chuckled.

"Only one way to find out," Pearl said, writing *Sheila* under the fruitcake column on their notepad.

31

#friendshipgoals

"Just as I thought," Pearl said, hanging up the phone. "Ain't no one at that salon. Just a prerecorded message on there sayin' that the business is closed."

"That makes sense." Sally dropped into Mike's chair and sighed. "If it weren't for this snow, all of this would be much easier."

Gavin cleared his throat. "I've got to hold down the fort here for the next little while," he said, "but Mike specifically asked me to make sure you stay close to the shelter while he's away in the mountains looking for those kids. Lots of folks in town will be there, either taking refuge or volunteering. It's probably the best and safest place to be right now, to be honest."

"We said we'd volunteer," Sally said, looking at Pearl, who was pacing in front of the jail cells. "I guess we have to make up for some lost time, don't we?"

"Or grab a cot," Gavin suggested. "You're tourists stuck here, just like everyone else. You deserve food, rest, and shelter."

"We got the energy to help, and ain't no one gonna stop us,"

Pearl said, stopping and turning to him with her hands on her hips.. "I ain't just gonna sit here when there are kids that need tendin' to. Maybe we could whip up some more cookies."

"You'd be in good company," Gavin said. "Every contestant in the baking contest is helping out in the kitchen to ensure all refugees have enough to eat. You should see some familiar faces."

Sally's eyes widened. "All of them were stuck here in town? Really?"

"Every single one," Gavin confirmed.

"That means them red-headed gals are still here," Pearl whispered loudly to Sally, who nudged her.

"That could be fun," Sally said to Gavin. "I'm sure we'll work well together now that there's not a prize on the line."

"You might see some fireworks. They tend to hold grudges," Gavin said. "But nothing erases all of that like a shared goal. It's a good thing you're all doing, and you should be proud."

Pearl waved him off. "Ain't it just what anyone would do?"

Near dusk, Gavin dropped them off at the high school, which, with its backup power generator and the priority it was given, had become a hub for the community. They only had their coats and purses since Gavin was strapped for time and hadn't been able to swing by Mike's so they could get a change of clothes. Even if he'd been able to, it wasn't as if they had a key to his place, anyway.

They were greeted at the door by a kindly man in a button-down shirt, his sleeves rolled up. "Welcome. I'm Gary, pastor at McKenzie Bridge Christian Church just down the road. We're glad you're here," he said, beaming at Sally and Pearl. "Please come in and help yourself to some of the scrambled eggs and toast. It's been prepared by some excellent professional chefs."

"Ain't here to sit and eat eggs and toast," Pearl said. "We're here to volunteer. What can we do to help?"

"Bless you both," the man said, sighing. "We can always use an extra set of hands. . You must be from out of town since I haven't seen you in my congregation."

"That's right," Sally said, "although I've missed church. I hope the roads are clear enough that we can attend this Sunday."

"You'd be most welcome," Gary smiled. "Thank you, ladies, again. If you would excuse me, I think that that news crew from Portland is trying to set up to report on this, and I know something about rigging mics in odd places. If you'll excuse me."

The pastor left to assist Brenda and Richard, who must have had an entire wardrobe in their trailer because they looked fresh and festive in matching turtle necks and puffy vests.

"Seems real nice that all sorts of folk can find it in their hearts to pitch in," Pearl said. "I ain't sure they even need us."

"Oh, don't," Sally laughed. "You heard Pastor Gary. They need more help and he is glad we are here."

"Yeah, suppose maybe that's true."

"Sally, Pearl!" a familiar voice called out from the kitchen, and both of them pivoted to look. It was Paul, beaming widely and holding up a soup ladle. "I'm so glad we get to see you again! Aren't you glad, Valerie?"

His baking partner grunted from her place at the stove, stirring a large stockpot full of mashed potatoes.

He waved her off. "She's still a little salty about the bake-off," he admitted. "I'm not, though. Those cookies were amazing."

"Fixin' to get a batch goin' tonight," Pearl said, rubbing her hands together. Paul flashed her a friendly thumbs-up.

"It kind of feels like the gang's all together again," Sally admitted.

"Then you'll be glad to know that Tillie and Millie are still here, too. So are Debbie and Denise, although Denise is doing some medical duty for frostbite and minor accidents when that's called for.

"Is anyone else helping in the kitchen?" Sally asked. "We wouldn't want there to be too many cooks."

"There's so much demand that I promise it won't spoil the soup," Paul assured. "We're shorthanded, and everyone needs to sleep sometime. Trevor Grassley and his girlfriend Sheila are also helping out, although he spends more time giving orders than cooking. She is a hard worker in the kitchen but isn't here quite as much as the rest of us. Believe it or not, she's doing hair for some of the people trapped here in McKenzie Bridge. Completely pro bono, too."

"Real angel," Pearl mumbled. Then her eyes lit up and she gave Sally a knowing look. "I don't suppose she could do my hair."

"It wouldn't hurt to ask," Paul said, donning oven mitts and retrieving freshly baked bread from the commercial oven. "Like the rest of us, her livelihood has been disrupted by this storm. She'd probably appreciate a paying customer at a time like this."

"Any free haircut ain't worth payin' for," Pearl said. "I'm gonna go find her."

"I'll come with you," Sally volunteered, worried about letting Pearl approach one of their suspects alone. "We'll both be back soon!"

"Take your time," Paul said easily. "While we're glad to see you, we've managed so far without you. We can manage another 20 minutes."

It wasn't challenging to find Sheila. She'd rigged up a salon chair by tilting a standard metal chair back in the gym's bleachers and padding the neck and head with lots of towels. She was using a blow dryer hooked to an extension cord to clear away the clippings, but it seemed to be working reasonably well.

"Do what you want," Sally said to Pearl, "but there's no way I'm putting my hair in her hands again." She absently fingered the green and red tinted ends.

"Oh phooey, your hair looks fine, ain't I told you enough times? I'll go. I ain't afraid of that woman." Pearl strode up to the bleachers. Sheila recognized Pearl from their quick shopping excursion and was happy to squeeze her in between appointments that evening.

Two hours later, Pearl and Sally sat a few yards down the bleachers, listening to Sheila chatter away as she styled one of the ladies from the city council Sally recognized from the parade awards. It seemed like all sorts were ending up in this gym refuge, unwilling to risk the roads to return to their warm, cozy homes, even if they were locals. It said a lot about how bad the storm was getting. Sheila finished the city councilwoman and dismissed her with a practiced smile and a goodbye Then she trotted down the bleachers towards Sally and Pearl.

Despite the grim and alarming situation they were all in, Sheila was in high spirits, wearing a shimmery red sweater with a white furry collar. "Ready for your Christmas makeover, Pearl?"

Pearl pursed her lips, muttering, "The things I do for you,

Sally Johnson."

Sally patted her knee. "You are on Santa's nice list this year for sure."

Pearl grunted as she pushed herself to standing. They hadn't figured out exactly how they would get a chance to go through Sheila's supplies. Maybe she didn't even have the chemicals she'd used to make cyanide with her. Still, they had to check, and at some point, Sheila would undoubtedly need to step away.

"Hey, Sally, are you still liking your hair?" Sheila asked. "More importantly, is *Mike*?" Sheila winked at her.

Sally touched the green and pink tips of her hair and forced a smile past the blushing that overwhelmed her cheeks. In a moment of uncharacteristic mischief, she said, "Of course I like my hair, and Mike's crazy about it, too. In fact, it's gone over so well that Pearl was just telling me how much she would like the same thing for *her* hair." She stopped and looked at Pearl, who was scowling at her, and then looked back at Sheila. "Do you think you can do that for her so that we can be twins?"

Sheila clapped her hands together, "Oh, I love you guys. You're *#friendshipgoals.*"

Pearl leaned over and whispered through gritted teeth, "I'm gonna kill you if we get out of this alive."

"Maybe you should've thought about that before you made fun of me for the last few days," Sally said, squaring her shoulders in righteous if playful, indignation.

Pearl huffed as she followed Sheila back to her set up and settled back into the tipped metal chair, nestling her neck against the pillow of clean towels.

"You can sit over there if you want," Sheila said, pointing Sally to a bare spot on the bleachers. Sally nodded and shifted a few inches to the side. Everything about this high school gym microcosm they'd created was surreal, sad, and maybe just a bit funny.

"What happened to my music?" Sheila mused, plucking her phone from the bleacher a level above Pearl's head. After a few taps on the screen, Christmas music was being pumped through the phone's tinny speakers into the immediate area of Pearl's ears.

Pearl grimaced as gracefully as she could. "Don't worry," Sheila said. "My playlist only has completely secular songs for the season. I did that so it wouldn't offend anybody. I've got 'Let it Snow,' 'Jingle Bells,' and, of course, 'Sleigh Ride!'"

Pearl tried to hide her long, pained groan in a very involved clearing of her throat.

Sally raised her hand slightly and said, "Hey, I missed break-fast. Do you, by chance, have any more of those apricots?"

Sheila turned to look at her, frowning. Then she seemed to remember herself and smiled brightly. "I'm fresh out. You know, only so much I could bring over from the salon. Maybe one of the kitchen volunteers could bring you a plate of something."

"Nah, they got enough mouths to feed. Sally ain't gonna starve," Pearl said as Sheila fastened a cape around her neck.

"Sorry about the kink you're probably getting in your neck," Sheila said. "I miss my salon, but the whole resort is shut down until they can clean everything out."

"I've bunked down in rougher places," Pearl replied sto-ically.

"I have, too, but I can't wait to have a real salon someday." Sheila sighed and looked around at the crowded, fairly bleak high school gym. "It's funny how 'someday' always seems a little further away."

Pearl caught Sally's eye and raised her eyebrows, mouthing, "Do somethin'."

Sally bit her lip. How were they going to get Sheila to leave so they could search her makeshift station and duffle bag full of beauty supplies? Sally couldn't let Pearl end up with red and green-tipped hair. While it would be hilarious, Sally would never hear the end of it.

"Before you get started, would it be possible for you to run down and get the two of us a cup of coffee?" Sally asked.

"Great idea. I'd better use the facilities before you get started, anyway," Pearl said, sliding off the chair and hustling down the bleachers and over to the restrooms before Sheila could answer.

"So now I'm a waitress?" Sheila grumbled after Pearl. "I'm doing this out of the kindness of my heart, you know. Aren't you two volunteering with the kitchen?"

Sally folded her hands on her thighs. "Every time I've ever gotten my hair done in a nice place, my stylist has offered me coffee," she said innocently. Sheila stood there, a comb and scissors in her hands. Sally glanced toward the bathrooms Pearl was walking into, watching from the corner of her eye as Sheila tried to decide if they were serious about sending her on a coffee run. Sally's mouth went dry, and her stomach flipped, but she made herself sit still and steady in the uncomfortable silence.

Sheila dropped the supplies from her hands onto her cart, threw her hands in the air, and walked down from the bleachers. Sally could hear her feet clumping across the gym as she headed towards the kitchen and their several drip-coffee dispensers.

As soon as the sound of her footsteps were out of range

and her back was turned, Sally whirled around and leaped across her spot on the bleachers. She stood on the floor next to Sheila's cart, unsure what to do next. Drawers. She would start there. She yanked open the drawer of Sheila's cart, the motion causing combs and scissors to clank around inside. Red threads next to a pair of unwashed shears caught her eye. She leaned in to get a better look. When she caught a glimpse of motion in her peripheral vision, she screeched and jumped, whirling around to find Pearl standing there.

"You're jumpier than a cat in a room full of rockin' chairs."

"Never mind that. Hurry up and get over here, because I found something."

She pointed at the red threads, and Pearl narrowed her eyes. "Wasn't that the color of the harnesses holdin' those reindeer in place?" Pearl asked.

"I think so," Sally said. So many things in McKenzie Bridge were green or red. It was genuinely difficult to keep track.

"Don't that beat all?" Under the cape, Pearl dug into her pocket and whipped out a plastic sandwich baggie. Using it to cover her thumb and index finger, she retrieved the red fibers from the drawer and turned the baggie inside out before sealing it. Then she handed it to Sally. "Put these in your pocket. I don't wanna accidentally get discovered while she's doin' my hair."

"You're still going to let her do your hair?" Sally asked, staring.

"Of course I am. Gonna question her like a one-armed bandit while she's at it."

"What does that even mean?"

"If you'd come from the south, you'd know."

Across the gym, Sheila, with two coffees in hand, started to clack here way back towards them. Pearl slammed the drawer shut, and they both grimaced at the noise. Sally raced back to her spot on the bleachers, pretending to peruse her phone while keeping her breath steady. Pearl climbed into the tilted-back metal chair she had abandoned earlier.

Sheila held out the disposable cups. "All they have left is decaf. I hope that's okay."

"What happened to all the good stuff?" Pearl asked, fluffing the cape out around her.

"I guess a tree knocked down another power line just outside of town, so a lot of townies came in for breakfast." She stood behind Pearl and smiled at her brightly. "These accommodations don't affect my know-how, though. What kind of look are you going for? Sexy, sassy, modern woman?"

Pearl tucked her chin into her neck. "Is that French for 'tramp?'"

Sheila froze for a second, then burst into laughter, shaking a comb at Pearl. "You're so funny. Maybe we should give you a mohawk."

Pearl pulled at the collar of her cape and started to climb out of the chair. "Oh, hell no."

Sheila put her hands on her shoulders, "I'm just kidding. We'll just do a trim and a nice blowout unless you have something else in mind. But first, I've got to wet it down a bit. Sorry, there's no sink."

Sally watched as Sheila spritzed Pearl's hair with a water bottle, chatting casually about her style. What were they going to do on the investigation front, though? They needed to find the chemicals Sheila had used to synthesize the cyanide. Sally slid out of the bleachers and wandered around the small space, pretending to look at volunteer lists posted nearby with rotating duties. She doubted it would be that easy, especially with the town in chaos, but Sheila had been careless about leaving the apricots out. Maybe she would be obvious with the chemicals too. Sally glanced over her shoulder at the cart, bottles of developer and color lined up in rows, and the other side was stocked with styling products. No suspicious chemicals. Sally looked at Pearl, now in the chair with Sheila holding a section of her hair up while snipping the ends, and shook her head slightly.

What were they going to do? Sally tried to check in with Lauren, but go no response. Great. Mike was off trying to save the world, Lauren was lost in transport, and they were failing miserably at solving this crime.

32

Speaking of Drama

"Well, that was a bust," Pearl said, her chin in her hands after the appointment.

"It wasn't quite a bust," Sally insisted. "We found those red fibers and saved some without getting our fingerprints on them. Besides, you got your hair done, and it looks pretty nice."

"Ain't what we were looking for, though, and that chaps my behind. She probably ditched the apricots with the flood to backtrack on that evidence that would incriminate her."

"Hey," a woman's voice said suddenly. Sally and Pearl glanced up from their cots, surprised to see the approach of none other than Millie and Tillie from the baking contest.

"We need to talk," Tillie said, planting her hand on her hip.

"We won that contest fair and square," Pearl said flatly.

"That's not it," Millie said, rolling her eyes. "We owe you an apology."

Sally blinked. "Why?"

Millie sighed. "Seems you got caught up in some old rivalry between us and Paul. Last year he thought it would be funny to

223

CHRISTMAS, CABERNET, AND CHAOS

unplug our oven during the competition. This year we returned the favor. "

"Only I couldn't tell which cord was his, so I unplugged both," added Tillie. "Even if that competition was a disaster for us, we shouldn't have hurt your chances on purpose. So, we're sorry."

Pearl sat up and swung her feet over the edge of the cot. "So you cheated and still got beat?"

Millie chuckled, "We deserved to lose. Your cookies were amazing, and we all know how ours turned out."

"Our competitive nature got the better of us, and we hope you'll accept our apology," Tillie added, looking at her sister and then at Sally and Pearl.

Pearl stood and faced them. "I appreciate that. Pretty sure Sally will agree with me that you got what you deserved already."

Sally moved to sit on the edge of the cot, then pushed herself up. "And it made for some great television."

Millie slung an arm over her sister's shoulders. "We can always be counted on for some drama."

"Speakin' of drama," Pearl said, "do you gals know anythin' about Sheila?"

The sisters exchanged glances.

"Actually," Millie said, "she tried out for the first reality show we were ever on. She was in San Francisco at college. She didn't make it past the first round, but we spent eight hours in line with her."

Tillie continued, "We felt bad for her, being so young and seeming so desperate." Both sisters nodded. "All she talked about was wanting to get out of this town. We thought it sounded charming, personally. She invited us to come to visit, and we did. Now we visit here every year."

"Do you remember what her major was?" Pearl asked curiously.

"That's the thing. We were shocked when we learned she was doing hair. Back then, she was majoring in chemistry," Millie said. "She's so much smarter than she comes across. She got great grades and was always on top of things, but she sort of burned out in her senior year. She said she wanted to find a rich guy to marry so she could be taken care of."

Sally sucked in a breath of air. "Did you say that she has a chemistry degree?"

"No, she dropped out. She doesn't have a degree unless she went somewhere else. Seems she went to beauty school instead," Tillie said. "When we got cast on the second show we had to move to New York and lost touch."

Pearl, as always, could be counted on as the direct one. "We got our suspicions about her. Her boyfriend's aunt thinks someone is tryin' to kill her, and cyanide turned up in some tests."

"Sheila is smart as a whip and smooth as a snake, but not sure she's a murderer," Millie said. She leaned in, "Saw the interview about Mexico, maybe we can help you solve the crime this time."

Sally bit her lip, not wanting to let the opportunity go to waste, but unsure how to ask for something she was too afraid to do.

Fortunately, Pearl jumped right in.

"Reckon you could swipe her purse, or find a way to rifle through it?" she grinned. The sisters exchanged glances, which turned into mischievous smirks.

"Get us a decent diversion, and if there's anything suspicious in there, we'll find it," Millie said.

Sally and Pearl sat at one of the cafeteria tables waiting for dinner to be served. "Fancy another game of bridge?" Pearl asked, shuffling her cards. "I'm pretty sure I could rope in some other players."

"No," Sally replied. "I can't stop thinking about Millie and Tillie. What if they're in danger getting mixed up in this whole thing?"

"Then I say they're grown-ass women, and they can handle themselves," Pearl replied. "Don't worry so much. They done survived two reality shows, they'll be fine."

"I just don't want anything bad to happen to them," Sally said, pulling at the hem of her shirt.

"Stop that. They know what they're about," Pearl said shortly.

"Is that-" Sally started.

"Wait," Pearl said, standing. A little girl with long black hair and a red beret was crossing the gym towards them, waving her little hand.

"Hi," Noël said, swallowing hard, her eyes red-rimmed.

"Everythin' okay?" Pearl asked, brows furrowing.

"Not really," Noël trailed off, sniffling. "Um. We can't get to the cabin because the roads are bad. Now we have to stay here. My mom's really mad abut it." She glanced miserably at her family's little triangle of cots with their luggage in the middle.

Pearl frowned. "It ain't so bad. Where's your fleet of guardian angels, anyway? Ain't they helpin'?"

Noël sniffled deeply, pulling deeply into her nose as her eyes filled with tears she refused to shed. "My parents got rid of them. They said I didn't need them... they said we didn't need charity. I checked the trash, but then Mom told me that she took them to the church's donation bin."

"Those sons of-" Pearl rocketed to her feet, hands clenched at her sides. "Gifts are gifts! Your folks had no right."

"My folks are getting a divorce," Noël said softly. "It's a sure thing." She looked over at her parents, who were sitting on cots, staring at their phones. "My dad's moving out when we get home. Why did they have to throw away my only present?" Noël's face crumpled into contorted pain. Her shoulders curled, and Pearl reached out to hug her.

"Now, you listen. I don't mind about those ornaments, you hear? They're just porcelain and plastic. They ain't angels, just look like 'em."

Noël sobbed into Pearl's side. "I want them back. I don't understand why I couldn't keep them."

"Shhh." Pearl reached out an arm to hug Noël. "It'll all be okay. I promise."

"I need my angels," wept the little girl.

"The roads are all blocked off and we're in here for a reason, but I'll do my best," Pearl promised fiercely. "You get back to your folks before they worry. Stay warm. Try to stay happy."

"How can I," Noël wept, "when Christmas is ruined?" After one more hug from Pearl, she ran back to where her parents were sitting and flopped onto her cot, burying her head in her hands.

Throughout dinner Pearl seemed preoccupied when Sally wanted, more than anything, to formulate a plan with her.

"Can you please try to focus?" Sally asked, pinching the bridge of her nose. "I can't do this alone."

"Can't stop thinkin' about that kid," Pearl muttered. "Can't

227

believe her parents would donate those angels I gave her. Of all the heartless nerve."

"Listen, if traffic is all blocked, the pickup for donations is probably stalled," Sally said encouragingly. "If there's no way they've moved from the church, I'm sure you'll be able to help her get her angels back, but in the meantime, can we please focus on who's trying to kill Birdie?"

"Those redhead sisters seem alright to me," Pearl confessed. "So do Paul and Valerie, for as much of a wet blanket as she is."

"Leave the redheads on the list," Sally said. "If they'd sabotage other bakers, it shows a pattern of dangerous behavior."

"Reckon it's possible," Pearl muttered. "Don't forget about that florist and the dozen other people who might want revenge."

Sally nodded, but rolled her eyes. "We never even wrote down Birdie's florist as a suspect. But, of course, there's Sheila. Sweet as a sugar cube, but she's also a hairstylist, trained chemist, and wants to get engaged to Trevor, who stands to inherit all of Birdie's money and has tried to gain access to it already."

"Motives all around," Pearl commented. "Guess we should keep our options open if we wanna come out ahead."

It was more difficult to be discreet about it in the gym, but Pearl insisted on making her famous list of suspects with markers and a poster board. Some supplies, at least, weren't too difficult to come by in a snowed-in high school in Oregon.

"I'm still not convinced that Trevor is innocent," remarked Pearl. "He stands to gain the most from Birdie's passin', and it could all be an act that he's too much of a pansy to do her in."

Sally nodded, writing his name on the board. "How do we

feel about Millie and Tillie?"

"Well, Birdie done said the fruitcake was different, and they're also willin' to help us out with Sheila."

"So Sheila's still the primary suspect?" Sally asked, drawing a new box with her sharpie.

"I'd say so. She's countin' on that money to get outta this town, and maybe she got sick of waitin'."

"But Trevor has fallen out of Birdie's good graces since the failed conservatorship," Sally pointed out.

"Ain't that all the more reason to be desperate? Sheila's pushin' thirty, ain't gonna get younger even with all those Instagram filters."

Sally sighed. "We have Millie and Tillie, Trevor and Sheila. And a town full of people who have a grudge against her, but obviously the whole town isn't *really* out to get Birdie." She paused. "Do you think they really will manage to shake down her purse and find something we can pin on her?"

"Only if we give them a decent diversion," Pearl winked.

"Gather 'round, kiddos! Cookies and carolin', we've got cookies and carolin'!" Pearl strode through the gym and repeated the announcement close to families, and children bored of waiting for outlets to charge their devices were eager to hop up and join.

"It's not just for kids!" Sally added, scanning around for Sheila. *Come on, take the bait.*

"All ages welcome," Pearl added, hopping up on the bleachers for more attention and visibility and accidentally upsetting some of the supplies on Sheila's cart. The younger woman glanced up from the magazine she was reading in annoyance.

"Oh shoot, I'm so sorry," Pearl said, clapping a hand over

her mouth. "Let me help you clean all that up." She crouched down and started scooping things into her hands, and Sheila was so preoccupied watching to make sure Pearl didn't get her hands on anything that she didn't notice a hand reach from under the bleachers to grab her Gucci purse.

Sally's heart was pounding in her chest. After less than a minute, the purse reappeared right where Sheila had left it, and Sally released a breath she didn't even realize she'd been holding.

Sheila turned, squinting at the purse. "Did anyone...?"

"Don't reckon so," Pearl said, as Sheila frowned at the bag and straightened it slightly on the bleachers.

"Weird. It must have tipped over," Sheila mumbled.

"Come on, Pearl!" Sally said. "We're about to start! Who knows 'Hark! The Herald Angels Sing?'" She was so relieved that the purse had made it back without Sheila's notice that her nerves were nothing. Leading the kids and Pearl in caroling was easier than even the most relaxed possible karaoke night for her.

After they were finished, Sally and Pearl went looking for the red-haired sisters, but they were approached first.

"Any luck?" Sally asked, pressing her lips together.

"This came out of her purse," Tillie grinned, handing Sally a folded up piece of very thin paper. "I'd call this pretty lucky. Not for someone... but for you, definitely."

"My stars," Pearl said, taking the slip and unfolding it. "You're faster than a couple of mongooses."

"You gave us a good opportunity," Millie shrugged. "Read what's on it."

"She bought ethanol and diethyl ether," Pearl said, squinting. Sally's eyes widened.

"Pearl, remember what we read at the police station? To make cyanide, she'd need to boil the apricot pits in ethanol, and then add diethyl ether. This fits. This is the missing piece. Even Mike would have to agree with this, right?"

Pearl nodded. "I reckon we might need his help to arrest her, unless we just want to sit on her legs until he gets back."

"Good point," Sally said, brows furrowing. "It might be a good idea to hold off until tomorrow to reveal her. It's getting late and it's better if she doesn't suspect we're onto her."

33

Christmas Eve

December 24

Sally and Pearl stood in the girls' locker room in front of the mirror, brushing their teeth. Even with everything happening, Sally couldn't help but embrace the tingle of excitement. Secretly, she had always loved Christmas Eve, with the magic of anticipation still buzzing in the air, just a little more than Christmas Day.

"All I want for Christmas is a confession," Pearl said before shoving the toothbrush back into her frothy mouth.

"All I want for Christmas is my kids," Sally said. Then guilt washed over her, thinking about Pearl's children, who wouldn't ever be coming home. "Sorry."

"Don't you worry about me. I know how much you were countin' on them comin'."

Sally nodded and cupped her hands under the faucet to rinse her mouth. She needed to stop dumping on Pearl and focus on the task at hand. "We have to make sure we do this right. Even if she doesn't confess, the evidence needs to be so solid that it doesn't matter what she does or doesn't say"

Pearl met her eyes in the mirror. "You know this ain't my first rodeo."

Sally bit her lip. "I'm just saying we need to be careful."

"I know. Hurry up. We gotta go help with breakfast."

Sally dried her face and followed Pearl to their cots, where they dropped their bags off before heading to the kitchen. Paul was scrambling a huge skillet of eggs, humming a Christmas song. Valerie rolled out dough for cinnamon rolls. She smiled at Sally and Pearl and said, "Merry Christmas Eve."

Sally echoed the greeting and shared a look with Pearl. Since when did Valerie become so cheery? "What can we do to help?" Sally asked.

"We have oatmeal almost ready for the volunteers, and the rest is easy. Would you be willing to round up the kids and entertain them for a few minutes to give their parents a chance to clean up?" Paul asked.

Pearl said, "Sure. I'll whip 'em into shape with the threat of Santa showin' up with coal."

"That's not nice," Sally admonished.

"But it works, " said Valerie. "I used the Santa threat for two months each year leading up to Christmas. Nothing got my kids in line faster than a threat of being on the naughty list."

"See, that's real parentin'," Pearl said.

"Come on," Sally said, "Let's go find something for the kids to do. There's a real chance that they'll be stuck here on Christmas Day without their presents, and I don't want them to think that it's because they were naughty."

After digging through the tubs of donations, Sally and Pearl assembled a craft table so the kids could make ornaments as presents for their families. Sally went and rounded up the children from their grateful parents. Pearl marched around the table, giving out orders and monitoring progress.

Twenty minutes later, Valerie walked out of the kitchen with two bowls of oatmeal topped with chopped apples and brown sugar. "Sally and Pearl, come eat. I'll take over for a bit."

Sally sighed. Her hands were covered in glue. There was more glitter on the gym floor than on the ornaments. They made a quick pit stop to the bathroom to wash off as much Christmas craft mess as possible and headed for the volunteer table. Making their way across the gym, they saw Kelly waving them down and met her in the middle. "I was looking for you. Mike is back. He and Gavin are on their way over with some news."

Sally's heart lifted. She hadn't realized the weight of worry she'd been carrying. It had been a long 24 hours without him. Kelly nodded briskly, heading off to give Valerie a hand with the kids.

Pearl paused at the volunteer table and then turned towards the kitchen door. "I've got a hankerin' for a sweet roll. Gotta see if they're done. Anythin' else I should grab?" Pearl asked.

"Oh, that sounds good," Sally said, smiling as she slid into the bench seat. "One for me as well, and I'll ask one of the runners to grab us coffee. We're going to need caffeine to get through today."

The oatmeal smelled delicious. *Apples, brown sugar, and almonds.* When Pearl returned, Sally raised her coffee cup in a playful toast before picking up her spoon.

"Stop!"

Everyone in the room whirled to look in the direction of the person shouting. Mike was running towards them. "Don't eat that food."

"What in the world?" asked Pearl.

"Mike, what's wrong?" Sally asked. Mike's eyes were wild as he grabbed the two bowls in front of Sally and Pearl and lifted them away, setting them on an empty table. It was only then that Sally noticed Gavin right behind Mike, unpacking a poison testing kit next to their food.

"I know who poisoned Birdie," Mike said, winded from running.

"Sheila," Sally and Pearl said in unison.

Mike, breath slowing, nodded soberly. "Don't worry. We apprehended her when she tried to escape out the kitchen's back door, and we're shutting down mealtimes until we're sure what's safe to eat." His eyes were full of fear as he met Sally's gaze, and they both realized just how close they had come to disaster.

Sally nodded, feeling stricken. She could have been just like that raccoon, frothing on the ground, then dead. Mike stepped closer to her and put a hand protectively on her shoulder.

"When I was in the mountains, I got a call from Gavin. He filled me in on the fruitcake and the raccoon," Mike explained. "By that point, we'd found those lost kids, but it was slow progress getting down that mountain through the snow. I'm glad I made it back in time."

"What led you to think that it was Sheila?" Sally asked. He couldn't know about all the evidence she and Pearl had gathered.

"It started with fruit for my morning oatmeal," Mike admitted. "I like to switch it up to keep it from getting boring, so I'm familiar with the produce selection in Harry's Country Store. Harry rarely has apricots in stock, but one person in McKenzie Bridge always has a full bowl of them on hand and, according to all of her recent clients, asks for the pits back."

"How did you know about Sheila's apricots?" Sally asked.

Mike shuffled his feet, pushing his hands into his pockets. "Before you came out, I got a haircut from her. When I got the call from Gavin, I remembered that full bowl of apricots because I thought it was an odd thing to offer someone in a salon. I went by her shop, still shut down, and confirmed that was where she was making the cyanide. She has a portable burner and a ton of-"

"Ethanol and diethyl ether?" Pearl grinned.

Mike's eyebrows shot up. "You girls have done your research."

Gavin tapped Mike on the arm, "I'm heading to the kitchen to double-check the rest of the food." Mike nodded. Gavin took the bowls and his kit with him, disappearing behind the double doors.

"That ain't all. Did a little extra diggin' for insurance," Pearl admitted, handing over the receipt. Mike looked at it and whistled. "This is hers? You're sure?"

"It came out of her purse," Sally confirmed. "But we were careful. I don't think she would have known we were investigating her."

"Something must have tipped her off," Mike said, rubbing his forehead. "We aim to find out more about this at the station. Regardless... I'm sorry that I doubted you. Things wouldn't have gotten this far if I'd just listened to you when you were sure something was wrong."

Sally reached for his hand, squeezing it reassuringly. She was trying to formulate a response when Gavin stuck his head out of the kitchen, holding up two blue test strips, along with several white ones. Mike nodded to acknowledge him.

"It was just your bowls," he said. "I thought so, but we

needed to be sure."

"Can't believe I almost got fed poison," Pearl said, seething, her fists clenched on the table in front of her. "I wanna give that gold diggin' hussy a piece of my mind and find out how she knew it was us lookin' into her cyanide spree."

"I can make that happen," Mike said. "I think you girls would be a great help."

Even though the snow was deep and still coming down hard, Mike's truck plowed through the few blocks to the police station, where Sheila was locked up in one of the cells, sitting with her head drooping towards her knees.

"Did she get her call?" Mike asked the attending officer.

"She sure did. She contacted–"

Though he was cut off mid-sentence, it became almost immediately apparent who had received Sheila's one call. Hair in disarray and face red with fury, Trevor burst through the door of the station, slamming it behind him and glaring at the holding cell.

"What did you do?" he demanded shrilly, almost shaking with fury.

Sheila sniffled and pulled her arms closer to herself. "I'm innocent," she insisted softly.

"That's not how it looks. Apricots? Chemicals in the salon to make poison? What the hell, Sheila?"

"I'm being framed," she said, eyes wide under her dark bangs. "That stuff was planted on me. Your aunt never liked me. She's always made me feel unwelcome in your family, and you care so much about what she thinks that it's kept you from proposing all this time."

"I'm not ever proposing. In fact, we're done, Sheila. You

used everything I ever told you to try and hurt my Aunt Birdie, and I can't forgive that."

"No, not everything!" she pleaded, shooting to her feet and clutching the cell's bars. "Just the things that could hurt us, like when you said you overheard those nosy wannabes sniffing around. I had to throw them off our trail."

"*Your* trail," Trevor said icily. "And by poisoning their oatmeal? Get this through your head: we're very different people. I would never hurt anyone, especially my aunt. Yes, I was concerned that she might be slipping. Yes, she was getting obstinate and looking for conspiracies around every corner. But *killing* her? That's all you."

He turned and started to storm away, but Mike put a hand on his shoulder.

"Could I ask you to stay for questioning, Trevor?" he asked softly.

"Yes," Trevor said stiffly, straitening his collar. "Of course. I have nothing to hide."

The snowfall and the coffee supply both dwindled over the course of the morning and well into the afternoon. Trevor cooperated, admitting that he had overheard Sally and Pearl's conversation with Birdie the night they'd come to collect the evidence.

"I was just telling my girlfriend about something strange that had happened," he said, drumming his fingers on the table in front of him. "I always thought she was just concerned about my aunt, asking questions about the house and her activities, so it didn't seem unusual."

Mike nodded, adjusting the tape recorder on the table between them before concluding out loud that they didn't have any reason to think that Sheila and Trevor had been working together.

Sheila's questioning was a lot messier and far less cooperative. She was stony and seething, her arms crossed tightly across her chest as she sat low in her chair with her back curled.

"Why did you do it?" Mike finally asked after walking through the details of the case, the evidence she couldn't deny, and the ugliest possible motive.

"I wanted to get out of this town," she said flatly. "I wanted to have a life that was finally perfect. Is there anything so wrong with that?"

"There's a lot wrong with 'perfect' when you go about it like that," Pearl said. "Reckon we're just about done here, Mike? Sally and I got some turkeys to roast for those shelter folks for their Christmas Eve dinner, and it looks like the snow's lettin' up."

Mike nodded, concluding the questioning and leaving Sheila in the care of the other officers. Blue sky and sun started to peek through the clouds, reflecting brilliantly off the drifts of pure white snow that had finally finished falling.

34

Get a Grip

"Ladies and Gentleman." Mike's voice boomed across the gym that evening. They'd returned from the police station just in time for Sally and Pearl to pitch in to roast the turkeys. "I know you're excited about a marvelous dinner tonight, but I have a few quick announcements first. I am happy to report that the downed lines are being repaired as we speak, and the snow plows are hard at work. By tomorrow morning, those without power should have it restored, and the roads down the mountain will be open. You'll be free to head home."

Cheers echoed through the gym. Families began chattering among themselves and corralling their children.

"Hang on, folks," Mike continued, and the joviality faltered. Mike gestured for Gary, the pastor, to step up onto the bleachers for an announcement.

"The McKenzie Bridge Christian Church has put together a breakfast for you on the way out of town. Please feel free to stop by in the morning and get a to-go box or share the meal and our community in the Fellowship Hall. We'll have a service starting at 10 and would be honored if you joined us. Merry

Christmas."

A smattering of applause broke out, and people began to move again.

Sally beamed. With the roads open, maybe at least Joel would make it down. As she looked around the gym at the families celebrating the chance to go home, a sense of peace settled over her. Even if her kids didn't make it, she would be okay. She was so proud of Mike. He knew exactly how to keep people calm. He was, indeed, the police chief that McKenzie Bridge needed in a crisis. Her face flushed with heat, and her stomach tingled. She cleared her throat and rolled her shoulders. *Get a grip on yourself.*

She glanced over at Pearl, slumped in a chair and drinking coffee from a disposable cup. The exhaustion on her face mirrored Sally's.

"Up and at 'em," Sally chuckled. "There's more coffee and more work. We've got to get these folks their Christmas Eve dinner."

They carved and plated the turkey, scooping out mashed potatoes, cranberry sauce, and some canned string beans they'd done their best to spruce up. The stuffing was boxed but seasoned well, and the gravy was canned, but Sally hoped everyone was too hungry to notice. She didn't want to think of the tourists as choosing beggars, not when they'd been so grateful and friendly to the volunteers. Many families who had come here for relief had even pitched in themselves, especially with the highly demanding cleanup process after meals.

Mike headed back to the station to take care of some paperwork but promised to be back soon.

"Hardly the vacation I thought we'd be takin'," Pearl said, finally settling down on her cot next to Sally after dinner. "At least no one got shot at this time."

"I'm glad you can count your blessings," Sally laughed lightly. "Do you want to smear some leftover mashed potatoes on our faces and pretend we're getting a facial in a nice spa?"

"Don't be silly. We got gift certificates to a nice spa," Pearl joked, digging in her purse to flash the gift certificates to services at the spa upstairs in the resort with the clogged pipes. Sally snorted. She imagined they'd be down for a while until they found some replacement staff.

Just then, two individuals rushed up to them. Their faces were familiar, but their unity was such that Sally had to blink and check herself to ensure that it was Patrick and Kiyomi.

"Have you seen Noël?" Kiyomi asked softly, her face pale. "We can't find her."

"Did she come here?" Patrick echoed, gray-faced. He looked like he hadn't had any sleep in ages, the bags under his eyes dark and heavy.

"Haven't seen her. She's your kid, and you don't want her talkin' to me anyway, remember?" Pearl said without looking up, her focus on stuffing the gift certificates back into her purse.

"We thought she'd gone to bed, but she's not there," Kiyomi blurted out. "Her boots and her coat are gone. We just wanted to see if perhaps the two of you knew anything at all about it."

"Aw, heck," Pearl groaned. "She probably wandered off to grab a cookie. I'm sure it's just somethin' like that."

Patrick took a deep breath. "We don't want to be over-dramatic about this, but we're starting to get worried."

"Did you check the rest of the school?" Sally asked, her brow furrowing.

"Every inch of it. We even got some of the other volunteers

to help out, but we can't find her," Kiyomi said, wringing her hands.

"We know the police chief. I'm sure he'd be happy to help sort this out," Sally said gently. She knew how they were feeling and didn't want to cause more panic or pain. Henry had gotten lost in the mall once, and it had been awful.

"We wanted to check with you first before going right to the police. I hoped maybe she would have come here since she's so fond of Pearl," Kiyomi stammered, her gaze dropping to the floor.

Pearl swallowed, tightening her lips. "No one was oversteppin'. Think we learned our lesson from the last time we all talked."

"We're sorry about the ornament shop," Patrick said, shaking his head. "Passions were high already, and I guess things just escalated. We were wrong to take it out on you."

"I reckon it wasn't me y'all were takin' it out on," Pearl said stiffly. "I wish she'd come by this evenin', truly."

"I do, too," Kiyomi said, looking miserable. "Will you please tell us if you find out anything?"

"'Course I will," Pearl said. "Hope you find her soon."

"Let's keep looking," Patrick said, nodding his sheepish appreciation before turning with Kiyomi to set off across the gym.

"Keep us posted," Sally called out after them. Even though the storm had ended, the cold and the sheer amount of snow on the ground would be dangerous for a grown adult to be out in, let alone a little girl.

When they were out of earshot, Sally met Pearl's eyes. "What if they don't find her?" Sally asked, tugging the hem of her shirt. "If she's out in the cold..."

"She was mad at her parents. Every kid's done about the same at some point. It's natural." Pearl tipped her head back and closed her eyes. "Why's it gotta be McKenzie Bridge after the storm of the century, though?"

"There's a reason she didn't just go hide in a different part of the school without her coat and boots," Sally mused. "A kid who just wanted to sulk would have probably done the warmer and safer thing. She doesn't seem like the type who would pull a dangerous stunt just to worry her parents." In fact, they'd seen her doing the opposite, falling over herself at the light parade to put on a bright face and encourage harmony.

"She's hurtin', though. They took her gift and donated it, so-" Pearl smacked her forehead. "Ain't it obvious? She probably went back to the church to look for the donations so she could find her angels." She looked around for Patrick and Kiyomi, making an exasperated sound when they appeared to be nowhere in the gym. "Heck, by the time they find Mike and we find them, it might be too late."

Sally pulled out her phone, making two calls. "No answer at the police station, and Mike's cell is going straight to voicemail," she reported.

"We might be the ones who can get to her fastest," Pearl said. "Even with these old legs, we gotta chance it."

"Let's hope the plows have at least cleared those streets," Sally said, pulling on her boots and coat and topping it with her pink puff-ball hat.

"Even if they have, the temperatures are gonna keep droppin', and half of the town has still got no power. Church might not even have heat." Pearl also scrambled to pull on her cold-weather gear, complete with her chunky peacock-blue scarf.

"I guess we'll see when we get there." Sally stepped out into the snow, and sure enough, there were small footprints along the path that, despite being shoveled earlier in the day, had another eight inches of snow.

"Shoot. They must not be prioritizin' around the high school because they know folks here are safe," Pearl muttered. "She must be freezin'. Keep an eye out for any sign she fell."

"Okay," Sally said, squinting against the sea of white. Even if the snow had stopped coming down, there were almost three feet of it on the ground in places, with drifts even higher. Fortunately, she didn't see any signs that anyone had fallen in it, and she thanked God that it wasn't snowing anymore. Otherwise, it might have quickly covered the footprints and any sign of a body.

"We're in some luck, at least," Pearl said. "Looks like the plows have been through Main Street." Sally peered ahead, nodding in relief. After they made it through the high school parking lot mess, it looked like it would be a clear and relatively straight shot to the church.

"I wonder if they called the police," Sally said.

"Doubt it. Those highfalutin' folks keep their business private. Surprised they told us. Must be real shook."

"I hope she's alright," Sally murmured, wincing as snow overflowed into her boot and melted against her sock, soaking her ankle. She would text Mike if they didn't find Noël at the church.

"She'd better be. If a whole fleet of guardian angels couldn't help her, old Pearl's gonna have to work extra hard."

35

Lost Then Found

The sanctuary was dim, exterior lights shining through the stained glass windows. Sally rubbed her hands together, grateful to be out of the wind. There was no sign of Noël.

"It's gotta be the charity part of the church," Pearl said. "Volunteered at enough of these things to know. Usually off towards the back, wherever it ain't heated in the winter or air-conditioned in the summer, and people can pull their cars up and drop their donations right off inside. That's where they stick volunteers."

"Pearl," Sally said uncomfortably, "I don't know what churches you've been to, but that Baptist tag sale is always held in the nice fellowship hall."

"Yeah, but that's not where they store all the crap for you to buy."

"You shouldn't be so negative about the church."

"I call it as I see it. I know my morals, and I'll talk about such as I please."

Sally decided that it would be futile to argue and merely followed her friend as they wound down the darkened hallways of the church. When they finally came to a part of the building that did seem unusually dreary and cold, they opened the door to what seemed more like an oversized open garage than a room. There were boxes piled high with donated goods.

"Don't let that door shut," Pearl warned. "Looks like it's locked from the inside." Sally quickly unlocked it, propping it open with a door jam for good measure in case it locked automatically when it closed.

Sally and Pearl picked their way through the maze of boxes, and then Pearl's flashlight beam fell on a little black boot.

"Noël!" Pearl exclaimed, dropping her flashlight and rushing forward.

The little girl seemed to be asleep, Sally thought, but she wasn't dressed nearly warmly enough for this chilled and drafty area that was practically an open garage, let alone the punishing walk from the shelter at the high school to get here. Pearl was already stripping out of her peacock-blue scarf and her jacket, pressing them around Noël fretfully.

"Is she alright?" Sally asked, hardly daring to breathe, scared of the answer.

"She's breathin', I think," Pearl said, her voice shaking. "Hard to tell when my hands ain't real steady. She's got those angels in her arm. Reckon this is all my fault."

"No," Sally said fiercely, dialing 911 on her phone. "*No*, you are not allowed to say that, Pearl. Can you lift her? We should get her inside where it's warmer."

"All I ever wanted was to do right by a kid." Pearl's mouth twisted as she scooped up Noël and hugged her close. "I had two and blew both chances. They slipped through my fingers, and there wasn't nothin' I could do. Christ, she's cold."

Sally held the door for Pearl as she cradled the phone between

247

her shoulder and her chin. She told the 911 dispatcher where they were and the situation, speaking as quickly and clearly as possible. She hurried to join Pearl's side, following her to the sanctuary. She took off her coat and spread it over the chilled little girl, who they tucked in between them on a pew for warmth and waited for help.

"Grief is love with nowhere to go," Sally said steadily, locking eyes with Pearl. "But your love has so many places to go. It goes to my family and me. It goes to the children whose lives you touch wherever you travel. It goes to your heart, soul, and memory, Pearl, and yes, it goes to your children. Your children are still a place your love can go. I believe that they know where they are and that your angels send all their love back to you."

Pearl shook her head, hugging Noël.

Sally hugged both of them while Pearl trembled and Noël barely shivered as they waited for emergency services to make it through the snow. They stayed that way in the church's sanctuary for what seemed like an eternity until finally, paramedics burst through the door, followed closely by Noël's worried parents.

It took a bit to get Pearl to let go of Noël. She wanted to cling to the point where it seemed almost instinctual, and Sally had to work hard and speak soothingly to pry her hands away.

"You gotta tell me she'll be okay," Pearl said breathlessly as the paramedics bundled up Noël and loaded her into the ambulance.

"We think so, ma'am," a young paramedic offered, but Pearl made a dismissive noise with her lips that made it sound like she was completely blowing him off.

"Won't believe that until I see it. I need some kinda reassurance, dang it!"

Kiyomi's hand reached out to touch Pearl's shoulder. The older woman stiffened suspiciously. "What do you want?" She demanded, but Kiyomi's hand was lightly placed and gentle.

"I want to thank you," Kiyomi said. "And to apologize."

"What are you sayin'?" Pearl asked from the floor, sounding like she wasn't sure she'd heard correctly.

"Thank you," Kiyomi emphasized. "You saved her. She's alive. She might have frozen to death if no one had found her, and she's our life."

"Does she know that?" Pearl asked, swallowing thickly.

"We both would do anything for her," Kiyomi confirmed. Patrick nodded in support. Pearl curled, crossing her arms over her chest.

"Let her keep those angels she loves."

"Done," Kiyomi and Patrick said in unison.

"And you need to get your house in order. What about couples' counselin'?"

"Well... I..." Kiyomi fumbled, seeming to find the words supremely awkward.

"It's what she wants more than anythin' in the world for Christmas, I guarantee it."

Patrick hung his head, nodding sheepishly. "I guess we could have been better parents to her all along, however well we manage with each other. Or don't manage," he said, shoving his hands in his pockets and sighing.

"You think?" Pearl asked sarcastically.

"This is difficult enough as it is," Kiyomi sniped, but Sally moved in to embrace Pearl, resting her forehead against the other woman's.

Patrick and Kiyomi were herded into the back of the ambulance by the paramedics. The doors slammed, and sirens wailed as they left for the medical center.

Pearl hardly heard any of it as she buried her face in Sally's shoulder. "I'm so proud of you," Sally whispered. "You're like a patron saint of keeping children safe. There's no life I wouldn't trust you with."

"Aw, hell," Pearl snuffled. "I ain't worth that trust."

"Yes, you are," Sally said fiercely. "I believe in you. I'm in awe of everything that you give, Pearl."

Sally held Pearl as the other woman cried. There was something bone-deep and guttural about the sound. As Sally rocked and shushed Pearl, she realized that she was hearing all of Pearl's wounded pain, all of her loneliness, and all of her misery over decades.

That's okay. You're my best friend. We can share this, Pearl, so you don't have to do it alone.

"I miss them," Pearl choked in Sally's arms. "I miss them so much. They had all my love, and then they were gone, just like that."

"Say their names," Sally said softly on an impulse.

"Can't," Pearl gasped.

"You have to. What are you afraid of?" Sally asked. "Say their names so we can remember and honor them, Pearl. Say their names so they can be here on Christmas with us."

Pearl's breath shuddered. Her shoulders curled stiffly, but the names *Peter* and *Mary* were discernible in her tortured exhalation.

"I love you, Peter and Mary," Sally said, rocking Pearl like a small child as she held her in her arms. "I love you, darling children, because you belonged to my best friend. Thank you for being hers. Goodbye, Peter and Mary."

"Goodbye," Pearl wept. "Goodbye, Peter and Mary. I love you. Goodbye."

36

Merry Little Christmas

December 25th

"Hey there." Mike turned from the coffee he was pouring into the *I'm on Mexican Time* mug Pearl had bought him for his birthday. He was dressed in navy pants and a gray sweater. "You and Pearl became heroes twice in 24 hours. Are you sure you don't want to apply for a job at the station?" He smirked.

Sally chuckled. Mike had come to get them at the church the night before, and instead of driving them to the shelter, he'd opted to risk the mountain road to his house. They'd had a chance to sleep in comfortable beds, warm showers, and clean clothes.

"You look nice," Sally commented. "Especially considering you've been tromping around in the wilderness and saving women from getting poisoned left and right."

He looked down at his outfit, grinning. "Thought I'd dress up for church, it being Christmas and all."

Sally smiled and moved forward to make her own cup of coffee.

"Any word from your kids?"

Sally shook her head, her smile faltering, "Lauren sent me a text late last night saying they might have a flight out of Salt Lake. I haven't heard any updates since. Joel was waiting till the roads were confirmed clear. So it might just be us today."

"You okay with that?" Mike asked carefully.

Sally shrugged, then took a deep breath, "I'm glad to be here with you and Pearl. That's enough for now."

Mike sipped his coffee and asked, "Is Pearl awake yet?"

"She's showering now. She woke up grumpy as a mule, but I told her she had to come with us this morning. Surprisingly she didn't fight me on it."

"You better take her some coffee then. We need to leave in thirty minutes." Mike turned and leaned against the counter, watching Sally reach into the cabinet and pull out two mugs.

Sally knew he was watching her. She swallowed a smile as she added milk and sugar to the mugs. "I'm just glad they were able to pull together a service. It wouldn't be Christmas without church." She watched steam rise from the cups as she poured coffee. "I'd better make sure Pearl doesn't crawl back into bed." She turned, and Mike pushed off the counter to stand in front of her. Sally froze, her throat going dry. She looked up at him from under her lashes.

When he spoke, his voice sounded husky. "Merry Christmas, Sally."

Sally swallowed, looking down at the steaming mugs in her hands, then back at Mike. "Merry Christmas. Thank you for everything, especially..."

He shoved his hands in his pockets and rocked on his heels.

Sally cleared her throat. "I should get this coffee to Pearl."

"Oh, right." Mike stepped out of the way, the mood of the moment dissipating. "Uh. Sally, we'll talk later, Okay?

253

Tonight, after dinner. Just us, after everyone else has gone to bed?"

"Um. It's a date," Sally agreed, cringing at the way that had sounded. She padded across the wood floor to where she could hear Pearl's blow dryer going.

They pulled into the church parking lot with fifteen minutes to spare. Pastor Gary stood just inside the doors, waiting to welcome people as they entered the church. He leaned over to Sally and Pearl and said, "Heard about what you two have done for this town. God bless you both."

Sally smiled and thanked him. Soft piano music filled the sanctuary. Poinsettias lined the front riser. A beautifully lit Christmas tree twinkled gently in the corner. The windows had been covered with cheery wrapping paper made to look like gifts. The church was packed, and the trio worked their way around the pews to the opposite side of the sanctuary, where chairs had been set up along the wall for overflow. Sally recognized several faces in the crowd and exchanged smiles and waves. This was how it should be in a small community.

After singing "O Come, All Ye Faithful," Pastor Gary stood and opened with prayer. Then he began to speak. "It's been a rough week for our little town. With power outages, road closures, lost hikers, and stranded families, there has been no shortage of struggle. Despite all that, Christmas has come. We are so glad you chose to join us on this peaceful morning."

Mike reached over and took Sally's hand. She looked down at their woven fingers woven, feeling the warmth of their palms pressed together. Mike was smiling and looking straight ahead at the pastor.

"In this life, we are promised there will be trouble. Peace on earth isn't something we can achieve. We cannot strive, fight, or work for peace, at least not lasting peace. True peace is a gift to be experienced. God is peace; he came to earth as a baby in a manger so that you might experience him. Amid a broken world, peace is found in Jesus."

Sally sensed Pearl shifting in her chair. Sally knew this was hard for Pearl. Not just Christmas, but being in a church. She sensed that her friend had been angry with God for a long time. And it had been an emotional week for all of them. She leaned over and whispered, "You okay?"

Pearl nodded, "Just tryin' to get a better look at my girl up there."

Sally followed Pearl's gaze to see Noël sitting in the second row between her parents. Sally smiled. That little girl looked healthy and happy. She was an angel from God, sent just for Pearl. "I think you did it, Pearl," Sally whispered.

"I did not," Pearl whispered fiercely, "Wait, what are you accusin' me of?"

"Your heart. It grew three sizes."

"Oh, shut up," Pearl said, elbowing Sally playfully.

Pastor Gary went on. "The Wise Men brought gifts for baby Jesus. All he asks of us is that we come freely to him with an open heart. And in exchange, he binds up our wounds, restores families, builds communities, and brings peace."

Sally watched as Noël turned around and waved at Pearl. Her mom turned as well and smiled at Sally and Pearl. Sally smiled back and squeezed Mike's hand. What a difference a week could make. At the end of the sermon, Pastor Gary offered a benediction.

"May the Lord bless you and keep you. May his face shine upon you and be gracious to you. May the Lord turn his face toward you and give you peace. Now, under your seats, you will find a candle. Please locate yours and hold on to it until the flame is passed to you. Parents, please hold a candle for both you and your child so we don't burn the place down."

The parishioners chuckled as Pastor Gary pointed to a rambunctious little boy in the front row.

Sally reached under her chair for her candle, and when she stood, she saw that Noël had joined Pearl. Pearl covered Noël's hand with her own as they cupped the candle together. "You sure your parents are okay with this?" Pearl whispered.

Noël nodded, "It was Mom's idea."

Sally looked to where Noël's parents each held their candles with one hand; their other hands joined in promise.

"You know what I want for Christmas?" Pearl whispered.

Noël tipped her head back to look at Pearl.

"For you to write me a letter or draw me a picture for my refrigerator. Could you do that when you get home? Then maybe I can write you back?"

A smile broke out across Noël's face just as the lights were dimmed and the opening bars of "Silent Night" began. "Anything for my guardian angel," the little girl whispered.

The congregation sang along with the hymn as the flame was passed from candle to candle, lighting the darkness. Tears pricked Sally's eyes. She wished her kids were here to see this.

After the service, they hung back to wait for Noël's parents.

"Thank you for everything you've done for our family," Kiyomi said before hugging Sally and then Pearl.

"Wasn't no trouble," Pearl said, patting Noël's red beret.

Patrick reached out to shake their hands. "Please stay in touch. We would all love that."

Pearl narrowed her eyes. "I will be keepin' my eye on you

two."

Patrick smiled, slipping an arm around his wife. "We would expect nothing less." Then he turned to Noël and said, "Come on, kiddo, we should hit the road. I think some presents are waiting for you under the tree at home."

Noël turned to Pearl and looked at her with weepy eyes, "Bye, Pearl."

Pearl pulled her into a bear hug and whispered, "Just for now, honey."

When they parted, Pearl wiped her eyes and sniffed. When Noël and her parents were gone, Pearl turned to Sally and Mike, "Let's get outta here before Pastor Gary tries to get me baptized."

They returned to Mike's house shortly after noon, settling in with a cup of coffee to enjoy the sun glistening on the brilliant white snow outside. The sound of car doors opening and loud conversation broke the peaceful atmosphere. "What in the world?" Mike asked, heading to the window.

Sally followed, and her mouth dropped open at the site. Several rental cars were parked on the driveway. Out tumbled both the source and elixir for Sally's holiday grief. It was like a perfect Christmas card illustration as Sally watched her children and their families pile out of their vehicles, gifts in tow. Sally ran out into the snow in stocking feet, throwing her arms around Lauren before scooping a fussy Amelia from her dad's arms. "What are you doing here?"

Lauren beamed. "We finally got a flight and miraculously found rental cars in Eugene."

"It was fate that drew us to this marvelous haven," said Windsong in her ethereal lilt. She stood off to the side in a

257

vintage wool pea coat, arms wrapped around herself, gazing dreamily at the mountains.

"Merry Christmas, Mom," said Henry, stepping forward to wrap his arm around Sally's shoulders and, looking at her feet, said, "Did you forget something?"

Sally looked at her wet socks and laughed. "We better get inside before I lose a toe to frostbite. You must be starving."

"We hit the only open Mcdonald's on the way out of town," Joel said. Then he turned to Tom, who was opening the trunk and retrieving bags of presents. "Thanks, honey."

Tom somehow looked like he had just shown up for a fashion shoot in an upscale outdoorsy catalog. He closed the trunk and headed towards Sally, flashing a brilliant smile before he kissed her cheek. "Merry Christmas."

Sally wasn't sure she had ever been happier than at that moment, with her entire family and best friends gathering for Christmas. Once inside, she reluctantly passed off Amelia and ran to the bedroom to change socks, a grin on her face she couldn't hide even if she tried. When she returned, boots and coats were piled by the front door. Mike was handing out cups of coffee to the group gathered around the Christmas tree, sharing their epic adventures in travel.

Sally slipped into an armchair and watched the scene unfold in quiet bliss. The fire crackled, and light snow fell outside. Pearl caught her eye and motioned for her to follow.

"I know you ain't had time for buyin' gifts on account we weren't sure they were even gonna show, but I got an idea." She filled Sally in on the plan. Sally sneaked into the den and borrowed some supplies from Mike. When she peeked her head out into the living room, she saw that her kids were listening to Mike tell stories about their time in Mexico. Amelia was asleep in Lauren's arms.

A few minutes later, they returned and nonchalantly deposited the presents under the tree.

"Mom, you didn't need to do that. We are exchanging gifts later," Joel said.

Sally ignored him and Pearl waved him off, "You mind your business. You're mama can do as she pleases."

Tom patted Joel's knee and smiled.

"You tell them about the naked hippies you rescued during the storm?" Pearl asked with a twinkle in her eye.

"We need to hear that story," Henry said.

Mike laughed and recounted the story, correcting Pearl's hyperbole.

Amelia's eyes fluttered open, but she snuggled in her mom's lap. Eventually, she wandered over to start examining the presents. Lauren watched her and smiled, "Should we open presents? Amelia may start without us."

"I'm afraid there's something you should know about the gifts," Sally said, tugging at the hem of her blouse. "We planned to do a lot of shopping in McKenzie Bridge."

"But between the murder attempts, bakin' contests, runaway reindeer, and town square Christmas trees tipsier than the night before Thanksgivin', we didn't have much time," Pearl said bluntly. "So, anyhow, Merry Christmas to y'all from Sally and me."

"It's the thought that counts," said Brad.

"The spirit of peace and harmony is all that matters," said Windsong, sweeping her wrists in circles.

Mike played Santa, handing out presents and then pausing to watch the recipients open their gifts.

"Wow, Mom," Lauren chuckled as she and Brad unwrapped

Sally and Pearl's coordinated aprons from the baking show. Lauren slipped it over her neck and smiled.

Brad said jokingly, "Maybe now you'll cook once in a while."

Lauren playfully punched him in the arm, "You got one too. Maybe *you* can cook."

Amelia squealed as she unwrapped the baking contest trophy, then immediately dented the edge by banging it against the stone framing Mike's fireplace. Lauren winced and looked at Sally, who was hiding a laugh behind her hand.

Windsong lifted the thunder egg out of the gift bag and examined it. Sally watched her attempt to figure out what it meant and said, "There are crystals inside. You have to open it with a hammer. Thought it was right up your alley."

Henry held up the autographed glossy photo of Brenda and Richard, raising his eyebrows. "I assume there is a story behind this?"

Pearl smacked her leg and roared with laughter.

Joel and Tom both chuckled as they opened a pair of gift certificates to a local spa they could certainly never use, reading the words written on each in sharpie: *I.O.U. A gift certificate in an equal amount to anywhere else on earth!*

They laughed together over the odd assortment of gifts when a sharp, prim knock sounded on the door.

"What in the world?" Mike asked, frowning. "I'm not expecting anyone else." He opened the door and let out a low whistle. "Mrs. Grassley," he greeted. "What can I do for you on this fine Christmas Day?" He sounded slightly apprehensive, as though he was already trying to think of ways to tell her that a rogue ice rink could wait until tomorrow.

"A little bird named Trevor told me that Sally and Pearl are staying here," Birdie said, peering into the house and waving her gloved hand. She looked rather cozy in her luxurious fur coat and matching hat. On her arm, Maximillian was tucked inside a custom-made, fur-lined handbag. "You'll be glad to know I can keep a secret, unlike some people I know."

"Hello, Birdie," Sally said, waving back. "It's wonderful to see you. Merry Christmas!"

"I had a feeling you'd say something like that," Birdie said. "And after spending so much of your Christmas vacation on me, I wanted to return the favor. Would your family please come to the window?"

Sally and Pearl stood, mystified, and led the group to peer out the large front windows. Amelia squealed with delight first, clapping her hands, and Sally's mouth dropped open.

Steve had harnessed his reindeer up to a sleigh, and they trotted into view on Birdie's signal. He tipped his hat and waved jovially at them. He slung a sack full of gifts out of the back, hauling it up to the door and handing it over to Mike.

"Merry Christmas, Chief Cunningham!" he said.

"Birdie!" Sally exclaimed. "You didn't have to-"

Birdie waved her off. "Neither did you," she said. "But in a world full of people who *didn't*, you and Pearl did. Consider this my sincerest thank you."

They quickly invited Birdie inside, and she admitted that while she didn't know everyone's names or much about them, she had done her best to plan for all sorts. She directed Mike on where to deliver various gifts, and by the time the bag was empty, they each had a nice assortment of presents in their laps.

Amelia was delighted by a beautifully crafted dollhouse with detailed-yet-sturdy furniture and a family of little cloth rabbits. It looked handmade and outrageously expensive. All the adults received a set of cashmere gloves and slippers, as well as soft fair isle sweaters for the men and designer scarves for the women. Pearl and Sally received gift cards to a chain store known for selling fancy kitchen supplies, and Sally blushed when she noticed the amount.

"All this time, we thought she was a grinch," Pearl whispered to Sally as the others thanked Birdie for her kindness. "Turns out she was actually Santa Claus."

"Birdie, I don't know what to say," Sally said. "This is so generous." She paused. "Where's Trevor this morning?"

"Taking some time to reflect on what his girlfriend tried to do," Birdie said. "He's a poor judge of character, but I feel vindicated that I was right about him not having the stomach for murder."

"He'll get over her," Pearl said confidently. "Maybe find a nice gal next time who keeps a bowl of apples in her salon instead of apricots."

"You can make cyanide out of apple seeds, too," Sally groaned. "Didn't you read that when we were researching?"

"Papayas, then."

"Well, let's all hope he finds his papaya princess." Birdie smiled, standing. "It's been a pleasure, but I should get home."

"Wait. Birdie," Mike said, "what do you think of bringing Trevor by for dinner tonight? We would be so pleased to have you."

"There's plenty to eat," Pearl added. "Not to mention some more of those cookies."

"Oh, well." Birdie seemed to take a few moments to think it over. "Yes, I suppose that does sound lovely. We'll bring a bottle of wine and a cherry pie."

Sally beamed. No one should be lonely this Christmas,

except maybe the hairdresser who had used all of her talents, determination, and resources to get rid of a woman with a surprisingly big heart.

Even though Sally tried to believe no one deserved to be lonely, she decided to make an exception in Sheila's case.

37

Holly Jolly Visit

"You all outdid yourself," Lauren said as they sat around Mike's table. They had to add a folding table and pull in every chair they could from throughout the house, but it worked. A larger table, of course, would have been perfect, but Sally had long since given up on perfection as a goal. What was the point when everything had turned out beautifully despite all the bumps in the road? All that mattered is that they were together.

"How did you glaze this ham?" Pearl asked, tapping the brown and glossy sugar coating with the tines of her fork. "Gotta say it turned out great."

"Believe it or, I used a propane torch from my workshop," Mike chuckled. "Don't worry. I cleaned it well."

"Hot dang," Pearl said. "You're always figurin' out ways to solve problems. It's a good thing this town's got you."

"A very good thing," Birdie agreed, sitting at the table beside Trevor and spreading cranberry sauce on her cut of turkey. "Of course, you've gotten much better at your job lately."

"Thank you, Birdie," Mike said politely.

"Here's to growing long after we're grown," Joel said,

raising his wine glass in a toast. The adults were quick to join him.

"May we never stop growing," Sally said. She smiled and surveyed the table of people she loved. "I'm so happy you're all here. Knowing what it took to get all of us around this table makes it even more special."

"Is it as perfect as you dreamed?" Pearl teased, setting a tray of warm cookies on the table. They were shaped like angels and decorated haphazardly.

"Better," Sally replied, reaching out to take one.

Birdie reached for one, too, frowning slightly when she took a bite. "They're delicious, of course, but different from the cookies that won that contest."

"We shook things up a bit," Pearl said. "This time Sally baked the cookies, and I did the decoratin.' Ain't too shabby, if I do say so myself."

"Amelia loves them," Brad chuckled, giving one to the baby and watching her immediately bite into the angel's wings.

"I'd like to propose another toast," Sally said, standing and raising her wine glass. "My friend Mike opened his home to us during our entire stay in McKenzie Bridge, not just today. He baked and served a beautiful ham after expertly handling the worst crisis he's seen yet as this town's chief of police. I want to thank him from the bottom of my heart for his amazing ability to fix things and his incredibly generous heart."

Mike ducked his head modestly as the table began to clap for him.

"Speech!" Tom said, clapping his hands loudly above his head. Mike stood and cleared his throat.

"I want to thank my dear friends Sally and Pearl for bringing excitement and their spirit of adventure to our quiet mountain town and for filling my home with laughter and light on this very joyous Christmas Day. But I owe a special thanks to Sally," he added, glancing sideways at her. She froze, eyes fixed on his face. "Thank you for standing for what you knew was right. You've got the instincts of a great detective, and I'm a lucky man to have you at my table."

Sally blushed as the table clapped again. She looked up at Birdie, who was nodding her quiet approval.

"Trevor, go start the dishes," Birdie said, and her nephew nodded, hopping up to pitch in and help. "Would you all like a family photo to commemorate this day? I would be glad to take it."

"Thank you," Sally said, handing over several of the family's smartphones and helping to arrange everyone on and around the couch.

"Get in here, Pearl!" Sally said, and after a moment's sheepish hesitation, Pearl came and sat next to her.

Something still seemed to be missing, though.

"Mike," Sally said, meeting his eyes. "Would you like to join us for our family photo?"

Mike blinked. "Are you sure, Sally?"

She held out her arm. "Come over here. Of course, I'm sure."

Mike took a seat on her other side. They were sitting together just as they had in his truck, and Sally, Pearl, and Mike joined hands and linked arms as the kids leaned in and smiled, Lauren cuddling Amelia close and Tom and Joel sharing a kiss.

After hours of beautiful conversation and easy laughter, when Amelia had fallen asleep with the baking trophy in one hand and a fistful of the little dollhouse rabbits in the other, Birdie announced that she and Trevor were taking their leave.

"You don't have to leave so soon, Birdie," Mike said. "It's

been a real pleasure having you here."

"I make it a rule never to overstay my welcome," Birdie said. "But this has been very nice. Next time, we'll invite you and anyone who might be staying with you for my famous homemade lasagna." She smiled at Sally, and Sally was struck anew by just what a sharp and perceptive woman Birdie actually was.

"I can't wait," Mike said warmly, seeing Birdie off and waving as Trevor walked her back to their car.

As the evening wore on, Sally's children peeled off gradually to head towards the Hoover House, which was still available after Mike had secured it for their use. Lauren put Amelia in her car seat, and after a few sleepy hugs and kisses, each car disappeared down the road. After the long delays and the doubt that had swept in with the snowstorm, everything had turned out wonderfully.

With the house silent and only Sally, Pearl, and Mike remaining, Pearl was the first to go to bed. Though she yawned widely, she made it a point to approach Sally, who was nodding off on the couch with a glass of wine in front of her.

"Just wanted to tell you that I'm real glad I came here with you. It might not have been the vacation I wanted, but I reckon it was the vacation I needed."

"Thank you for saying that, Pearl. I worried so much that you weren't having fun, even before the snowstorm turned everything upside-down."

"Sometimes fun ain't what the heart needs," Pearl said. "Just sayin', there was somethin' here that I needed, and I wouldn't have found it without you hangin' off my ear like a piranha and chewin' on about Christmas this, perfect that."

"Can you say that you like Christmas a little bit better now, at least?" Sally asked. Pearl crossed her arms and hummed noncommittally, but her eye had a mischievous glint.

Sally patted the couch cushion next to her. "Sit with me for a while. We can watch one of the old holiday classics and finish this bottle. Then, maybe we could open a new one?" she suggested slyly.

"It's a temptin' offer," Pearl chortled. "Especially the wine. I'm just plum-tuckered out, though. Wouldn't want to take up one of those couch cushions when I'm just. So. Tired!" She made a point of yawning exaggeratedly between the words, then pretending to fall asleep while standing. Sally laughed.

"Why are you worried about taking up a couch cushion?" Sally asked, raising an eyebrow.

"No reason," Pearl said evasively, in a sing-song tone. "Gotta fall into bed before I fall into the fireplace. Goodnight, friend."

"Goodnight," Sally beamed. "Merry Christmas, Pearl."

"Bah, humbug," Pearl joked. "Aw, fine; Merry Christmas to you, too, Sally." Pearl shuffled off towards the stairs as other footsteps traveled the other way, approaching Sally.

"Pearl said I'd find you here," Mike chuckled. "Do you mind if I join you?"

"I don't mind at all," Sally said, sitting up a little straighter and smiling in surprise. Pearl must have set this up. So this was why she'd insisted on slipping off to bed when she could have put away more wine and stayed up with Sally.

Pearl was a fantastic friend.

Mike rested his elbows on his knees after sitting beside Sally on the couch, setting a clean wine glass on the rustic coffee table in front of them. Sally was quick to fill it with a half-empty bottle of cabernet.

"Do you really forgive me for not listening to you right away about Birdie?" Mike asked.

"Of course," Sally answered. "Do you forgive me for not appreciating how much stress you were under during the snowstorm?"

"Yes," Mike said. "Not that I think it warrants an apology. It's like you said. Birdie matters just as much as anyone else in this town and probably only wanted to feel like she mattered all along."

"I think everyone wants to feel like they matter," Sally said, reaching for his hand and squeezing it.

"You matter to me. I hope you know that," Mike said. Sally's eyes widened as he shifted closer to her on the couch; this time, she didn't stop him or turn away.

"You've worked hard to prove it," Sally said, tilting her head.

"Did it work?" Mike asked, leaning towards her.

"Perfectly," Sally answered a moment before their lips met.

38

Pearl's Secret Sugar Cookies

```
Preheat Oven to 375 F

Combine:
1 C butter
3 C sugar
2 C sour cream
3 eggs
2 t vanilla

Add Slowly:
1 t salt
3 t baking powder
3 t baking soda
7 1/2 C flour

Chill dough in the fridge
Roll and use cookie cutters to shape
Bake for 5-6 minutes
Allow cookies to cool on rack
Frost with powdered sugar icing
```

Acknowledgment

As a girl who loves Christmas as much as Sally, this book was pure joy to write. Creating the fictionalized version of McKenzie Bridge seemed like the perfect way to pay tribute to the spunky little village tucked in the mountains above Eugene, OR.

Thank you to my editor, Alexis A. Wright. Your love for the story and ability to see my vision is extraordinary. I couldn't have done this without you.

Thank you to my family, who indulged my endless hours of writing and editing in trying to finish this in time for Christmas.

To my parents and grandparents, thank you for instilling in me a true love of Christmas. No matter what was happening in our family, Christmas was always wonderful.

To my Keller Williams community, thank you for supporting my writing passion. It is such a blessing to be part of a great organization.

And thank you to whoever is reading this. As an independent author, it isn't easy to get a book in front of the right audience. It has been so wonderful introducing you to Sally and Pearl.

About the Author

Wendy Day lives in Michigan with her patient husband, four kids, two dogs, and one very entitled cat. She is a mediocre painter and terrible cook. When not writing, she's likely to be found daydreaming in a rowboat or curled up in a cozy chair with a glass of wine and a good book. She has written several books featuring spunky female characters.

You can connect with me on:

🌐 http://www.readwendyday.com

Also by Wendy Day

Mexico, Margaritas, and Murder

After her grumpy husband dies, Sally throws out his thread-worn plaid recliner, cashes the life insurance check, and lets her spunky best friend, Pearl, drag her to Mexico for an all-inclusive vacation using their Senior Citizen's discount.

They kayak, sing karaoke, and spy on the next-door nudist resort. Sally's not sure if it's the sun or tequila, but she is truly having fun for the first time in her life.

That is, until a fellow guest turns up dead.

While Sally fearfully packs her bags for home, Pearl insists they stay and get to the bottom of what's happened.

Together, they become crime-fighting seniors who refuse to let the bad guys win.

Killing Cupid - Book 1

Callie Mcguire thought it would be easy to find romance in Chicago. Big city, great nightlife, and a fabulous roommate to bash about town with-her Jane Austen dreams were bound to come true. After her boring boyfriend does the unthinkable, she is drawn to a mysterious and seductive dating website offering a $1 million guarantee.

When she becomes suspicious of her new love's motivations and the otherworldly man behind YourLove4Life.com, it opens a world of supernatural secrets and danger. Callie must save her friends by untangling the mystery of the irresistibly handsome man who calls himself Cupid, then destroy his power forever.

Does Callie have the heart to defeat a powerful nemesis and claim true love as her own?

Hera's Revenge – Book 2

At 24 years old, Kat Phillips has a stable job, an apartment, and her favorite taco place on speed dial. She should be happy, but she's not. When she realizes her life might be stuck in neutral forever, Kat goes into full panic mode. She jumps in her car and heads south to the one person who she knows will understand.

With her grandmother's advice comes revelations that rock Kat's world. generational secrets come to light, and a shocking possibility sends Kat on a thrilling search for answers before her next birthday.

The clock is ticking. With her life on the line and handsome, mysterious Jace Woods tempting her heart, Kat will have to challenge fate and change her destiny.

Dethroning Dionysus – Book 3 – COMING 2023

Standing Water - Available Now Kindle Vella

She survived the collapse of America. Now she just wants to live.

Nineteen-year-old Jamie dreams of adventure far from the small town where her family took refuge during the virus and subsequent war of 2027. Ten years later, the country is beginning to rebuild, and she even has a map hanging on her bedroom wall with push-pin plans.

But when her dad is suddenly dragged out of their farmhouse by government officials, Jamie's world is rocked again. Her mom is in denial, and her little brother looks to her for answers.

Can she rescue her father and protect the town she is so eager to escape? Or will this adventure cost her everything?

Made in the USA
Monee, IL
09 April 2024

56689957R00166